Anything

Michael

Baron

T0150062

THE
STORY PLANT

This is a work of fiction. Names, characters, places, and incidents either are the product of the author's imagination or are used fictitiously. Any resemblance to actual events, locales, organizations, or persons living or dead, is entirely coincidental and beyond the intent of either the author or the publisher.

The Story Plant
The Aronica-Miller Publishing Project, LLC
P.O. Box 4331
Stamford, CT 06907

Copyright © 2011 by The Fiction Studio
Cover design by Barbara Aronica-Buck
Print ISBN-13: 978-1-61188-021-2
E-book ISBN-13: 978-1-61188-022-9

Visit our website at www.thestoryplant.com

All rights reserved, which includes the right to reproduce this book or portions thereof in any form whatsoever , except as provided by US Copyright Law. For information, address The Story Plant.

First Story Plant Printing: October 2011

Printed in The United States of America

Also by Michael Baron:

When You Went Away
Crossing the Bridge
The Journey Home
Spinning

For my wife,
who makes anything seem possible

Acknowledgments

Special thanks to Michael Peck for his tremendous help in developing this novel.

Thanks to Barbara Aronica-Buck for the beautiful covers she always provides.

Thanks to Danny and Heather Baror for taking Michael Baron out into the world.

Thanks to Jackie Baron McCue (no relation) for her wise editorial input. There are fewer howlers in here because of you.

Thanks to LuAnn Morgan for catching what the rest of us missed.

Thanks to the bloggers and reviewers who have embraced these books. Your willingness to spread the word has been a true gift.

And thanks, as always, to my supportive and inspiring family.

I know two things now that I didn't know when this all began.

The first is that there are forces far beyond what most of us think of as reality – and believe me, I am the last person I thought would ever say something like that – and these forces can have an overwhelming effect on your life. It doesn't matter whether you choose to believe that these forces exist or even if you have proven to yourself beyond doubt that they don't. Again, I didn't buy into *any* of this stuff until recently.

Now, though, I know that there truly is magic in the world.

The second is that, while phrases spoken to lovers like "I would do anything for you" are bandied about in the best talk-is-cheap fashion, you can't ever know this for certain until you are tested. After I fell in love with Melissa, if someone were to ask me whether I would do anything for her, I probably would have responded, "Absolutely. As long as I don't have to give up football or potato chips." That was a lifetime ago.

Now I know without a doubt that I would do anything for the woman I love.

Anything.

Chapter 1

Should Have Been Preserved

"You have to let go of me," Melissa said, looking down at the grass.

"Impossible. I'm physically incapable of doing it."

She glanced in my direction. Melissa was all business. Except when she wasn't. A smile slowly emerged. That "you'd be pretty frustrating if I didn't love you so much" smile. Melissa had so many expressions, always complex, always bearing multiple meanings. This one was among my favorites. It spoke volumes about our relationship.

She laughed. "Come on, Ken. I have to set up the blanket."

"No, I'm sorry. I'm never going to let you go. I've decided I like this much too much." I squeezed her waist a little more tightly and she finally turned around to face me. Slender fingers caressed my cheek and she gave me a kiss that would have buckled my knees if I wasn't already kneeling down. Out of the corner of my eye, I saw a passing bicyclist grin at us from under his white helmet.

"In eleven days and twenty-four minutes, you and I are going to be together until death do us part," she said. There is no chance that either of us is ever going to *let go*. At the moment, though, there's the matter of the blanket. And, sadly, the ticking clock. I have to go back to the office to make sure that life as we know it continues."

"I wish you would take your job a little more seriously."

She smirked at me. "To those of us who have *evolved*, this *is* serious. The oil companies have somehow convinced the White House to let them drill in an Alaskan wildlife refuge. We have to lobby Congress to stop them before it's too late."

"You weren't including me in that 'we,' were you? Might be tough. I think my firm is representing the bad guys. This very picnic could be a violation of any number of the firm's policies."

"Remind me again why I'm marrying you."

I finally released her and allowed her to spread the picnic blanket. I sat back on the lawn to admire her at work and allowed myself to take in the vibrancy of this gorgeous day. May is that special time of year in Washington, D.C. when the weather settles for a brief time between April chill and June humidity. The grass celebrates by tickling your nose with the scent of life. And everything is in synchronous motion, from birds flitting among the budding trees to office workers shedding their pinstripe skins. This is about as right as the world gets.

The Mall is an oasis of green nestled among concrete canyons. Around us was the cultural heart of the nation, the Smithsonian museums ringing the narrow, rectangular field. At one end of the rectangle, white tents rose. There was always a festival on the Mall, and this week it was a festival of Native American culture. Tourists entered in T-shirts and left with colorful clothes and Styrofoam trays of buffalo meat and frybread. Next week it would be something Asian and there would be something Latin or African or Martian after that. We were definitely at the crossroads of the universe.

Tour buses bursting with the spring harvest of tourists circled the Mall in an endless merry-go-round. From an open bus on the other side of the field, a tour guide worked overtime extolling the virtues of the seat of power of the free world. Picnickers and sunbathers sprouted like mushrooms in the grass. Mothers rested on benches, content to let children wear themselves out chasing each other. Outside the park, the sidewalks of Washington hummed with lunchtime crowds buzzing around food stands. A novice rollerblader seemed intent on breaking the sound barrier, though he was more likely to break his arm. Bicyclists were being only slightly more careful as they wove between pedestrians ambling on the dirt paths.

The pale yellow blanket was now settled precisely as Melissa wanted it. She sat and curled her feet under her. She looked spectacular in her white business suit. Nicole Miller, I think. I wore Hugo Boss. Gray, of course. You didn't work where I worked if you were interested in pushing the limits.

She smiled warmly. "If I recall correctly, you were a lot closer a minute ago."

"That's before you shooed me away."

She held out her arms. "Very, *very*, temporarily."

I moved to her and kissed her tenderly, adjusting our bodies afterward so she leaned softly against my chest. She tapped my leg and nodded toward our left. Against a tree sat a young couple, the man with a heart tattooed on his wiry shoulder, the woman with buzz-cut hair and a rose etched in her ankle. They clapped as their blue-clad toddler mastered the art of walking, and falling, and walking again.

"Cute, isn't he?" she said.

"Really cute." I snuggled her closer. "Ours will be cuter."

"Goes without saying."

The toddler gurgled at a thin man in a dark suit sitting on a bench, his high-domed forehead taut with concentration and his large ears propping up glasses through which he studied a thick black binder. I don't think he noticed the kid at all. I wouldn't have either a couple of years ago.

I looked down to see a wistful half-smile play on Melissa's mouth. I knew she was thinking about the children we would have. I thought about it often myself since she'd agreed to marry me.

After a while, she leaned her head back. "Did you bring the sandwiches?"

I held a thumb and forefinger to the bridge of my nose. "I was supposed to bring them, wasn't I?"

"That *was* the plan."

"Blew it. Sorry."

It was to Melissa's credit that she never got exasperated with me, even when I was being my most exasperating – or at least pretending to be. She patted me on the leg.

"I guess I'll have to go to one of the vendors and get a hot dog for you and a pretzel for me. It's a pretty safe bet they don't have veggie burgers anywhere around here." She looked up at me and offered a mock scowl. "Or anything approaching the fabulous sandwiches I made for us before we went to bed last night."

"That's the problem, you know. You distracted me in bed. Consider this a compliment."

She reached up and kissed me again. "Do you think you're going to charm your way out of this?"

"Sorta."

She smiled and leaned her forehead against mine. "I suppose anything is possible."

I kissed her hair and looked out to spy the bicycle deliveryman approaching us. "Let's forget hot dogs and pretzels. I feel like Chinese food."

"I wish," she said with a little moan. "I really don't have the time, though."

"I guess I'll have to conjure a little magic then."

No more than ten seconds later, the deliveryman stopped in front of us. On top of his red helmet was a little illuminated sign proclaiming, "Tony Wong Delivers."

"Mr. Timian?"

"That's me," I said, not even trying to avoid smiling at Melissa's stunned reaction. "Any problems finding us?"

He grinned like a freshman at his first frat party. "No, sir. You said to look for the beautiful dark-haired woman in the white suit." Both he and Melissa blushed at this, guaranteeing a huge tip. He unzipped an insulated red pouch in his basket. Out came two paper bags. I paid him and he dipped his helmet in my direction and smiled at Melissa before heading off. Melissa still hadn't said a word.

I placed the bags on the blanket with a flourish. "Your table is ready, Madame. Lunch is served."

Melissa shook her head. "You never cease to amaze me."

"If I ever stop, you can toss me on the trash heap." I began opening cartons: eggplant in garlic sauce for Melissa, Peking Duck for me, vegetable fried rice for both of us.

"Nah, I'll keep you around even when you're old and boring."

"You're such a romantic." I handed Melissa her carton and a pair of chopsticks and set the rice between us.

"Mmm," she said. "And I was all set to eat a stale pretzel."

"I really wouldn't have forgotten the sandwiches. Even with the *distractions*." This was another thing that had become completely different in my days since Melissa.

We ate quietly for a while. The duck, the day, the woman of my dreams. I had everything I needed right here on this blanket.

When we finished eating, I held her close to me. "You know, I could probably get out of work the rest of the day."

She kissed my forehead and then my nose. "That sounds incredibly tempting, but I really can't." She pulled back and reached into one of the bags. "Fortune cookie?"

Melissa pried open her cookie and removed the small slip of paper. I crushed mine between my fingers and plucked out the message.

She read hers first. "'A major change is coming.' It must be talking about the wedding."

"Or something like that. These fortunes are so vague. They can be taken to mean anything. It's like those psychics on TV who magically know callers are stuck in bad relationships, because anyone desperate enough to call has a good chance of being in a lousy relationship. The 'major change' could mean that we're going to switch long distance carriers or that you're going to wear a different pair of shoes tomorrow. My fortune says, 'Your heart will show you the way.' *That's* really going out on a limb."

"Were you expecting profundity?"

I took a bite. "I was expecting a better cookie. Mine tastes like plaster of Paris."

Fortunes forgotten, we lay against each other on the blanket. Melissa's face was as placid as the turquoise sky that extended dreamily overhead. I knew that her work responsibilities were going to intrude again in a matter of minutes, but I was thankful for this little respite. We never had enough of these moments together.

"Oh, I didn't tell you," she said, propping herself up on one arm, "Kate managed to pull the right strings so she could get out of that business trip and come to the wedding. Solo, I'm afraid. She and Chris called it quits."

"That's great that she can make it. And kind of great that she isn't with Chris anymore. It's difficult to believe her self-esteem was really that low."

"I have had that conversation with her thousands of times over the years." Melissa shook her head sadly, pondering the romantic fate of her childhood friend. "I'm so glad she got out of that trip, though. It would have been terrible if she wasn't there."

"Definitely wouldn't have been right." In addition to knowing Melissa since they were kids, Kate Jordan was a former lawyer at my firm, and the person who'd introduced Melissa and me.

"I have something for you," Melissa said, fishing in the backpack she'd brought the picnic blanket in. Her hand emerged with a shiny object. She held it before her eyes for a moment as if communing with something inside. The pocket watch spun gently on its chain, first toward me, then toward Melissa, like a dog uncertain of its master. "I had it engraved yesterday," Melissa said.

She lowered the watch into my palm, the chain folding on itself like a golden cobra. On the front was etched a cloverleaf. Flipping open the round case revealed an old-fashioned watch face with black Roman numerals on a white dial. KEN + MELISSA FOREVER proclaimed the letters engraved on the inside.

"It's beautiful," I said.

"It belonged to my mother's father. Mom said it's supposed to be a lucky charm."

I looked at her with arched eyebrows. That was a very un-Melissa-like thing to say. "Lucky charm?"

"I know. It's silly." Her eyes were huge and slightly moist. I'd never seen her like this, though, as we got closer to the wedding, I noticed certain signs of sentimentality that had never been there before. I drew her into my arms again.

"It's fabulous. Thank you."

I held out the watch to examine it and Melissa ran a hand over mine. "Do you really like it?"

"Of course I do."

"I love you."

I kissed her. "I love you. Forever."

Like a diamond in amber, that moment should have been preserved. Washington is a town that runs on the nervous energy of its self-importance, though, so there was no chance of that. A police car hurtled past in a blur of lights and sirens, followed by a black limousine and then another bodyguard of screaming police cars. This broke the mood and reminded Melissa that she was a citizen of the real world. She sighed and then looked at her cellphone, which was much less elegant than my new watch.

"I have to run," she said regretfully, kneeling. She kissed me quickly on the lips and stood. "I have to finish briefing Pam before she goes on the Hill. I'll see you tonight. I love you."

With that, she was gone. I saw her striding purposefully through a lunchtime crowd that parted like peasants before a queen. I felt a little cheated. I wanted to hold her at least a little longer. I knew, though, that this level of responsibility was one of the things that made Melissa who she was. Would I have loved her as much if she didn't take her job so seriously?

I shook my head at the ridiculousness of that question. I would have loved Melissa as much regardless of what she did for a living.

I stood up and threw out our trash, then knelt to gather up the blanket, realizing that the backpack would be making the trip to my office with me. As I lifted the blanket, our two fortunes fluttered to the ground.

A major change is coming.

Your heart will show you the way.

Who knew that true messages could be packaged in such an inane way?

Chapter 2

Not Breaking Contact

Dusk was my favorite time to return home. It wasn't very often that I got here early enough to watch the sun set fire to the horizon. Tonight the flames were orange in a pink sky. I probably wouldn't have rented this twelfth-floor unit in Arlington if not for a shrewd rental manager who arranged for me to tour it at sunset, with the White House and Capitol Hill spread out beyond the living room windows like a wide-angle postcard. The vision was as staggering as the rent check.

I stared out the window for several minutes. I rarely took the time to truly appreciate this view. But more often over the last few days I felt the need to slow down a little. It must have been the impending wedding. I hear huge transitions can do that to a person. So in this moment, I simply watched the city go by without me, content to see it from above rather than being part of the fray.

Finally, I turned back toward the living room. Sometimes, when I got the chance to look at the place with fresh eyes, it still surprised me to see how thoughtfully appointed the apartment was now. Every now and then, I expected to find the pizza boxes and mismatched furniture that had decorated my home before Melissa moved in. I, of course, complained when she had Goodwill pick up the old stuff – some of it cost a huge amount of money even if it wasn't tasteful – but I think both of us knew that I was only doing this out of some sense of bachelor obligation.

We wouldn't be living here much longer. When we returned from our honeymoon in Taormina, it would be time to start looking for a bigger place. Not a condo, not a townhouse, but a real home with offices for both of us, and a guest bedroom, and a backyard where Melissa could raise a garden. Melissa would get to decorate each room as she desired with her innate sense of how things went together. My only caveat was that the den would be mine and I could fill it *my* way, with a pool table, jukebox and the 1950s Coke machine that a friend promised to sell me. Maybe a basketball hoop on the driveway also. That was as far as I went, though. Even I understood that I wouldn't want to live in a house that I decorated. The truth was that I never really *lived* in this place until Melissa came along.

I deposited the mail on the coffee table and grabbed the remote, flipping to CNN. Wars on multiple fronts, some of which the US was involved in and some we were only being implicated in, more bracing news about the economy – and then a feature about a juggling chimpanzee. They all looked vivid (the wars perhaps too much so) on my sixty-inch flatscreen. The decor was Melissa's, but the electronics were mine, from the video system to the audio system to the computers. Mine, too, were the papers littering the floor in the spare bedroom that served as my office for now. Friends would ask why the door to the room was closed and I would tell them it was by order of Inspector Melissa of the Health Department. A full quarantine was in effect to prevent contagion to the rest of the apartment.

I walked into the kitchen and drew copper-bottomed pots from the cupboard. In this household, cooking was governed by a simple rule: whoever came home first made dinner. I didn't always enjoy cooking. Why slave over a hot stove for two hours to create a meal you eat in ten minutes, when a simple phone call brings whatever you want to your door in fifteen? If the task was more enjoyable now, it wasn't just because home cooking tasted better, but also because it was fun to cook along with and for Melissa. Sometimes we entertained friends at dinner, and sometimes we just entertained ourselves. But it was in fact, now, entertaining. There were even times during the day when I thought about what I might make us to eat that night.

I stopped a minute to go back into the living room when I heard an announcement of live footage of police officers chasing bank robbers. The entire thing was really a pointless exercise; the robbers stood no chance of getting away, especially if HD cameras were following them. But I guess this was their fifteen minutes of fame, something to share with the other inmates years from now.

I went back to the kitchen and started chopping garlic. The local farmers markets opened the week before, bringing fresh tomatoes for marinara sauce instead of red supermarket rocks. I knew Melissa would be able to tell the difference.

While I got things started, the cat came into the kitchen. "Hello, Wizard," I said to the animal who contemplated me with perfect feline indifference. "Don't worry. Mommy will be home soon." Wizard was my cat, a stray my friends somehow convinced me to take in; a temporary lapse of reason on my part. I never liked cats much, and this stuck-up little dictator, for whom I had to pay pet rent to the apartment complex, didn't change that point of view. Somehow, though, we managed to coexist until Melissa moved in. Between them, however, it was love at first sight; I even felt a little jealous over Wizard's affections for Melissa. Life is nothing if not complicated.

Wizard rubbed against my leg, leaving a piece of his furry self on my pants. "Understood, master," I said as I filled his bright blue bowl with food. The cat ate and then slinked off. I had served my purpose.

About forty-five minutes later, Melissa opened the door and inhaled the aroma of simmering tomato sauce. "Mmm," she said in an exaggerated swoon as she came over to kiss me. "I love a man who cooks."

"That's funny; my mother always told me women love men who eat."

"And you certainly have a natural talent for that." She nuzzled my neck. "Although it doesn't show."

Not breaking contact, I put the pasta into a pot of rapidly boiling water and then squeezed her close to me. "I may not look so good in a few weeks. I'm going to have to live in the gym after all the Italian food we'll be feasting on."

"I'll just have to make sure you get your aerobic exercise while we're in Italy," she said seductively.

"Promise?"

"Absolutely." She gave me another kiss on the neck and then a feather-light one on my ear. The water on the stove boiled over and Melissa chuckled. "Temperature too high?"

"I'll say."

It wasn't a bad meal. I can boil spaghetti with the best of them. As usual, I finished my portion first and went back for seconds. Melissa continued to chew hers slowly. She cooked with gusto, but she always ate very deliberately.

"I'm really looking forward to getting a bigger kitchen," I said over a forkful of pasta buried under a snowfall of Parmesan. "I can't wait to get rid of this apartment. No more apartment living ever. No more elevator rides where we stop on every floor. No more upstairs neighbors' kids jumping up and down and shaking our ceiling."

When Melissa had something important to say, she shook her hair like a cat drying itself, then brushed away the hair piled on her shoulder. "Ken, we keep talking about buying a house, and a big one sounds nice. But I've decided that it's not that important. It's not where you live but whom you live with that counts. I don't want our marriage to be founded on material things. This apartment is more than enough for us. I can live in the back seat of our car."

"Melissa, you may marry me for better or worse, but one thing I can promise you is that you will never end up sleeping in the back of a car. Not to mention that our car happens to be an Audi A7."

She smiled and looked a tiny bit embarrassed. No one would ever accuse Melissa of crass materialism, but she did like nice things. I saw nothing wrong with that.

If you gave as much to the world as Melissa gave, you had every right to surround yourself with as much luxury as you could afford. Still, I sometimes think she believed the eight-year-old Saturn she used to drive before we got together was more appropriate for her than the car we drove now.

After dinner, Melissa loaded the dishwasher. That was the other part of our deal: whoever didn't cook cleaned up. I wrapped my arms around her while she did so and kissed her shoulders while she attempted to finish the job.

"I've been hungering for you since lunchtime," I said.

"Only that long?" She turned to face me, running damp hands through my hair. I drew her as close to me as I possibly could, pressing myself against the curves and grooves of a body I had memorized completely. She shifted slightly and even this tiny movement sent my senses reeling.

"No, not only that long. I've been insatiable for you since the day we met."

Slowly, she began unbuttoning my shirt. My hands reached under her blouse and ran up the smooth contours of her back.

"Insatiable," she said in that dreamy voice that told me that passion was beginning to overtake her. She pulled my shirt free of my waistband and ran a hand down my chest. I tried to think of something clever to say and then realized that doing so was absolutely pointless. I too was now somewhere else entirely. Her fingernails played across the lower regions of my stomach and my mind reeled. I kissed her deeply and let myself fall into her. Nothing ever felt as fulfilling as surrendering myself completely to Melissa.

Later that night, as she lay in my arms sleeping, I wondered how it was possible that this had happened to me. I never dreamed of a woman like Melissa. I never believed it was possible that a person could make me feel the way she did. As I kissed her hair and settled my head against hers, though, I knew one thing for sure. I could never live without her. Now that she was here, now that she showed me what life could be like with a partner who thrilled me and challenged me and inspired me, I could never be satisfied with anything else.

I pulled her just a little tighter to me and felt immensely thankful that we would always be together.

Chapter 3

A Light All Their Own

Why was there never anybody here?

Normal businesses have customers, casual shoppers, and little bells that ring when someone enters the store. I had visited Stephon's for two years, and in all that time I never saw another soul shop there, or even venture to peek in the window. It was as if the Flying Dutchman reached port and went into retail. It was more than a little spooky, but that spookiness also conferred an aura of buried treasure waiting to be revealed. Stephon's was a special secret, one we never shared with friends. We always deflected questions about the beautiful jewelry Melissa wore by saying things like, "We picked it up here and there."

We discovered Stephon's at the end our third date when, well-fed and content, we wandered the Adams Morgan section peeking at the menus taped to the windows of ethnic eateries. The savory smell of stewed lamb drew us to a Greek café, and a gleam of metal attracted my eye to a gold plate in the window of a shop tucked into a hole in the wall below it. The plate was hypnotic, engraved with an intricate design of squares and circles that appeared random but formed a sophisticated pattern hovering at the edge of recognition.

"Let's check this place out," I said.

Melissa peered down toward the shop. "Is it open?" The windows were dark and dusty, although there seemed to be faint light inside.

"Let's find out."

"If you want."

Something in her voice made me look at her. At this point, we were still learning to pick up each other's signals. "Is that okay? You told me you liked handmade jewelry."

She wrinkled her nose. "This place seems a little forbidding."

I looked back at the store. It was dingy, which probably meant there was little more than junk inside. "You're right. Let's keep walking."

I started to move, but Melissa held her place. "No, let's go in."

"You sure?"

She smiled. "There *probably* aren't any demons in there."

We made our way down the steps, our shoes crackling on discarded potato chip bags. Something sticky tugged at my soles. As I opened the door, I expected a dark interior and a musty smell.

So where did the light come from?

It wasn't the bright fluorescence of store lights that leave green rings when you close your eyes. Nor little spotlights that artfully illuminate the contents of display cases. The display cases in this shop didn't need lamps. They shined with a light all their own.

We passed through an enchanted metal forest of gold, silver and jade, every object shining with its own radiance. Bracelets and necklaces lay beside plates of great age and polished with even greater care. Was I in a jewelry store or on an archaeological dig? A white square on the wall caught my eye. It was like ivory but whiter, inlaid with some smoky blue stone that might have been lapis lazuli. The stones spelled a name in rough letters; STEPHON'S, it read. I turned to Melissa and saw that her gaze was as transfixed as a pilgrim at the foot of a shrine. It was then that I learned just how much Melissa really loved jewelry. I already knew she looked down on ostentatious displays of wealth, but to her, a gold bracelet was *necessity*.

"I think I'm in heaven," she said with wonder.

"We're definitely not on Earth," I said sarcastically, though I had to admit to myself that I was fascinated. Very few stores ever affected me this way. Browsing was a way to pass the time, not an avocation. This was someplace special, though. I knew I wouldn't be leaving here without buying Melissa something.

It turned out to be something small – we were only on our third date, after all, though I already knew in my heart that this was the real thing – just a simple pair of silver earrings. Melissa beamed and put them on immediately. When we left the shop and continued our walk, she stopped in several windows to get a look at her earrings in the reflection.

"Am I shimmering?" she said.

"You light up the night."

She turned to me and touched me on the cheek. "I might just hold on to you."

My first birthday gift for Melissa came from Stephon's, as did her first Valentine's Day gift from me, and gifts for just about every occasion imaginable, including a few I invented on the spot. I went back there enough times to fill Melissa's jewelry box like Fort Knox and send Stephon's kids to private school.

That morning, wedding plans swirling in my mind, I ducked into the low doorway yet again, pausing for a moment to let my eyes adjust to the singular light. As always, Stephon was absorbed in some task, this time bending over a table behind the rear counter as he polished a stone necklace. He looked up at me and smiled, his long, narrow face bisecting as he did so. Though he probably wasn't any older than fifty, Stephon always struck me as wizened. He needed several good meals. A little sunlight probably wouldn't hurt him either.

He turned back to his necklace and I began my search. For a store with no customers, inventory had a way of appearing and disappearing almost in the blink of an eye. It was absolutely impossible to guess what you would find there, and pointless to go to the store with a particular item in mind. So I carefully peered among the tall display cases glittering with silver in the center of the shop. I bent over the gold in the counter showcase. Shapes and colors twinkled and beckoned. Through the sunken front windows, passing cars flickered in reflections from the display cases.

I would know what I wanted when I saw it. But what would it be? Among these bright baubles was the last gift I would give Melissa before we said our vows. I wanted it to tell her how much I cherished our courtship and how much I welcomed our marriage. Of course, she knew these things already, but I wanted something that would mark the passage, something separate from the ring I would place on her finger in less than two weeks.

"You always look so fascinated," Stephon said. I turned to find him regarding me carefully from across the counter.

"It's hard not to be when I'm in here."

"Thank you."

"You're very welcome." I walked over to a display of carved onyx.

"And what is today's occasion?"

"Melissa and I are getting married the Saturday after next," I said, not taking my eye off the display. Not a single one of these items had been here the last time I visited the shop. "I want to get her one more pre-wedding gift."

"Then this is unquestionably a very special occasion."

"Which makes picking something out just a little more of a challenge."

Stephon laughed softly. "Take your time. Take all the time you need. Excuse me a minute."

I looked up to see Stephon walk into the back room, then my eyes lit on a sapphire necklace. Blue, like the depthless blue of Melissa's eyes. I imagined her wearing the necklace and how her eyes would sparkle as a result. It was a curious image. Melissa's eyes were warm, thoughtful and wise, but I didn't recall ever seeing them sparkle. She was too put together to sparkle.

Stephon emerged from the back a short while later with two cups of cappuccino. He approached me and proffered a cup with a perfectly manicured hand. I took it and thanked him, a little surprised by the gesture. The cup and saucer were a delicate shade of robin's egg blue, inlaid with golden doves. Stephon sipped and then I did the same. The cappuccino was delicious.

This entire exchange was unusual. While Stephon had always been pleasant on my many visits, he had never done anything like this before.

Stephon took a second sip, then peered up at me thoughtfully. "Nothing has caught your eye?"

"Dozens of things have caught my eye. I find it amazing how this store reinvents itself every time I visit and yet still always fascinates me."

"Like a great romance."

I chuckled. "Yes, I guess so."

"But you still haven't found anything for your special present." Stephon took one more sip of his coffee and I did the same, finishing the cup. "Why do you think that is?"

I shook my head and looked around the room. "Like I said, we're getting married. Of course I'll buy Melissa gifts when we're married – trust me, you'll get a steady stream of business – but this is the last chance I have to buy her a gift as her fiancé. Don't ask me why, but that puts extra pressure on this. I'm going to spend the rest of my life with Melissa, but I'll never again get to present her a gift not as her husband, but as someone who *wants to be* her husband. That requires something even more special than usual. Something fantastic."

His eyes grew just a tiny bit wider when I said that, and for a moment he glanced down at the floor. When he looked back up, his gaze held me as though he was seeing me in an entirely different way. "Something even more special than usual, you say. Something fantastic." He nodded, as though he just imparted great wisdom on himself. "You do realize that you have a very special relationship with Melissa, don't you?"

Of course I did, but Stephon's saying so still made the hairs on the back of my neck stand up. I didn't realize he'd been watching us that closely when we came in. "Yes, I do."

"I'm glad that you do. You can only imagine the number of troubled relationships I encounter on a daily basis. It's a rare pleasure to see the two of you together. It's the kind of thing I wish I could see just a little more frequently."

I began to feel a tiny bit uncomfortable. A little bit naked.

"I can understand why you would want to celebrate this love with something very distinctive." He looked off in the distance and didn't speak for a very long time. Then his eyes caught mine. "Tell me; is it necessary that you buy this gift for your fiancée today?"

"I was planning to. Why do you ask?"

"As you yourself said, I get new things in here all the time. I have some thoughts about items you might find suitable for this present, but they aren't here. If you can return in two days, I may be able to offer you something extraordinary."

Two days? I was planning on giving Melissa her gift that night, though I didn't have a particularly strong reason for doing so. Considering what Stephon was capable of acquiring, it seemed silly to stick to such a rigid schedule.

"Then I'll be back in two days," I said. I smiled and pointed a finger at him playfully. "I'm counting on you to come through for me big time, Stephon."

Stephon nodded once slowly. "I promise to do my very best. I do have one request of you, though. When you return, answer this question for me: what is the greatest fantasy you have of your future wife?"

I was a little abashed by the question and I'm sure it showed on my face. "You don't mean...."

Stephon laughed heartily. "No, certainly not. I am anything but a *voyeur*. I'm talking about a fantasy of the heart. A fantasy of your love. What is your wildest wish for your life with Melissa?"

I smiled. "I'll have to give that some thought."

"Give it a *great deal* of thought."

I had no idea what he meant by that, but he'd already gotten me thinking. I would, in fact, give this a great deal of consideration – and I really looked forward to seeing what he had for me when I returned.

Chapter 4

This Evening's Entertainment

I was blinded by the light.

Down went the night setting on my rearview mirror, but my side mirror glowed incandescent white in the glare of high beams. It was an SUV or a pickup, judging by the height of the headlights. My pursuer edged closer until he was within spitting distance of my bumper.

"Ignore him, Ken." Melissa said. She leaned over from the passenger seat and rubbed my shoulder.

I squinted against the halon light and focused on my speedometer. I had dared to drive forty-five in a forty-mile-per-hour zone, and now some fool who'd had a hard day at the office was taking out his anxiety on me. Or maybe he was somebody who worked on Capitol Hill and truly believed the country was at serious risk if he was late to dinner. Speed limits were for non-essential personnel.

A horn bellowed. I lifted my right hand off the steering and flexed my fingers. Melissa grabbed my hand in a grip surprisingly tight.

"Don't do it, Ken."

My mirror faded from white to silver as the SUV surged into the opposing lane and zoomed past me, its driver slowing to give me a middle finger. *Same to you, buddy,* I muttered silently.

Hadn't there been a time, though, when I was at least as heavy on the pedal as this guy? When I would have sent my car hurtling down the road, trusting in my skill as a driver and the speed of my airbags? The day I bought my A7 was the day someone's Hyundai nearly went into a ditch. Speeding made Melissa nervous, though, so I didn't do that kind of thing anymore. Like so many other things that seemed central to my existence before her, I didn't miss it in the least, and I'd even come around to seeing things from her perspective.

Spots were just beginning to fade from my eyes when another pair of headlights appeared, closing fast. I saw a little red sign on top and braced myself for a ten-minutes-or-it's-free banzai charge. This vehicle stayed its distance, though, covering our tail until we turned off the road to the shelter of the street that led to where Melissa's parents lived.

We were in McLean, home of the CIA and more wealth than most developing nations. It was the sort of place where you could judge the money and importance of people by how far back their homes were from the road. We passed mansions hidden behind trees, their roofs silhouetted against the skyline like castle battlements.

It was Wednesday night, and Wednesdays meant roast beef and potatoes with Mr. and Mrs. Argent. We had a million things to do to prepare for our wedding, but not even the impending marriage of their daughter was going to interfere with the Argents' Wednesday tradition.

I pulled into a quiet side street that was probably affordable when Melissa's parents bought their home thirty years ago, before housing prices rocketed and then went stratospheric during the first Internet boom and stayed relatively high through the economic crisis. It was the sort of street every suburban child should grow up on, where the homes were large and the trees plentiful. As we passed a yellow "For Sale" sign, I calculated that our combined incomes could afford us a house here. The neighborhood was getting younger again, as pensioned government officials retreated to the carefully pruned comfort of Florida retirement communities. Where once big, lumbering American sedans called these streets home, shiny BMWs now sat in driveways. Melissa's parents could make a fortune selling their house and moving to a sunnier clime, but Mrs. Argent said the Marine Corps had moved them enough when they were younger, and that she was determined to stay in the home they'd settled in.

I parked before a white house with rose bushes blooming and tulips standing sentry in parade-ground platoons of yellow, red, and white. Sitting in the driveway was a four-door Ford Taurus, spotless and shiny as the day it was bought. On the back windshield was a sticker emblazoned with the red eagle-and-globe of the Marines.

Though dusk had barely begun, the porch light was on. Melissa's mother greeted me at the door with a hug that dented my ribs. "Welcome, son-in-law," she said. Mrs. Argent was a 1950s TV wife come to life. She was a short, cheerful woman with a gray perm, rosy cheeks, and a way of calling me "dear" as warm as a January fireplace. She wore an old-fashioned apron over a red-checked dress. She was a bit of a cliché, an outmoded one at that, yet I liked this woman, housewife exterior and all. She was kind to me from the day Melissa brought me to dinner for the first time. Loyalty to family was everything to her, and that I so obviously cared deeply for Melissa meant that I was okay in her book.

A big, rough hand grasped mine in an ex-Marine grip. I squeezed back firmly, feeling the muscles in Mr. Argent's fingers and knowing that anything less than an iron handshake invited his disfavor. Melissa's father was tall and lean, his skin a reddish tan under hair crew cut and gray. His lined face was a souvenir of years of sun and rain from Vietnam through Desert Storm. Tonight he wore a red polo shirt and tan slacks, but I always thought of him in camouflage fatigues. I didn't know his exact age, but once I made the mistake of joking that I could do more pushups than an old man, and this wiry soldier with a washboard belly matched me until my arms collapsed. He then did an extra twenty. He retired from the military to become an executive at a defense contractor, and then to the serenity of his garden. It was his reward for a lifetime of hard work, though he still arranged those flowers with the thoroughness of a rifle company at drill.

"Hello, Ken. You still taking good care of my daughter?" His deep, quiet voice maintained just a hint of the Tennessee hills. It contrasted dramatically with his wife's patrician Massachusetts accent. Melissa claimed she had no accent because her parents cancelled each other out.

"I know what will happen to me if I don't, Mr. Argent." I was only half-joking and he only half-chuckled through the long-stemmed pipe protruding from his lips like a periscope rising from a sea of weeds. I had to remind myself not to call him "Colonel." His orders were that he had given and received enough salutes in the Corps, and he didn't need his son-in-law doing it. On the other hand, he always was – and always would be – Mr. Argent to me. I just could never imagine calling this man "Dad."

We only got a foot inside the door before we ran into a roadblock. Wolfgang, the hundred-pound Alsatian and Mr. Argent's special pet, sprawled over half the living room floor. He wore the calm, sleepy face and languid eyes of an even-tempered animal. Yet his breed had been known to be vicious, and I took care to stay on his good side.

Melissa knelt on the floor and rubbed the dog's flanks vigorously while he whimpered with delight.

The Argent home was larger than it appeared on the outside. Perhaps it was the relatively sparse furniture, as if the Colonel expected a call to ship out to Afghanistan tomorrow. Yet Melissa said her father turned down some plum overseas assignments at the end of his career so his family could stay in Washington and his kids could stay in one school district.

There were reminders of a life led on foreign shores. A carving of a camel stood on a bookcase. An Asian vase of deepest blue, emblazoned with ornate red and yellow flowers, sat on the fireplace mantle, which itself was etched in red, green, and gold. In the winter, it reflected the firelight as if the fire burned within.

We sat down punctually, as always, and ate roast beef, as always. Chicken would have been heresy, lamb an act of rebellion, and vegetarian cuisine the first salvo of a Communist invasion. My fiftieth roast beef meal here would have been tedious if I didn't love roast beef and if Melissa's mother was not such a good cook. I enjoyed two helpings of meat, earning a smile from Mrs. Argent and a grunt from the Colonel, who would likely get to his third before dinner was through. Melissa filled her plate with side dishes as she did every time we ate here. She gave up explaining vegetarianism to her parents after they failed to receive her vivid description of cruelty in slaughterhouses well. I think she still held out some hope of persuading me to become a vegetarian, but I think she also understood that her chances were slim. Yet she loved me still.

In this house, there was one commanding officer, and he sat at the head of the table and dictated the conversation. Tonight he expounded on the sexual innuendo and coarse language that pervaded the airwaves. We all nodded our heads, and I neglected to mention that I found shock jocks a guilty pleasure and even occasionally amusing. I did this more out of respect for Melissa and her mother than out of any sense of intimidation – no need to get into some unpleasant argument. Though, to be entirely honest, Mr. Argent *did* intimidate me a little.

We offered to help wash up after dinner, knowing that Melissa's mother would insist we relax in the living room.

"You're going to be spoiled from now until the wedding. You kids have enough to deal with."

"Exactly," her father said solemnly. "Enjoy it while you can. The hard work comes after the honeymoon."

"Be quiet, Harold," Mrs. Argent said. I don't know whether he intimidated her or not. Certainly there were occasions when she got away with putting him in his place, which I found fun to see.

Melissa and I sat on the living room sofa and listened to the splash of water meeting cutlery in the kitchen sink. She leaned on my shoulder while I stroked her hair. "A good dinner," I said, sighing. "In a nice house with nice furniture. When we buy a house, we'll make a home like this."

"That sounds wonderful."

"We'll need to get a lot more stuff than we have now, though. Maybe we'll even get a piano to take up space."

"I don't want a piano, Ken."

A warm, sweet smell floated out of the kitchen.

"Oh, yes," I said eagerly. "Here come the gingerbread cookies."

"If you keep eating like this, you won't be hungry again until we leave Italy."

"Don't worry about my appetite. Besides, your mom loves when I make a pig of myself. And if the cookies are coming, that means it's time for the next stage in this evening's entertainment."

"Ken, don't tease her this time."

Mrs. Argent really would be a TV character if she didn't have any flaws. Some women were afflicted with the need to knit afghans that no one wanted. Melissa's mom's vice was photo albums. She had dozens and dozens of them. Her collection was as big as the *Encyclopedia Britannica* and just as enthralling to spend time with. It inundated the living room bookshelf with rows of black volumes.

Like everything else in the Argent household, this was a ritual as consistent as the phases of the moon. First came roast beef, then the smell of gingerbread baking, and then, invariably, the photos.

Melissa's mom made wonderful cookies, but not even hot gingerbread compensates for the tedium of leafing through somebody else's pictures. I liked seeing what Melissa looked like when she was a little girl, but we'd gotten to those pretty early in our relationship and had since moved on to volumes that didn't include her at all. It's bad enough when friends insist on showing them, and you have to feign interest in fuzzy shots of Rome or zoom-lens pictures of someone's kids trashing a campground. But how do you tell your mother-in-law that her cherished memories are a bore? I flexed my lip muscles for a session of obligatory smiling.

Endurance was the key when Melissa and her mother got started on one of these little Kodak trysts (yes, Melissa actually seemed to like doing this). The Colonel always retreated after dinner, mumbling that he had to walk the dog, even if Wolfgang was sound asleep. Wolfgang's leash was as wide as a vacuum cleaner hose, but I would rather have tried to restrain him than nod at the umpteenth snapshot of the Grand Canyon.

That we would look at photos was a certainty. However, I never knew which album Mrs. Argent was going to choose. Tonight she walked over to the bookshelf and paused, her forefinger fluttering over the rows of volumes. My mind locked onto her hand, willing it to follow my suggestion. *Go for the book from your time in Cambodia – at least the art is interesting.* For a moment, her forefinger hovered over one volume with a capital

M carefully drawn in red ink. She put her hands on her hips and turned to us.

"You are not going to believe this, Melissa. Do you remember how we lost that album with your teenage pictures? Remember how upset I was? It's the strangest thing, but I was clearing out the attic for the neighborhood garage sale next month. An old coin rolled behind the chimney in the corner. When I bent to pick it up, I found the album wedged in there. I can't imagine how that happened. It must have fallen in when the roofers fixed the attic years ago."

"You mean you have more pictures of Melissa?" I said, almost clapping.

Mrs. Argent beamed at my expression of interest. "Yes, Ken. I know how much you enjoyed her baby pictures and the scrapbook of her college days. But we haven't seen these other pictures in nearly fifteen years. I almost forgot we had them."

This was not going to be the same old evening after all. I found it absolutely fascinating to look at pictures of the early Melissa. It filled in the blanks for me. No matter how much we talked about our past – and admittedly it wasn't much beyond the traditional old boyfriend/old girlfriend stuff – I found myself wanting to know more about her. This woman who meant so much to me had had decades of life before we met, and I wished I could have shared every minute of it with her. She was especially vague about her teenage years, disposing of any questions I had with dashed-off references to acne, braces, and unmanageable hair. Clearly it was an awkward period for her and she didn't have any interest in revisiting it, but I know I would have loved Melissa even if she had a zit the size of Everest on her nose, and this new "discovery" from her mother was like striking the motherlode.

I turned to Melissa. Her head had withdrawn from my shoulder and her smile had faded. "Your mom found some more old photos of you."

"I heard."

"Where should we start, dear?" Mrs. Argent said to me. "Do you want to look at the new album, or should we go back to Melissa's baby album first?"

"Let's start with the baby album," I said enthusiastically. We might be here all night, but I did not want to miss one image. These weren't lifeless stills of heartless mountains or ancient relatives. These were pictures of life itself.

Mrs. Argent plucked a binder from a shelf and sat beside me on the couch. She smoothed her skirt and opened the album. Inside the plastic sheaths were photos of different sizes. At the top were two small studio portraits of Melissa as a toddler, in a pink suit and showing the first twists of golden curls. In one picture, she held a little doll and in the other a stuffed lamb.

"It was a chore getting her to pose for that one," Melissa's mother said. "It took two lollipops. She was always such a good baby, but when she was determined not to do something, she didn't do it. I'll bet she's still the same way."

I grinned at Melissa. Her lips twitched in a half-smile, and she mumbled something. I shifted my attention back to the album. Melissa's mother turned the pages. Now the girl in the picture was taller and darker-haired. She danced in a tutu, her face glowing with the same carefree energy that she'd had as a toddler. This was a child that loved life.

"Melissa used to be so exuberant," her mother said proudly. She glanced thoughtfully at her daughter.

A short while later, Mrs. Argent retrieved a second album. The pictures changed, revealing a girl taller and more beautiful by the year. The first shot was of young Melissa walking along a stream, clad in one of those sleeveless winter jackets that resembled body armor.

"Melissa belonged to a student environmental group that cleaned up trash from wildlife preserves," Mrs. Argent said. "Harold had difficulty understanding why young people worried so much about picking up soda cans. I explained to him that it was just like soldiers policing trash on the grounds of a military base. He always took extra care that his rifle company kept their bivouac spotless."

I glanced at the adult Melissa. Her face was now buried in the front section of the *Washington Post*. She turned the page, and I could see she was reading a story about a toxic waste dump. Still the same Melissa, eager to make the world a better place.

We got to the last page of the album. Melissa stood on a stage, receiving a certificate from a smiling man in a gray suit. I squinted at the picture. The award seemed to be for community service. Melissa's face was proud and confident, her eyes bright as jewels.

Mrs. Argent's nose wrinkled. "Oh, dear; I think the cookies are burning. I'll be right back." She rose gracefully, moving purposefully but without haste toward the kitchen.

"Excuse me," Melissa said as she also rose from her seat.

"Are you okay?"

She nodded as she climbed the staircase. "I'm just going to the bathroom."

A door slammed at the rear of the house, and then came the clink of metal passing by the front. Mr. Argent was out walking the dog again. Suddenly the house was quiet. I hefted the album and flipped through the pages, images passing before my eyes like an old newsreel. My future wife's life, frozen in the artificial and faded colors of old processing. The Melissa in these pictures was only a shadow of the original – a pale reflection of a vivid flesh-and-blood person.

What would it have been like to have known her then? To see her first baby steps or her first dance recital with my own eyes instead of the camera's? Ever since I met her that night at Kate's party, I'd wanted to know everything about her. She was a novel whose plot became more interesting as I delved deeper into the book. But my book had its first thirty chapters torn out, with only stories and a few illustrations to fill in the details.

Stephon had asked me that very day what my fantasy with Melissa was. I wasn't sure then, but now it was incredibly clear to me. In my mind's eye, I would be an invisible observer watching her grow. From my imaginary vantage point, I would see her giggle as she played in a sandbox. I would see her brow furrow with determination as she mounted her first bicycle. I would experience her past with her and by doing so know her as completely as I possibly could. I couldn't imagine a more fulfilling fantasy.

Melissa came back downstairs and slumped in her chair. Waitresses after a double shift looked less exhausted than she did.

"Are you feeling all right?"

"I think I ate something that didn't agree with me. My mother must have roasted the potatoes in the same pan as the meat again. She always forgets."

"Next time we'll bring some of that soy beef. You always tell me it tastes just like real meat. I'd love to see if your father could spot the difference. If he did, he'd probably grab one of his rifles and hunt rabbit in the suburbs until he came home with a real meal."

She laughed slightly. Her face looked freshly damp, as did the fringes of dark hair over her forehead. I put down the photo album.

"Hey, you're not embarrassed about looking at these pictures, are you?"

"I don't know why we always have to look at pictures. They belong to the past and they all look the same after a while. I wish sometimes we could just play cards or Scrabble. Or just all sit down in the living room after dinner and talk. That's what other human beings do."

Moments passed while I tried to understand where this was coming from. "What are you talking about? You always enjoy looking at pictures. I'm the one who thinks those travel shots are excruciating." A clatter came from the kitchen, and I lowered my voice. "Now you're complaining? I was actually having fun with this for the first time in months."

I didn't lose my temper with Melissa often, and my annoyance shocked her. She thought a moment, then tried to smile. "It's okay, Ken. If it makes you happy looking at my baby pictures, go ahead. I'll even make baby faces if you want." She stuck out her tongue and I tossed a pillow at her.

Mrs. Argent returned and walked over to the bookcase again. She lifted a manila envelope lying on the middle shelf and held it aloft like a trophy. "I forgot to mention I also found this behind the chimney, dear. High school photos of you on the tennis team. She was a good player, Ken."

"I've seen her play." She'd beaten me on the court a few times.

"There are also a few pictures of Melissa taking piano lessons. I thought you might like to see them as well."

Melissa took piano lessons? If they were anything like my saxophone lessons in junior high, there was little wonder why she'd never mentioned it.

"Absolutely," I said. "Melissa was just telling me how happy she is to relive these memories." I turned to her and winked. She had turned pale.

"I don't know how these photos ended up behind the chimney as well," her mother said. "Melissa, I thought I gave them to you to put in an album. But you never lose anything, so it must have been those roofers again. It's a good thing they did a better job with the roof than they did preserving our family treasures." Suddenly Mrs. Argent stopped and looked at her daughter, concerned. "What's the matter, honey?"

This made me look as well. Melissa was rubbing her temples.

"I have a headache, Mom. Maybe it was something I ate, or all the pollen in the air, but it's a really bad one. Ken, I think we should go home. I feel like I need to lay down."

I stood up. "Yeah, of course. Mrs. Argent, can we borrow those pictures? We'll bring them back next time we're over."

"Of course you can." She neatly secured the clip on the back of the envelope and handed it to me.

Melissa rose and took the envelope from my hand, tossing it on the couch. "Actually, I think we better leave them here. They were lost once already, and I wouldn't want that to happen again."

I opened my mouth to protest, but Melissa was already headed for the door. Mrs. Argent and I shared confused looks. Melissa obviously had a *hell* of a headache.

"Don't you want to say goodbye to your father?" Mrs. Argent said reprovingly.

"He's not back from his walk, Mom. Just tell him goodbye for me."

As we walked out the door, Wolfgang led Mr. Argent up the front walk. The dog sniffed at us and squatted on the concrete. I made sure to pet him.

"You're leaving in a hurry," Mr. Argent said calmly, the sweet scent of his pipe tobacco mingling with the smell of newborn leaves. His face remained immobile, but his eyes aimed at Melissa and then at me.

"Melissa isn't feeling well, Mr. Argent. I'm going to take her home."

"Hmmm." Mr. Argent puffed his pipe. He paused and tilted his cheek, waiting for a kiss. Instead Melissa brushed past him. I could see her father's eyes tracking us as we walked to the car.

Once we'd driven away from the house, Melissa seemed to relax a little. "Feeling better?" I said.

"My head still hurts. I'll be okay."

"Chamomile and a neck massage?"

She leaned back on the headrest. "That would be great."

"You're on." We drove a short while in silence. "Hey, what was the deal with those pictures tonight? Why didn't you want to take them with us?"

"I just didn't want to misplace them. They've been lost all these years. With everything going on with the wedding and all, they could wind up in some file that we'll never open again. I'm not sure my mother could survive that."

I chuckled. "Yeah, you're probably right. We'll look at them the next time we're over there."

"Mmm, can't wait," Melissa said, rubbing her temples again.

I reached out and gently massaged her shoulder. "We can skip the chamomile if you want."

Chapter 5

Diminished By Not Being With Her

I had a curious feeling when I walked into Stephon's a couple of days later. This wasn't surprising, since Stephon's was a curious place, but that wasn't the source of the strangeness I sensed. Instead, it was the incongruous fact that I had a response to Stephon's even more incongruous request: to return with my greatest fantasy for Melissa. If I could remake the laws of physics, if I could wrinkle the fabric of time, I knew exactly what I would do with such power.

Of course, there were no customers in the store. Stephon always dressed well, if casually, and he had a fortune of jewelry in this small space. He had to get his money from somewhere. Was the store a front for some illegal operation? Did he think it was funny that I actually came here to *shop*?

Stephon offered me a friendly nod when I came in. "Good to see you again, Mr. Timian."

"Thank you, Stephon. As promised."

"As promised."

"Do you have something fabulous for me?"

He smiled as broadly as his narrow face allowed. "I very well might."

I smiled as well, getting a little excited about what was to come. "That's great. Let me see what you were able to find."

Stephon turned and walked toward the back room. Just before he entered the doorway, though, he stopped and faced me again. "I had a request of you, didn't I?"

In some ways, I had hoped that he had forgotten. I wasn't sure I could say what I was thinking out loud. "You did, yes."

"A fantasy for you and your fiancée."

"That was what you requested."

"And did you think of one?"

I suddenly felt very uncomfortable. This seemed like such an intimate thing to share with someone I barely knew. "Is this really necessary?"

Stephon's shoulders relaxed and he tilted his head to the side. He walked back toward the counter. "Of course it isn't. If you haven't come up with something or if you'd rather not tell me about it, I understand. It's just a little question I ask from time to time when I *see* things in certain people. I thought it might enhance this whole transaction for you."

Why that didn't sound incredibly creepy to me, I don't know. The entire experience had become fairly surreal. Just to make things a little more Dali-esque, I suddenly found myself wanting to share this with my jeweler. My eyes landed on a silver phoenix brooch where a golden elephant had been two days before. I shook my head briskly and then looked up at Stephon.

"This is probably going to sound ridiculous to you," I said.

"I think that's very unlikely."

"It's pretty outlandish."

He nodded.

"My fantasy is to be able to go back to the beginning of Melissa's life and watch her become the person she is today."

"You mean travel back in time?"

"I guess, but not really that. I don't want to be an orderly in the nursery or her third grade teacher or anything like that. I'd just like to be able to *see* her. Like in a home movie, but in three dimensions and with all five senses."

Stephon nodded more broadly now.

"It's pretty silly, huh?" I said.

"Oh no, I don't think so at all. Why do you want this?"

I looked up at the ceiling and then around the room. "I don't know. I just feel like I missed out, you know? I mean I have never even come close to feeling about another person what I feel about Melissa, and when I looked at her baby pictures the other night, I just got the strongest sense that I've been, I don't know, *diminished* by not being with her for her first thirty years. I really want to hear the first words she spoke as a baby. I want to see her having a tea party with her dolls. You asked me to come up with a fantasy and then only a few hours later, this popped into my head. Now that it has, I can't get it out."

"That's a very good fantasy, Mr. Timian."

"Not that I can do anything about it."

Stephon shrugged.

"What was that?" I said.

"What was what?"

"That little gesture. Why'd you do that?"

Stephon held my gaze firmly. I truly don't think I could have looked away. "Sometimes," he said, "the impossible isn't *entirely* impossible."

That was when the experience became creepy for me. "I think I'd like that piece of jewelry now, if you don't mind."

Stephon shrugged again. "It's in the back room; let me go get it."

He turned away.

"Wait," I said with more force than I intended. "You aren't suggesting that you could...fulfill this fantasy, are you?"

"That depends on how much you want it. Though I think I've already determined that."

I was like Alice in the Lewis Carroll novel. Like Neo in "The Matrix." There was absolutely no chance I could walk away from this. "You have a time machine?" I said, trying to sound skeptical.

Stephon chuckled. "It isn't a time machine."

That wasn't the response I expected. "What are we talking about here?"

He looked at his hands and then for some reason glanced toward the front door. "This comes as much from you as it does from me, but if you really want this fantasy – and I see that you do – I can help make it happen."

My fingertips went numb. I was either having a heart attack or I'd just stepped into a parallel universe. "You can send me back into Melissa's past?"

"In a manner of speaking. I can give you the opportunity to observe the life of your Melissa. She would not know you were there and of course you couldn't touch her or anything else."

"That makes sense," I said, the remaining rational part of my mind mocking me for such a ridiculous comment. "Do I have to eat or drink anything? I'm not putting any controlled substances into my body."

"There is nothing hallucinogenic about this. I merely have the ability to help send you on this little excursion. It's really that simple. It is your choice whether you want to do this or not."

A screaming ambulance siren drew my gaze to the window. It jarred me, and I appreciated that. On the other side of the door was a world of rules that clearly stated the impossibility of what Stephon was offering. I stopped believing in Santa Claus when I was seven. I knew my mother was the "Tooth Fairy" right off the bat. And I certainly didn't believe in magic. Yet this little suggestion from Stephon was so seductive – and it seemed so real.

The more I thought about it, the more I realized how much I really wanted it. If there was a chance that I could experience Melissa in this way, then I would have to try.

"Okay, Stephon, if you can do this – I can't believe I'm saying this – I would really like to take you up on it. How much will this cost me? Before you answer, remember that even though I'm an attorney, I still have a wedding and a honeymoon to pay for."

He seemed truly offended by this question. "I sell jewelry and antiques, Mr. Timian. The service I offer you now is priceless. Therefore I charge no price for it."

"And there are no *strings* attached?"

He laughed. "You mean like selling me your soul or promising me your first born or something like that? No, no strings. Sometimes a favor is really just a favor."

And I thought the cappuccino had been a big deal. Stephon definitely knew something about fostering customer loyalty.

I smiled. "So what do I have to do?"

"Nothing. The process is not mechanical in nature. I will take care of everything. You will suddenly find yourself in another place. Again, no one will hear or see you, nor can you touch anyone or anything. I must warn you that what you see can be very informative or amusing, but also very disconcerting. How we imagine the past always differs from the actual history, just as our memories of our own pasts distort over time. You must always remember that you are an observer. You can neither cause nor influence events."

"I understand." Actually, I didn't. Why was he giving me such a lengthy disclaimer? Did he know something that he wasn't admitting?

I suddenly felt a little weird about this. Exactly what was I going to see? I didn't want to be some kind of peeping Tom with Melissa. Would I see her make out with her first boyfriend or take her first lover? How would I feel about that? How would *she* feel about that if she knew?

"Your heart isn't going to let you see anything it doesn't believe you should," Stephon said. I know I hadn't expressed any of my concerns out loud. If he meant to reassure me with that statement, he did not succeed.

I made eye contact with him. "This is a good idea?" I said.

"It's a good idea if you think it's a good idea."

I closed my eyes and tried to determine how I really felt about this exercise. It was harmless, right? I wasn't being a peeping Tom, I was being an admirer. This was like a Wednesday evening with the Argents only in 3D and with Dolby audio.

"Okay, let's do it. When can we set this up?"

"Right now, if you'd like."

"Right now?"

"Or not, if that makes you uncomfortable."

I was way past uncomfortable, but that wasn't the point. "No, right now would be good."

"If you have any questions upon your return, I will attempt to answer them."

"Oh, you mean *really* right now."

Stephon held up his hands as though to say, "Your call."

I shook my head briskly. "Yes, right now. Let's do it."

I expected Stephon to wave a wand or press a button or at least throw some fairy dust in the air. Instead, he simply stood there as a white fog shrouded me. The last thing I saw were his coal-black eyes.

Chapter 6

Uncharted Waters

I knew where I was.

It was different from Wednesday night. The familiar maroon tiles were gone, replaced by white linoleum etched with golden hexagons. White walls loomed over a black stove instead of yellow walls enclosing a white stove. The refrigerator changed from big and white to small and avocado green. Even the technology was different, like things from an old spinster's garage sale. The microwave and coffeemaker on the counter were replaced by a simple toaster oven and a transistor radio with an old-fashioned tuning dial. Where tall glass jars filled with pasta and rice once stood under the window, there were orange jars of Tang and pink cans of Tab. Overhead were fluorescent rods that reminded me of Darth Vader's lightsaber, though Vader himself was still a few years away.

I'm in the early '70s. How on earth did Stephon do this?

This was unmistakably Mrs. Argent's kitchen. In a cabinet on top of the refrigerator were the blue Wedgewood plates that she only used on Thanksgiving. Plastic apples and grapes still clung to the window sill, their vivid reds and purples not faded by time. Even the tacky "Bless This Kitchen" sign hung from the wall by the pantry, but again in more intense colors.

What happened to the parade-ground neatness, though? What did Mr. Argent think of this mess? Plastic toys were scattered in every corner. Pots and pans spilled out of cabinet doors. The air reeked of diapers, disinfectant, fried food, and a few other smells I could not identify. From the living room came a tune that I dimly recalled as the theme of the "Bozo the Clown Show."

I breathed deeply and learned lesson one of time travel: the world smells different. Not very different – fried meat smells the same wherever and whenever. But just different enough to be noticeable, like biting into an orange candy that tastes closer to tangerine. Aromas in the air mingled with aromas in my memory of my mother standing over a stove. Our kitchen was smaller than this, too cold in the winter and too hot in the summer. I guessed that the difference between this and the present was that you brought your own suite of memories to the past. Or something like that. I could hardly consider myself to be an expert on the subject with all of thirty seconds experience.

My stomach reminded me that I'd promised to feed it after I stopped by Stephon's. How long was I going to be here, anyway? I should have thought to ask. I looked around the kitchen. Powdered orange drink brought back memories of concoctions that seemed sickly sweet to me now. Diet soda had never been acceptable to me, and I couldn't understand why someone wouldn't just drink water instead.

An open package of chocolate chip cookies beckoned to me from the counter. The kitchen was empty and
though the TV was on, no one appeared to be around. I
looked over the row of cookies stacked like poker chips
and found one bulging with chocolate. I grabbed it –
and my hand felt a chilling cold. The cookie felt like a
slippery fog sliding through my grasp. I tried again, and
it was as if I were squeezing water. Stephon told me I
wouldn't be able to interact with this past. I guess he
wasn't kidding.

There came an infant's squall, beginning with a gur-
gle and ending with a scream. Through the open kitchen
door came a woman cradling a baby.

I never thought of my future mother-in-law as beautiful or ugly. She was simply my future mother-in-law.
However, in the flesh thirty-something years earlier,
Mrs. Argent was pretty, certainly prettier than the photo albums suggested. Her figure was slim, her hair a cas-
cade of brown shoulder-length shag. She wore a plaid
blouse and bell-bottom jeans that would have stood out
on the matronly woman I knew like a tutu on an elephant. What happened to the plump gray-haired lady
who served gingerbread? Was this the Colonel's frowsy
wife? The woman before me looked like a rebel in the
ranks. It boggled the mind to think that there was a time
when the Queen of Roast Beef was cool.

They say a mother knows her child even if they were
separated at birth twenty years ago. I wasn't a mom,
but even if I didn't know it was Melissa being held in
those arms, I would know who that baby was. Just like
her mother, the old photos did not do her justice. Melissa was round-headed with perfectly smooth cheeks.
Her hands were chubby and her hair was blonde,

with fringes curling into tiny question marks. She was dressed in a pink outfit with blue trim. I wasn't good at judging children's ages – they were either big or small – but I guessed she was somewhere between six and nine months.

Mrs. Argent gently lowered her daughter into her high chair and affixed a bib dotted with little rabbits as pink as her daughter's cheeks. Melissa bounced in the chair, her body fighting against gravity and the restraining tray table. Her mother opened the fridge to reveal a sea of little baby faces on jars dominating one shelf. Out came one filled with mashed bananas. The stuff resembled something they fed prisoners on the chain gang, but Mrs. Argent waved it before Melissa as if it were Bananas Foster. She grabbed a spoon from a drawer and bent over the squirming infant.

"Here come the 'nanas," she said in a singsong voice. "Aren't they yummy?"

I don't know what Melissa would have done if her mother gave her pureed beef, but she responded enthusiastically to the bananas. She smiled and banged her hands on the tray, and when her mother fed her, she ate so eagerly that the food smeared on both cheeks and dotted her nose.

I peered closer at the chubby, ruddy little face. "Hi, Melissa," I said in a whisper. Melissa remained focused on her mother. I whispered louder. Still no reaction. At this point, I'd come to believe everything Stephon had told me, but I still had to test it. Secure in my untraceability, I studied my future wife's infant face. She was so much more alive than in her baby pictures. The photos didn't capture the true sparkle in her eyes and the color in her cheeks. There was extraordinary vibrancy in this girl. My girl.

"Here come more 'nanas." When Mrs. Argent approached with the spoon this time, Melissa grabbed at it and then flailed wildly, flicking bananas into her mother's hair. I clamped my hand over my mouth to suppress a laugh, until I remembered that no one could hear me. My very disciplined fiancée was a baby-food-throwing anarchist. Her mother seemed momentarily peeved by the episode. Then she laughed at her daughter's antics, and I laughed some more. How could anyone look at that joy and that smile and not laugh? Even when Melissa's next trick was to rub the bananas all over her tray.

I longed to interact with this pair, to make myself a part of this precious event that took place several times daily throughout Melissa's infancy. But of course I couldn't, and in fact shouldn't. Would a camera work in this strange bubble of space? I wished I'd thought to bring one. But the craziness – the sheer impossibility – of what was about to happen clouded my mind from thinking of any such practicalities while I stood in Stephon's.

Even if I didn't have a camera, though, I had my memory. I stared at Melissa and imagined my mind was a video recorder that took in everything and saved it for posterity. The curls of her blonde hair and the button nose. The big smile and unimaginably bright eyes. These images would stay with me forever. This was *such* a good idea.

The house suddenly echoed with a heavy, measured tread. Mrs. Argent grabbed a napkin and hastily wiped her daughter's face. Melissa fought the cloth as if it would bite, but her mother persisted until the little girl's face was at least marginally clean.

"We want to look neat for Daddy, don't we, honey?"

Into the kitchen marched the Colonel. Only he was Captain Argent, the twin silver bars gleaming on each shoulder of a dark green Marine uniform blazing with ribbons across the chest. Fluorescent light gleamed back on itself as it bounced off the mirrors of his black shoes. His hair was thinly carpeted by a black crew cut instead of a gray one. His face was a little less weathered, his skin a little less red, but he looked as lean and mean as the first day I met him.

Mr. Argent bent over his daughter. "How's my little trooper?" he said enthusiastically. Melissa squealed and dropped banana on his perfectly polished shoes. He looked down and frowned before smiling at his daughter. Even the drill sergeant was easily charmed by her. "We'll get you squared away one of these days, pumpkin."

Mrs. Argent grabbed a rag and mopped his shoes. "They all do that, Harold."

"I know." He patted Melissa's head, careful to avoid any food that was lodged there. "She really has spirit. She's going to be a real hellcat. If she were a boy, I'd say she was going to grow up to be a real Marine."

Mrs. Argent finished cleaning her daughter up and then took her out of the high chair. "She won't be a Marine, Harold. She will be an artist. Or perhaps the first female President."

Captain Argent chuckled. "Not in our lifetime." He glanced down at the streaked high chair tray. "Looks like she had a heck of an experience with her food."

His wife peered at it and shook her head. "She's been a bit of a handful all day. When we went in the stroller to the park, she saw that brown dog that belongs to the family at the end of the street. You know, that German

Shepherd that barks all night? It's a nasty creature, and I have never seen anyone go near it. Somehow it got loose, and when Melissa pointed at it and squealed, it ran toward us. I turned the stroller around and walked away as fast as I could, but it caught up to us and put its paws up on the side of the stroller. I thought it was going to climb on top of Melissa and maul her and I was really scared. I took off my handbag and was about to give it a good whack. But then Melissa laughed and patted its head like they were friends. And the dog just stood on its hind legs – it must have stood there a full minute. When I wheeled the stroller away, it sat on the sidewalk and stared at us until we turned the corner. I didn't know whether to laugh or scream."

"It does appear that our daughter has some talent with animals. Maybe she'll become a veterinarian."

Mrs. Argent kissed the top of Melissa's head. "She'll become whatever she wants to become."

Mr. Argent grunted. Obviously the notion of a woman having that much freedom – even his own daughter – was still difficult for him to comprehend. But I could see from the look in his eyes that he believed that anything might be possible with this little girl.

Fog began to coalesce again, this time in shades of red flecked with gold like a Christmas decoration.

"No," I shouted. "I want more time." Through the mist, I could see Melissa sprawled against her mother's shoulder as her parents left the kitchen.

〜〜
〜〜

I blinked as the fog cleared. The white fluorescent glare mellowed into bright sunshine, and the air changed from stuffy to leafy. I stood in front of the Argent house, its blue paint fresh and smooth, bright in its newness. The cracks in the sidewalk were smaller and not as deep. A pothole where I nearly sprained my knee last winter didn't even exist. I rubbed my leg and looked around.

Leaves blushed brown and red before the advancing autumn. In driveways sat escapees from a classic car show. Everyone had big Chevy station wagons or boxy Ford Pintos, and who could fail to notice the lemon-yellow Volkswagen Beetle? In front of a neighbor's lawn lay a *Washington Post* in a plastic wrapper. I glanced down at the front page. President Carter was still trying to whip inflation and the Arabs had jacked up the price of oil again.

These were the years my father always said he wished he could erase, though I was no more than a toddler then. Those had been rough times where I grew up; my father's friends still talked about the shock of mass layoffs. This neighborhood looked well-fed and content, though. I noticed an oak tree in front of the house. Last year, the Argents cut it down in a mercy killing, but now it stood strong and proud, unaware of the fate that awaited it.

Something small and red came straight at me. I jumped out of the way as the tricycle sped down the sidewalk. The little girl in the pink jacket giggled as she rumbled over the cracks.

"Watch it, kid," I muttered as I hopped back onto the sidewalk. She turned around and came at me again. Again I sidestepped. For all I knew, she could knife right through me and I would never feel it. In the movies, ghosts love it when mortals put their hands through them, but corporeal or not, that experience seemed a little unnerving.

The girl paused, puffing happily. I looked at her more closely. Why hadn't I instantly recognized Melissa? Her hair was darker now, blonde sprinkled with brown like a sheaf of half-ripened wheat. Her face was more defined, strong with determination. She looked to be about three years old.

Again she pedaled up and down the sidewalk, trying to build up as much speed as her little legs could generate. When she returned, she stopped in front of me, panting. I knelt down beside her.

"Hello, Melissa," I said. It didn't matter that she couldn't hear me. "It looks like you're having fun. I wonder if Stephon can transport a tricycle from another dimension for me so we can ride around the block together all day."

A robin flew overhead and settled in a swish of wings on a bush in front of the Argent house. Melissa stopped and stared at the bird. Its pointed head swung every which way. Then it chose a new perch, with Melissa peddling furiously after it. She chased it until it settled on a tree branch three houses down the street. Melissa stopped again, looking up and gawking in wide-eyed wonder like a first-grader seeing her first dinosaur exhibit at the Smithsonian. The bird flew across the street and Melissa pedaled after it, her eyes fixed on the sky.

"Melissa, look out!" I leaped toward her, but I couldn't stop her from riding over the curb and falling off the tricycle. The trike toppled over on its side, handlebars twisted like the antlers of a deer felled by a fatal shot. For a moment, Melissa stared at the cut on her knee, which was bleeding heavily, as if contemplating the sensation called pain. Then she started crying.

"It's okay, Melissa," I said. I knelt beside her, the wheel of the tilted tricycle still softly whirring. "I'm so sorry, sweetheart. I wish I could kiss it and make it better. But now I know why you have that little scar on your knee. I always meant to ask you where it came from."

Melissa stopped crying. She looked around for a moment.

"You heard me," I said, my heart racing.

Her gaze was directed past me, though. A big black crow had swooped down on the sidewalk. Its hard, pointed face studied us as it determined whether we were food.

Melissa's brow furrowed in concentration. She stood and pulled her tricycle back on the sidewalk. The crow stared at her and squawked. She mounted the trike and put her feet on the pedals, ready to go off on another chase. A door slammed and her mother came running.

"Baby, what happened? I heard you crying. Did you fall down?"

"I fall," Melissa said, touching her bleeding knee.

Mrs. Argent came up to her, her face a mask of concern and sympathy. "Let's go inside and look at the boo-boo. We're going to need to put something on that." She shook her head in wonder. "I would think you'd be more upset with a cut like that. Your father is right. You *are* a trooper."

I had to do it. I ran up and kissed Melissa's cheek. My lips felt nothing but a cold mist. I didn't care.

"I'll see you soon, sweetheart," I said.

The scene dissolved again.

≋

I was shrouded in orange this time, a citrus fog that dispelled into gleaming patches of maroon and yellow. The aroma of sizzling grease stung my nose. The world resolved into maroon tiles, yellow Formica tables, and white plastic chairs bolted to the floor. On the blue walls were posters of cartoon chickens clutching knives and forks in their claws as they smiled at their impending journey to a frying pan.

The Argent family sat at a table, their heads barely visible through the forest of cardboard containers and soda cups. There had been three Argents at the beginning of my journey, but now Melissa's brother Tim had joined the family. Pigtailed Melissa seemed to be about elementary school age. It was hard to match the skinny figure of the boy next to her with the Tim I knew. The last time I saw Lieutenant Argent on leave at his parents' house, those tree trunks attached to his shoulders carried a small sofa into another room. Just as with Wolfgang, I took care to stay on his good side.

Mrs. Argent carefully removed fried chicken from a bucket spattered with grease stains. As she lifted each piece, crispy crust hung loosely like cholesterol-laden snakeskin. Mr. Argent and Tim received breasts, Mrs. Argent and Melissa thighs. Then Mr. Argent distributed French fries from a carton. Again, his plate and Tim's received the largest share.

Melissa grinned at her little brother, and I knew something was going to happen. I had been a little kid myself once, and a brattier one than Melissa could ever have been, and the expression was unmistakable. Sure enough, she began the war by stuffing a french fry

violently in her mouth. Tim took up the challenge and
retaliated with two french fries dangling from his mouth
like walrus tusks. Then Melissa gobbled three, and then
Tim ate four, washed down by a gulp of soda.

Something was different here. Something about
Melissa.

Mrs. Argent eyed with distaste the grease glistening
on her fingers. Then she noticed the War of the Fried
Potatoes.

"Melissa, Timothy, cut it out," she said sternly.

Mr. Argent continued eating his food.

Melissa gave her mother a beatific smile marred only
by a missing front tooth. Tim just pouted. As soon as
Mrs. Argent turned away, Melissa stuffed a french fry
in her mouth and threw a devilish grin at her brother.

Now I knew what was different about Melissa, beyond the chicken of course. She was fooling around.
The woman I knew was scintillating and invigorating,
but her actions were always tinged with seriousness and
responsibility. I couldn't think of a single time when
Melissa did something I would describe as "girlish."
I admired that she was the most "grown up" person I
knew, but looking at beaming little Melissa, I liked what
I saw. Why didn't she retain any of this playfulness into
adulthood? Maybe I'd try to cajole her with a french fry
sometime over the weekend.

〰〰

Even before the fog faded and my eyes took in the
scene, my nose rejoiced that it was no longer under attack from the aroma of fried fat. The air smelled fresh

and clean. The forest was cloaked in yellow twilight. A blue sky shone through, bright and clear.

Life was all around me, unseen shapes crawling and leaping and flying, their identities shrouded by under-brush. Melissa wasn't here. At least not yet. The woods remained quiet, the silence broken only by an occasion-al chirp and a sporadic dripping from the branches. A moist, earthy smell mingled with the leafy scent. The ground was slightly damp. It must have rained earlier.

I wrapped my arms around my body. The air was warm and still – could I even feel cold? – but there was something about being alone in a forest that's slightly chilly and creepy. My eyes and ears strained to pene-trate the silence. If anything made you believe in ghosts, it was a silent forest, and, at this point, I was open to believing in just about anything.

I heard a crackle behind me. I turned to greet Melis-sa, but instead found a cat standing about five feet away from me, ears flat against its head, tail puffed and body coiled like a spring. Scraggly whiskers twitched like ra-dio antennae in a strong breeze as they probed the air for danger. Hard eyes glared at me, their pupils black slits set inside yellow armor.

The cat was ginger with a wide face and a white breast. On a window sill or a sofa, with its throat purr-ing, it would have been beautiful. But the creature that fired bolts of malevolence from its eyes had damp, mat-ted fur with streaks of dirt on a once-pristine belly. Its head methodically swung from side to side as it scanned the clearing where I stood.

Regardless of my being invisible and untouchable, I instinctively moved a few steps back. The cat swiv-eled its head in my direction and sniffed. A low growl came from its throat. I moved to the left. Its head moved slightly in my direction, its whiskers quivering uncertainly. A sidestep to the right, and again a pointed nose swung tentatively in my direction. It couldn't see me, but it knew something was out there.

Birds chirped. The woods dripped. I felt like a gunfighter facing the villain in a Wild West movie. Was this animal going to spring at me? What would happen if it did? Maybe it was just *people* I couldn't interact with in the past.

Then I heard feet crunching twigs. Bushes parted to reveal two girls in tan Girl Scout uniforms emerging into the clearing.

"I think he's cute," Melissa said. Her voice was almost the one I knew, just a little higher pitched. She was almost fully grown, her hair raven-black and shoulder-length. The girl next to her was stockier, with straight brown hair and pudgy legs. She looked vaguely familiar.

"I think Jimmy is a total jerk," the second girl said. It had to be a young Kate Jordan. I'd recognize that cynicism anywhere.

Melissa suddenly stopped and stared through me. "There's a kitty over there," she said in a whisper. I glanced back at the cat. It looked ready to attack or bolt at the intruders in its space. A feral cat would have run away by now, but some residual memory or curiosity about humans made this cat stay, even if it looked ready to claw all of us to death.

As Melissa stepped forward, Kate took a step back. "Mangy-looking thing," she said in a loud voice surprisingly deep. "Wonder how he got out here?"

"I'll bet some campers brought him and he got lost. He could have been out here for months." Melissa knelt and extended her hands. "Psst, psst. Come here, boy. I won't hurt you."

"I don't know about this, Melissa." Kate was a mirror-image of the cat, knees slightly bent, head craning forward. "That thing looks pretty wild. He might have rabies. Maybe we should tell one of the forest rangers."

"By the time we get a ranger, he'll be gone. Besides, he looks scared to me, not dangerous." Her voice had that tone of compassion I knew so well. There were times when I criticized her for giving money to a homeless man who would only use it to buy a pint. Yet as I watched Melissa patiently extend her hand to a frightened, tired animal, I felt a thrill of pride.

"He's probably cold and hungry. His fur is all wet." Melissa moved slowly forward. "Psst, psst. Come here, kitty."

The cat bared long, sharp teeth and its eyes tracked the movement of Melissa's hand.

"He'll bite you," Kate said, picking up a long stick.

"Don't worry."

"If he jumps at you, I'm gonna whack him." Kate thwacked the stick in her palm and glared at the feline. For a girl who couldn't have been more than twelve, she had an intimidating stare. The cat spared her a contemptuous glance, then returned its eyes to Melissa.

"Take it easy, Kate. I think he's more scared of us than *you* are of him. I'll bet he hasn't seen any humans in a while. He looks like he hasn't eaten much, either."

The cat tensed until its leg muscles looked like they were about to pop out of its skin. Why didn't it run? "Get out of here, you stupid pest," I said sharply. The animal's whiskers twitched.

Melissa showed her open palms to the cat as if she were its prisoner. Then she slowly reached into her pocket. "I think I have some of those cheese crackers. I'll bet he's hungry enough to eat it." She pulled out a packet, opened a wrapper, and extracted a double-cracker with an unnatural orange filling. Melissa carefully slid one cracker off another, leaving cheese piled on top of the bottom cracker like paste stuck to a floor tile.

The cat rose slightly off its rear legs. Melissa was right – it definitely once belonged to someone. It was a big cat. Or it had been, judging by the folds of skin hanging loosely from its side. This was an animal that did not enjoy missing its meals.

Melissa advanced slowly. The cat hissed.

"It's okay, kitty. Come on. I'll give you some nice cheese. Then I'll take you home and give you some milk."

"Rabies, Melissa, rabies," Kate said darkly. "Do you know how they cure you? I'm talking needles the size of telephone poles."

"Psst, psst. He doesn't have rabies, Kate. He's not foaming at the mouth and he's not acting crazy. It's no wonder he's nervous. Look how hungry and dirty he is."

The cat's jaws opened wide and I thought I saw wetness around its lips.

"No! Don't do it, Melissa." I ran between her and the cat and spread my arms. She walked right through me.

"Come on, Kitty. Come with me out of the rain. I'll take care of you." The cat retreated a few steps. It limped on its right rear paw. "You've hurt your leg. Come here; I'll take you to a vet."

Kate grasped the stick grimly. "If it's injured, Melissa, it will attack you. If it does, move away as quickly as you can. I'll knock its lights out."

The cat mewed once, twice, in a cry of pain and despair. Then it inched forward as Melissa did the same. Melissa stuck out a finger. The cat sniffed it, then rolled on its side as Melissa reached out for its belly.

I braced for the scream of pain. How could she be stupid enough to rub a feral cat's belly in the middle of the woods? "Be careful, sweetie," I said with a cringe as I waited for a snarl and bite.

The cat rubbed its head against Melissa's hand and then turned its attention to the cheese.

"I don't believe it," Kate said, sounding disappointed that she wouldn't get to use her stick. She dropped it to the ground. "I thought he was going to bite you. How did you do that?"

"You just have to know how to deal with animals. Besides, it's a living creature. If we saw a person limping, we would help him without thinking, right?"

Kate shrugged, though Melissa didn't see this since she was still focused on the cat.

"Don't worry, kitty," she said. "You're coming home with me."

"You can't take him home. How are you going to convince your parents to let you keep him? You told me your dad hates cats. They drive your dog crazy."

Melissa grinned as she tickled the cat under his chin. "Don't worry. I'll convince them." She studied the cat. "What am I going to call you? I think I'll call you Ginger."

The fog that enveloped me was bright yellow...

≈

...and then it was as blue as the Caribbean at high noon. Now my world was bounded by tall curtains and a scuffed hardwood floor. I was in the wings of a stage, and when I stepped out into the center, I saw kids buzzing and chattering as they filled the rows of the auditorium. Through the open doors of the hall came glimpses of a corridor crisscrossed by rushing students bent under the weight of book bags. A buzzer announced that the next period had begun. A teacher closed the auditorium doors with a final thud. Above the doors hung a huge crimson banner inscribed with gold letters proclaiming PATRICK HENRY JUNIOR HIGH SCHOOL.

Over the roar of a student body in motion came heavy, precise footsteps. Slowly they climbed the stairs on the side of the stage, the footfalls themselves broadcasting a message of pure authority. I instinctively assumed a slumped teenage posture. Finally emerging from the stairs was a short, pudgy man with dark hair not his natural color. His jacket was gray, his pants were gray and his tie was laced with blue and black stripes. His mouth was deliberately expressionless. PRINCIPAL was metaphorically stamped over his broad forehead.

The principal slowly approached the podium. A teacher waved a boy in a Clash T-shirt to sit down. Off the walls echoed a wrenching sound as the principal lowered the microphone to his height. He gazed at the chattering students with a deep frown, and then cleared his throat. The chattering continued. He coughed into the microphone, while the teachers in the aisles strove to shush their unruly charges. Then a hulking, bald gym teacher pointed a thick finger at a skinny boy who'd just fired a rubber band at a spectacled girl in the next row.

I recognized Melissa in the front, sitting beside Kate. She hadn't changed much since the forest, except for a small pimple on her nose that must have had her rubbing acne cream on it every morning. Kate had definitely changed. She was slimmer now, her face evolving into the countenance of the pretty lawyer who would introduce me to the woman of my life. She whispered something in Melissa's ear that put a smile on her face.

The principal removed his glasses and polished them with exaggerated patience until they gleamed under the lights. It was a corny trick to establish control, but the kids began to quiet down until there were just a few whispers among the boys in the back row. All of them wore black T-shirts. Yes, the back row. Just like in my school, the future gas pump boys and penitentiary graduates sat together, drawing strength from each other's anger at the system that would spit them out.

The principal leaned over the microphone. "You may not believe this," he said. His voice was deep. Magnified by the microphone, it sounded omnipotent. He waited until all the noise finally died. "You may not believe this, but being the principal of a junior high school can be a tough job." Only the teachers chuckled, presumably remembering the words for their next contract talks. The principal smiled and shook his head, acknowledging the hard truth behind his own joke. "But sometimes my job involves more than sending students to detention. Being principal has some rewards, especially when I can bring you good news. Today I have the pleasure of introducing Melissa Argent, the new eighth-grade class president."

He looked down and smiled mischievously at a squirming Melissa. "I could torture poor Melissa by describing just how much of an outstanding member of our school she has been, but I know students hate it when I make long speeches about them. So I will just confine my remarks to saying that Melissa's accomplishments speak for themselves. She is vice-president of the Junior Honor Society, captain of the girl's volleyball team, a member of the school orchestra, and editor of the yearbook. And somehow she finds time to be co-chairperson of the Environmental Committee. I get tired just looking at her. Melissa, come on up."

Kate and the other girls in the front row cheered and waved. Most of the students dutifully applauded. The boys in the back rows booed and hissed. A gray-haired teacher pointed her finger at a boy with a red bandana around his neck. She gestured for him to stand up and whispered something in his ear. He grinned at his friends as he strutted behind her into the hall.

Melissa strode to the podium, dignified and regal in a white sweater and plain blue skirt. She shook hands with the principal, who gave an exaggerated bow as he gestured to the microphone. He patted her shoulder as Melissa placed a sheet of paper on the podium and looked out into the crowd. A gaggle of girls giggled in the second row, then abruptly fell silent at Kate's withering glare.

Melissa cleared her throat. "Thank you for that kind introduction, Principal Andrews." A few more boos from the back, and another delinquent-in-training was escorted outside. Melissa was unfazed. "And thank you, classmates and friends. Thank you for voting me to be your class president. Everyone says that today's young people don't care about anything except themselves. I get mad when I hear this. We all know that we face a world with many challenges, from drug abuse to pollution. I wish it was in our power to change everything that is wrong. But even if we do not have that power, this is not an excuse to do nothing. I tell you that we can do our part to make the world a better place. All of us together can accomplish great things. We can help clean up the environment so that when we become adults, we will inherit a better tomorrow. We can help our peers resist drugs so that they have the chance to grow up to become adults. I ask all of you to join me.

"I know that class presidents have been making speeches of this sort forever. And you know what else I know? Statements like these are usually a lot of garbage."

The principal's eyebrows raised and even the boys in the back began to pay attention.

"But there's something to be said for truly caring. For making a commitment and sticking to it. For having the strength of character to decide what you think is important and then going out and making it happen no matter how hard or crazy or unpopular it might seem. That's the real job for our generation and together I know that we can do it. It won't be easy, but if it's going to happen, it needs to start in this school. And I promise that I will do my best to make it happen with you."

Melissa bowed her head and the audience clapped appreciatively. It wasn't easy to stir a room full of adolescents. I, of course, was overwhelmed, as blown away by this as by any impassioned speech I ever heard my fiancée deliver. Melissa could rally nonbelievers. I knew this from personal experience.

Principal Skinner shook Melissa's hand vigorously. Then he took the microphone. "Thank you for that magnificent speech, Melissa. I think all of us can agree with those stirring words. They were a strong reminder that we can make a difference. Thank you again, Melissa. Assembly dismissed."

At the students filed out, Principal Skinner patted Melissa's shoulder and smiled. "That really was a wonderful speech. I have seen class presidents come and go for fifteen years, and most of them deliver some trite speech that no one cares about. But you spoke from the heart, young lady. I rarely see these students get fired up about anything, but you got them going a little today. I'll have to call President Reagan and tell him he had better watch out for his job."

Melissa stared at her feet as she always did when she was embarrassed. "No, I don't think I want to be a politician," she said shyly. "I'm actually thinking of becoming an environmentalist. Or maybe a musician."

"I am certain you will succeed at whatever you put your mind to."

"Thank you, sir. I meant what I said. I will do my best."

"Your best is going to be great, Melissa. I know it. Believe me, I also meant what I said. It's a treat to have a student like you. Now, you had better get on to your next class or I'll have to send you to detention."

He smiled and patted her shoulder again and left the stage. The door squeaked as he left the auditorium.

Melissa picked up her speech from the podium. She paused, looking out at the empty hall. Then she smiled proudly.

I simply applauded as she headed off for class.

≋

The walls were pink. So were the curtains and the furniture. Everything was pink except for the purple bed sheets. This was Melissa's old bedroom, which I recognized from some of the photos. Now it was the Colonel's den, painted and paneled over. The last time I saw it, it was decorated with a moose head and a captured Viet Cong AK-47.

Melissa lay on her bed with her neck on a fluffy pillow, flanked on one side by a fuzzy white lamb – maybe even the same one from her toddler picture – and on the other by a pink elephant. She held a pink princess phone in her hand – I'd never seen so much pink in one place before, and *certainly* never saw Melissa around anywhere near this much – and leaned her mouth against the receiver in the way that people do when they share a confidence.

"Don't tell anybody this," she said in a whisper, "but I think Tommy really might be the cutest guy in the entire freshman class."

A teenage girl's private conversation? I shouldn't be listening to this. But Stephon told me that my heart would avoid what it wasn't meant to witness. Besides, I had absolutely no idea how to exit a scene. I stood at the head of Melissa's bed and watched her face light up. She giggled. Gossip and giggling – my Melissa never did those things.

Melissa rolled from her back onto her stomach in a graceful motion. Her legs – and they were long by now – kicked up, the feet weaving short steps in the air like a duck waddling.

"No, Heidi, Greg is not cute. His ears are huge and his eyebrows meet in the middle."

She was talking to Heidi? About boys? Heidi called Melissa every few months now to complain about her latest disastrous relationship. She lived in San Diego, fleeing from the wreckage of her third marriage. If Heidi was advising her about romance, there was little wonder why I was Melissa's first serious boyfriend.

Metal flashed silver against pink. My eyes automatically locked onto the source. So these were the legendary braces. My fiancée had perfect teeth, but obviously she needed some external help – help that she was still self-conscious about today – to get there. She looked cute to me. I definitely would have asked her out if I was a boy in her school, even if I wasn't *the cutest guy in the entire freshman class* like Tommy.

Melissa put her lips against the receiver until she seemed to kiss it. "This is really secret, but Tommy asked me out yesterday. What? In the lunch room. He asked if I wanted to get some pizza or something with him."

My heartbeat soared. I'd always been a little jealous of the men in Melissa's past, even though I knew none of them took the place in her heart that I did.

"Of course I said no, silly." My heartbeat dropped below Mach I. "I don't know. Maybe I'll make him try a little harder. I don't want him to think I'm too easy. He should ask me two or three times." Her grin would have chilled any teenage boy. Then I laughed myself. Maybe she wasn't being kind to poor Tommy, but it was nice to see that she played hard to get. I didn't remember her playing hard to get with me.

Melissa's voice dropped to a whisper.

"She what? She offered you a joint? You didn't smoke it, did you? Good thinking. You really can't afford to get involved with that stuff."

This had to be a different Heidi. The one I knew spent three months in rehab after the breakdown of marriage number two. Melissa was right, of course; Heidi couldn't afford to get involved with that stuff, but I guessed it wasn't very long before she started doing exactly that.

Melissa's voice dropped lower still until I could barely hear her from two feet away. "No, I would never take a hit. Do you know what my father would do if he found out that I took drugs? He has a plan to win the war on drugs, and it involves nuclear weapons. Besides, I don't want to mess up my mind. Yeah, I know. That Matt Pizimot – he's a pothead. In gym class yesterday, the boys were playing basketball, and he just sat on the bleachers against the wall with a big smile on his face. He looked like such a doof."

Melissa turned her head, and noticed that her lamb was lying askew on her pillow. Her left hand reached out and straightened it until the lamb's head lay snugly in the center of the pillow.

"Ron offered you a beer? Don't tell anyone, but the Honor Society got together after school and we all shared a six-pack. Everybody thinks we're nerds, but see, we have some fun. No, Heidi, we really, truly aren't nerds, thank you very much." She sat up on her bed and glanced at the wall clock. "Anyway, I have to finish my homework soon. So, how long do you think I should keep Tommy waiting?"

A century will be fine, Melissa.

"Yeah, that's a good idea. If he really wants to go out with me, he has to sweat a little bit. He really is cute, though. I know Teri has her eyes on him. I can see it. After Tommy walked away at lunch, she gave me a look.

"Say that again? *That's* the kind of guy you like? No, thank you. Big muscles and a tattoo are okay, I guess, but that's hardly the man of my dreams. The man I marry will be good-looking and smart, and he'll really like me."

The jury was out on the good-looking and smart part, but I definitely really liked her. More and more every second.

〰〰

This time the fog was so deeply dark that it swallowed all light. I found myself in a hallway of dingy gray floor tiles and apple-green walls. The dismal colors combined with the odors of sweat, ozone and floor polish to reveal I was in a school. I looked around and saw a glass case filled with trophies and footballs and basketballs. The jocks at Thomas Jefferson High School had done well the past few years.

Two tall boys ambled down the hall in shorts and basketball jerseys. Once their footsteps faded, everything was strangely quiet, except for a faint murmur of voices from the other end of the building. Strange how I remembered high school as a noisy place, even after school. Now, echoes traveled down long corridors.

This hallway was lined with doors to classrooms. Some were lit and some were dark. I peered through a rectangular glass pane into a door. The room was dotted with black tables with little spigots rising out of them like sunflowers. A large chart on the back wall displayed the periodic table. Memories of chemistry class flooded my mind in a shower of *Hg*, *Au*, and *Cl* symbols. I shuddered – history and English were my favorites. Chemistry was just plain painful to me.

I noticed a clock on the wall. It was just past five, and most of the teachers and students were gone. A door opened down the corridor, and a green-uniformed janitor emerged pushing a wheeled bucket and mop. He was white-haired and stocky, with an anchor tattooed on his left forearm. He whistled tunelessly as he slowly pushed the bucket in that unhurried, timeless way of school custodians. I waited until he passed, then listened for a clue to where Melissa was.

A melody floated through the air, soft and incongruous in the impersonal, institutional atmosphere. I could not identify the piece, but whoever was playing that piano was blessed with a deft touch. A sudden suspicion led me to track the source of the sound. It came from behind a green door marked MUSIC ROOM. I bent down and peeked through the narrow window in the door, with a terrible feeling that the principal was going to see me and make me stay after school for a week. However, the window was covered with brown wrapping paper, no doubt to keep smart alecks from harassing music classes. *Not that I ever did anything like that*, I thought with a grin.

The piano tinkled again with a few random notes. I put my hand on the doorknob. It felt cold and vaporous. How do you open a door if you are not really there? Was I supposed to just walk through it?

The door abruptly opened, and out came Melissa. For the first time, I saw the woman I was going to marry. She was nearly fully grown now, with midnight-black hair trailing down to her waist. Her figure was slender and curvy under a red sweater. A red sweater? First pink and now this. Almost all of Melissa's sweaters were black or white. I always imagined her in high school with her collection of black sweaters growing, filling her closet month by month, year by year, until she'd personally depleted the world's supply of black wool.

Melissa drank from a water fountain and returned to the music room. I quickly slipped in before she closed the door. Folding chairs crammed the room along with music stands. Melissa sat at an upright piano and absently ran her fingers over the keys, stroking them like a favored pet. Then her fingers seemed to pluck at the keys at random, as if searching for a lost object that lay tantalizingly close. For the first time, I noticed how lithe Melissa's fingers were, long and supple like cat's whiskers. Why had I never noticed them like that before? It shouldn't take time travel for a man to notice the little things.

Melissa's fingers suddenly hovered over the keyboard, ready to pounce. She stared at a piece of sheet music for a few seconds. Then her face composed into a mask of pure concentration. Her back rose fully erect as she plunged her hands into the keyboard.

Rock-and-roll was my speed, not classical. I wouldn't know Brahms from Beethoven. But I knew Melissa's playing was special. Her sounds were transporting. They were stars in a ballet where the dancers were notes that floated like angels.

It's not the instrument that makes music beautiful – it's the musician. Revelation blossomed inside me as I watched Melissa merge with the music. She swayed to it as if the every note was an ocean wave. The concentration on her face evaporated, replaced by a look of contentment that could only come to someone who is truly expressing herself. I'd been surprised several times on this journey through Melissa's past, but nothing was more surprising than this. Even to my untrained ear, it was abundantly clear that Melissa was a truly skilled pianist. How could she ever give it up? How could she *never* have mentioned it?

I barely heard the door open. I turned to see a woman step into the room. Her thin, bony body was draped in a gray jacket as severe as her face. She paused to stare at the young woman playing so magnificently. As Melissa swayed again to a high-soaring note, the woman's tongue arced over her upper lip.

Melissa stopped and rested her head against the piano. Perspiration glinted on her forehead. She looked up and caught sight of the woman.

"Miss Hoffman," she said, flushing slightly.

Miss Hoffman marched to the piano with precise, high-heeled steps.

"Mr. Evans obviously knew what he was talking about when he called you his star pupil," the woman said. She put her hands on her hips. "I have trained many students and I can tell you that, for a mere girl of fourteen, you have great talent. If you cultivate it, it will take you far. Unfortunately, the taxpayers of your town do not allow your school sufficient funds to pay for my services on more than a part-time basis. I suspect that is why Mr. Evans left. Perhaps you should ask your parents about private lessons."

Melissa smiled shyly. "Would you take me on? We've only had two sessions so far, but I feel like I have learned a lot from you already."

Miss Hoffman nodded curtly at the compliment, as if it were too obvious to be mentioned. "You have the gleam in your eye, Melissa. I can see the music burns in your blood. So many of my pupils view the piano as a form of torture devised by their parents. It is a pleasure to meet a girl with a genuine love. Again, I must warn you that if you wish to cultivate your talent, you must devote the proper amount of time for study and practice. We must spend a *great deal* of time together."

Miss Hoffman was an odd bird. Anyone who bumped into her would probably turn to ice. Still, Melissa looked at her teacher with eager eyes. "I haven't told anyone yet, Miss Hoffman. But I've decided that I want to be a concert pianist. You're right. My parents made me take piano, and for a while it seemed like a chore. But now I feel like music is my life."

My invisible jaw dropped. Melissa never told me she'd planned to be a musician. Her mother's mention of it when she brought out those recently rediscovered photos was the first in my presence.

Miss Hoffman nodded understandingly. "Play for me as you played when I entered."

Sound again caressed my ears. Miss Hoffman closed her eyes and listened to the music, enraptured. When Melissa finished, the instructor wiped her glasses and flexed her fingers. Those digits were narrower than they should have been, curving slightly and tapering at the tips where sharp, scarlet nails gleamed. She looked her student up and down, appraising her more carefully than it seemed necessary. I didn't like anyone looking at Melissa that way.

"To play an instrument, you must be comfortable with it, yes? You are much, much too stiff. Here, let me help you."

She walked behind Melissa and rubbed her shoulders. Melissa closed her eyes and sagged against her teacher. "Wow, that feels really good. You have very strong fingers, Miss Hoffman." After a minute, Melissa sighed. "That's fine. I'm feeling relaxed now."

Her teacher kept one hand on her left shoulder and used her other hand to rub the center of Melissa's back. Melissa tensed as a flicker of concern crossed her face.

"I said I'm feeling more relaxed, Miss Hoffman," Melissa said, though it was obvious she was feeling anything but relaxed. Her teacher's face reddened. Her lips were pursed as if she were whistling. But no whistle came, just rapid gasps from her thin, heaving chest.

Melissa suddenly rose from the piano bench, and as she did her teacher shoved her against the wall.

"What are you doing?" Melissa said, sounding desperate.

"Hush, my darling. Listen to the music."

I grabbed at Miss Hoffman's neck, but my hand passed through cold vapor. *Damn you, Stephon.*

"No," Melissa said, her voice pitched, her face frantic. Everything happened so quickly. Miss Hoffman was in a frenzy, her face twisted and hands probing under Melissa's clothing. The teacher's own dress rode up her legs as she pressed herself and writhed insistently against Melissa's body, seeking out her perverted form of pleasure.

There was nothing I could do. I swear I tried to stop it. I yelled and cursed but no one heard. I vowed to dismember the woman piece by piece, but these thoughts did nothing to deter her. All I could do was pound the wall with an invisible fist and swallow the bile in my throat.

It was like watching Jekyll and Hyde. When the monster finished, heaving as she clawed at Melissa's most private places and pistoned against her, she straightened her dress and refastened the loose strands of her hair. Her face lost its flush and solidified into the stern visage of the severe piano teacher – all except for a faint smirk.

"That was very nice, Melissa. As I said, you have wonderful potential that needs only be developed. I will assist you in that process from time to time." The monster walked to the door and paused. "I suggest that you tell no one about our lesson today," she said without turning around. "They would not believe you. And you would not want me to be angry with my most promising student."

Melissa sat with her back against the wall. Behind the disheveled black hair shrouding her face, her mouth opened and closed in great gasps of breath as her eyes stared into space. She tried to rearrange her skirt, but her fingers wouldn't work properly. At last, she simply locked her hands around her legs and buried her face in her knees.

I knelt beside her and put my hand on her shoulder. I grasped cold nothingness, but I still squeezed as hard I could, as if I could bend the fabric of the universe into a bandage for her pain.

"I know you can't hear, Melissa, but I'm going to make this all right. You'll see. I'm going to make this all right." I kissed her cheek. Her head moved and her eyes looked straight into mine. Their deep blue was moist and dazed. Then she looked back at the door and sobbed.

Darkness spread merciful wings over the horrible scene, then dawned into the sparkle of gleaming metal. The next thing I could see clearly was Stephon standing behind his jewelry counter.

I let out a scream of anguish. I never felt more frustrated in my life. "Did you know?" I said, my voice a barely restrained growl. "Did you know about this?"

Stephon seemed a little intimidated by my ferocity. At that very moment, I didn't care. "I never know how these things are going to turn out," he said. "Did you see something disturbing?"

"I just saw my fiancée molested by a disgusting deviant. That's more than *something disturbing*."

He looked down at the counter. "I'm very sorry, Mr. Timian. As I warned you, these sojourns sometimes reveal unpleasant aspects of a loved one's past. I only hope that now you have more insight into why your fiancée is the person that she is. This knowledge can only strengthen your relationship."

"Strengthen our relationship? Do you think I can just live with this knowledge as if nothing happened?" I moved toward the counter and leaned against it. Stephon seemed a little taken aback that I was confronting him this way. "Stephon, I need to ask you something, and I desperately need for your answer to be yes."

He regained his composure. "As I told you before your journey, I will try to answer any questions you might have. But you don't even need to ask this one. The answer, I'm afraid, is no. I do not believe that it is possible for you to travel to the past to undo whatever terrible event you saw."

"You *don't believe*? What the hell does that mean? Can I or can't I?"

"I told you that what you ask is impossible." There was uncertainty in his eyes that made it obvious he wasn't telling the truth.

"You're a better magician than you are a liar."

Stephon seemed worried and more than a little confounded. "There was one occasion many years ago when I found a way to send someone back for a reason like this."

"Then do it again."

"You might think you want me to, but you really don't."

"Why, what happened?"

"I can't tell you. I guard his privacy as jealously as I will guard yours. But you are thinking about entering virtually uncharted waters, Mr. Timian. Think of time as a tapestry woven by the most skilled weaver imaginable. Its threads are so tightly bound that to undo one of them is to undo the whole tapestry. You wish to go back in time and change one event, but you cannot be sure of the outcome. Perhaps Melissa's life will be for the better, however you define what better is. Or it may be worse. Because Melissa has touched your life, your life may improve or it may become worse. A gambler would hesitate to take such chances, if he were clever. So perhaps it would be better for you and your future bride to continue on as before."

"Stephon, I saw something terrible happen to the most important person in my world. I would do anything to erase it. I would take any chance. Do you understand me?"

He looked at me carefully and for a moment I thought he was through talking to me.

"I understand how important this is to you. I strongly believe it would be a terrible, terrible mistake, but if you really want this, I will help you. But with one condition. You must go home tonight and tell your fiancée what you discovered and what you plan to do. Because it is her life that you wish to tamper with, you must obtain her consent. Then, if you still wish to embark upon this journey, return here tomorrow at noon."

"I'll be here. Trust me, I'll be here."

Chapter 7

From a Fading Sun

I made my way home in a daze. I couldn't go back to work, I couldn't walk around the city, I could barely drive. What Stephon showed me – and there was absolutely no doubt in my mind that what I saw had actually happened – so completely tore at me, so completely *changed* me, that I was incapable of functioning beyond the basest possible level.

My Melissa, the woman I adored more than any person I'd ever known, the woman who mattered to me more than anything in the world, had been carrying a traumatic burden her entire adult life. Did she think about it every day? Had she so completely sublimated it that she didn't think about it at all – only carried the weight of it? I felt horrible for her. I ached as though the ordeal was my own, while at the same time I realized that there was no possible way I could understand how terrible it was for her.

I should have known. I should have been able to see from the way Melissa carried herself that something deep inside of her was hurting. If I was really paying attention, I *would* have known. There were fundamental things about Melissa – her seriousness, her awkwardness around strangers in small crowds, her need to always make things right – that should have told me she had been marked by a darkness I couldn't otherwise see. When we made love in the early days of our relationship, there was a tentativeness to it that I perceived as Melissa's holding back, waiting for our love to deepen. Now it was impossible not to think of it some other way – that the very act caused at least a little bit of the darkness to return. If I really loved her as much as I said I did, I could have asked the right questions, allowed her to trust me enough to reveal this to me and in so doing maybe allow her to unburden herself.

But I didn't allow her to trust me enough. What did that say about us?

My little fantasy was meant to be a pure act of whimsy, a tiny pleasure cruise. I thought – though admittedly I obviously didn't consider all the ramifications – that maybe I'd find the source of some quirk of hers, some little thing she did now that she'd started doing when she was three and I'd chuckle about it to myself long into our marriage. However, if I'd found those things on my journey, I didn't remember them now. Nothing came from my trip to Melissa's past other than one, horrible, burning image.

Something I would absolutely never forget. Still, it couldn't come close to approximating the effect this event must have had on Melissa. I had to do something about that. I simply had to.

The light through the balcony window darkened with my mood. They say music soothes a troubled soul, so I rose and walked over to my iPod dock. I scrolled through some of my favorite bands, like Phish and the Dave Matthews Band. I realized, though, that crashing drums and wildly improvising musicians were the last things I needed right now. I went to the stereo cabinet and found a compilation of classical music still in its shrink wrap. I popped the CD into the player and watched the display flicker. Piano and violin flowed into the room, majestic and unruffled.

I sat back down and contemplated the ceiling, wondering what was tugging at my consciousness. Something *else* I should know. I finally realized that all of the music in this apartment was all mine. I had never seen Melissa buy music. I had never seen her play music. If I played it, she seemed to enjoy it. If I asked her to dance to it, she danced, and with a grace that I lacked. However, she'd never put on a song of her own volition. When she listened to the radio, it was always the news shows on National Public Radio. This made sense, of course. She was an environmental activist and she listened to the news like all the news junkies in Washington. But never once did she flip on the radio while we were driving and say, "I *love* this song." Never once did she put on a piano concerto and sit back enraptured the way she had that afternoon in the music room.

Of course not. Music was one of the many things that had been stolen from her that day.

Glass glinted from the wall opposite the balcony as the rays of the dying sun reflected off the casing of the photo montage on the wall. Melissa's mother had put it together from our photos and hers. There we were swimming in a Maine lake, frolicking like porpoises in the clear water nestled deep in the woods. There we were lying on a Bermuda beach, Melissa looking spectacular in her bikini and me with a face as red as the lobster I ate every night. In the center of the montage was my favorite picture. Kate Jordan snapped it soon after Melissa moved in here. It showed Melissa and me sitting on the sofa, my arm draped over her shoulder as Wizard lay contentedly in her lap.

As I stared at the photo, Melissa's eyes twinkled like tiny orange stars. But the light was not hers. The light that made them shine came from a fading sun.

The Melissa I knew was not the Melissa I saw on my journey to her past. The Melissa I would marry had the same passion and fire that her younger self had, but her inner light was gone, that special zest for living that made young Melissa such an extraordinary girl. A medical doctor could not restore it, nor could a psychologist. Not even a loving husband.

But I *could* do something. I could restore Melissa's inner light. She would continue to study piano, and develop her talent until she became expert. She would become a great pianist, her life a celebration of happiness and success contributing more to the world by far than she could ever contribute as an activist. She would find her destiny in Carnegie Hall, not Capitol Hill, and her influence would range across nations.

I could do that and I would. None of Stephon's caveats would stop me.

A key clicked in our lock and the door opened. I wasn't sure I was entirely ready for this moment. Melissa stood in the doorway clutching her briefcase. She looked puzzled for a second and then smiled.

"I didn't know you were going to be home early."

I didn't even attempt a smile. I was glad her eyes were invisible in the gathering dusk.

"I had some things to take care of."

"I know what you mean. I can't wait until all this planning is over and we can relax. Meanwhile, I'll be glad to get away from work. I had another briefing paper to finish before I left. It's amazing I was able to leave before midnight." She walked into the kitchen. "You didn't start anything for dinner?"

"I've been a little preoccupied."

"Do you want to order takeout tonight?"

I didn't get up from the couch. "Melissa, do you think you could come in here for a few minutes. There's something I want to talk to you about."

I'm sure the tone in my voice suggested something dire. A look of concern crossed her face as she sat on the sofa.

"Is everything okay?" She glanced at the stereo. "Where'd this music come from?"

I reached for the remote and shut the CD player off. The room was still for several long moments.

Melissa offered a nervous smile. "What's going on? You look way too serious. Did something happen?"

"Melissa, I know what happened to you."

She seemed very confused. "What are you talking about?"

"What happened to you years ago."

Her smile faded to bewilderment. "I'm really not following you."

"I know about the horrible thing that happened to you when you were a teenager."

Her expression relaxed a little. "This is about those pictures, right? You've drawn some ridiculous conclusion from the fact that I didn't want you to see what I looked like in high school."

"Not that. Melissa, you know what I'm talking about. You could have told me. You *should* have told me."

"Told you what? Ken, if you're going to talk in riddles, I'm not playing this game."

"I know about Miss Hoffman."

I braced for tears. For anger. I tensed my muscles to grab her if she fainted. Instead, Melissa gave me a look of incomprehension.

"Hoffman? I don't know any Hoffman?" She thought a moment. "Isn't that the name of the woman at the catering place? What does she have to do with anything?"

"I mean Miss Hoffman, your piano teacher."

Her expression remained puzzled. Then her face fell, imploding like a condemned building. She buried her face in her hands, and for a long time she didn't make any sound at all. It was almost as though she was trying to hide from me, hoping that when she finally lowered her hands, I would be gone and the world would be as it had been five minutes ago.

"Melissa, please," I said finally to break the silence.

"How could you know?" She spoke into her hands. Her voice was a deep whisper from her chest. Finally she looked at me again.

"I know."

"You *can't* know. No one knows."

"I know. How I know isn't important."

Anger flashed from her eyes. "Really? You uncover the ugliest, deepest secret from my past and you think it isn't important to me how you found out?"

"That's not what I meant. It's just that I'm not sure you would believe me if I told you."

"Let me guess," she said sharply, "a genie came along and offered you three wishes and you said, 'Tell me the most disgusting thing about my future wife.'"

I was feeling very uneasy, both because of Melissa's reaction and the fact that she wasn't all that far from the truth – though I *never* wanted to see anything like this. "It wasn't exactly a genie," I said, though it sounded ridiculous even to me.

Melissa leaped off the couch and paced across the room. "It wasn't *exactly* a genie? What the hell are you talking about?"

"Stephon performed a little…magic trick. I told him I wanted to see what you were like growing up. I saw a lot of things, all of which were wonderful. Until this."

She stopped pacing. "Stephon? The jeweler?"

I nodded.

"Magic trick?" she said, her voice wavering.

I nodded again.

She approached me with tiny steps. Her expression was unbelievably sad. I reached out to hug her. I wanted to hold her as long as I could. As long as she would let me.

Instead of coming into my arms, though, she slapped my face. I was stunned and my cheek stung.

"I didn't give you permission to spy on my past, Ken," she said bitterly. "It was none of your business. It was no one's business. Why did you have to pry into my life?"

I prepared for her to hit me again, but instead, she crumpled onto the couch and then buried her face in my chest, sobbing. I pulled her into my embrace and kissed her hair softly, allowing her to cry until she felt she could raise her head. She cried for a very long time.

"Tell me the truth, Ken. Did this 'magic trick' really happen? Or did you hear me talking in my sleep? I haven't had the nightmares for years, but maybe they're back."

"It really did happen. I never would have known about this any other way. And I *never* would have pried into your past. I just wanted to see if you were really as gorgeous with braces as I imagined you were."

She tried to smile, but it was a strained, painful-looking attempt. I reached out to touch her face and she took my hand and held it to her chest.

"I'm sorry I hit you," she said softly.

"It's okay."

"It's not okay. None of this is okay. I didn't want anyone else to know. Ever."

"You could have told me. I love you. There isn't anything you can't tell me."

"Not this. It was a long time ago. I buried it. Buried it so deep, I thought. So, so deep. After a while, the nightmares went away. It's amazing how you can forget something if you try."

"But you didn't forget."

She stared at me blankly for a moment, then lowered her face again. "No, I didn't forget."

"So what happened after that day?"

"I went home and told my parents I didn't want to study piano anymore. I told them the lessons were interfering with my school work, and that I wouldn't be able to get straight A's unless I gave up music. My father was about to leave for Okinawa and my mother was busy with Tim. My super-Marine brother had a couple

of scrapes with the law when he was a kid. But you'll
never hear about that from my family."

"You played so beautifully."

She looked at me with a mix of revulsion and sorrow.
"It didn't matter."

"You should have told someone. Why didn't you tell
the police?"

Her mouth twisted into something – someone – that I
had never seen before. Words spat out like poison darts.
"And let my parents find out? Tell my father the colonel? My mother the perfect homemaker? These things
don't happen to *nice girls*, you know. This couldn't happen to their perfect Melissa. They didn't want to hear
things like that. They would have blamed it on me."

"They wouldn't have. They were so proud of you.
They *are* so proud of you."

Melissa wiped her eyes. "Which is why I never wanted them to know about this." She offered me a look that
approached panic. "Ken, you can never mention this to
them. Never."

I shook my head in assent. "Of course not."

She sat back against the couch, her head tilted toward the ceiling. "Maybe I wasn't a nice girl. Maybe
I encouraged that woman somehow. Maybe I was pro-
vocative to her in some way."

"Melissa, I was there. I saw it happen. You did nothing wrong. There was nothing you could have done."

"That's exactly it, Ken. I couldn't have done anything. I can try to save the environment. I can save
wounded animals. I can fix dinner and fix a flat tire. I
pride myself on being a can-do person. But I couldn't
stop her. When she put her hands all over me, I didn't
know what to do. I should have fought her, screamed,

did something. But I was scared and confused. I just let her fondle me and rub herself against me until she had her fill. I should have pushed her away, but I couldn't."

I tried to put my arms around her, but she jumped back, animated again, frantic.

"I don't want to touch anyone right now," she said. "It has nothing to do with you. I have a horrible, horrible secret and somehow you've unearthed it. Now I need to hide it again. I won't live with this, Ken. I worked too hard to get rid of it. I don't want to be stuck in the past, Ken. We're getting married. That's all I want to think about. The future. The past is gone forever."

"And that's it? We just bury it under the carpet? Melissa, I heard you play. That woman was a monster, but she was right about one thing. You were born to be a concert pianist. You were cheated out of it."

"That Melissa is dead, Ken."

"She can't be dead," I said, moving forward on the sofa, wanting to get up myself, but not sure what would happen if I did. "There was too much life in that Melissa for her to be dead."

She shook her head sadly. "You're just going to have to live with the package you got."

"This isn't about me. I fell madly, irretrievably in love with 'the package I got.' This is about you. About losing more than anyone ever should."

"So what are you going to do about it?" she said combatively. "Go back to Stephon to perform another 'magic trick?'"

I leaned forward a little more. "What if I could?"

She covered her face in her hands again and then wiped at her eyes one more time. "Ken, please rejoin me in the real world."

"You didn't answer my question."

"It's a ridiculous question."

"It's not a ridiculous question. Really, I mean it."

She put her hands on her hips and stared at me. This was a Melissa I barely knew, one who ran from a fight, one who allowed the world to take her down. "Get over it, Ken."

"Like you've gotten over it?"

I didn't mean for the words to sting quite as hard as they obviously did. "Yes, just like I've gotten over it," she said. Again she stared at the floor, shaking her head. "I need to go out for a while." She turned and quickly exited the apartment.

I watched her from the sofa, wanting to chase after her, knowing that I mustn't.

I couldn't allow her to go on this way. Not when I could do something about it.

Chapter 8

Transfixed by My Own Power

"This is Melissa's wish, as well as your own," Stephon said the next day.

"Yes, it is," I said determinedly. I was convinced that it really was. That she would have said as much once she'd had the chance to think about it. She hadn't come home until late last night. I knew she wouldn't do anything to hurt herself and I also knew that she didn't want me coming after her, so I just stewed for a long time and then went to bed, though there was no chance I was going to sleep. When she came in, she snuggled up next to me and asked me to hold her, making it abundantly clear that she didn't want to talk and she didn't want me to ask her where she'd been. She was still asleep in the morning when I left.

"I feel the need to remind you again that there are significant risks involved in what you are doing."

"We've been through this already."

"I'm not sure you were listening."

"Trust me, I was listening. And trust me when I say that I've given *everything* – including everything you said – a great deal of thought. Can we please get on with this?"

Stephon seemed a little miffed, but he nodded. "Yes, we can."

"My plan is this: I go to the moment where Melissa is attacked. I have a very clear picture in my head of how I'm going to prevent that from happening. Then you pull me out. Everything will be the same, except that Melissa's horror will have been erased."

"Or not. There's no way of knowing how events affect one another."

"Are you telling me that you know something?"

Stephon raised his hands. "I'm not saying anything of the sort. I'm saying that things might not turn out exactly the way you expect them to."

"But there's an excellent chance that they will."

Stephon didn't respond.

"Regardless," I said, "Melissa will have this terrible blot removed from her soul."

"If you are successful."

"I will be successful. As long as I can touch things, interact with this world. That's really essential."

"That much is not a problem." Stephon held my eyes for a moment and I could see he was conflicted. Not that I really cared what he thought. "I must emphasize again that your decision is irrevocable. Whatever awaits you at the end of your journey will be permanent. Twice you have been given the opportunity to bend the universe to your will. I won't be able to allow it again."

"I understand and I'm ready for it. So what do I do now?"

"The same as you did before. You will suddenly find yourself at your destination."

"Will I be able to contact you?"

"I'll be here when you get back."

"You know that much?"

He offered me a half-smile. "I know that much. Do you have any other questions?"

Suddenly something flashed in my mind. "Just one. Why are you doing this?"

"You are *demanding* that I do it."

"But you still don't have to do it. I can't make you. Why are you going along with this?"

Stephon turned away from me and stared at a porcelain figurine of a princess that stood alone in a display case. "Because you are willing to. You obviously don't understand what a rare trait that is. Any other questions?"

I had dozens, but I was anxious to go.

"I think that's it. Thank you, Stephon."

He shook my hand firmly. "Good luck, Mr. Timian."

I took out my pocket watch. The time was 12:34.

Red fog descended.

≋

I strained to hear the sounds of piano as gray tiles and apple-green walls surrounded me. Last time those colors had been merely ugly. Now they were repugnant. I checked my pocket watch again. It still said 12:34, though I knew it was a different time here.

Piano notes tinkled from behind the door. The beautiful sound made by the woman I adored and the girl I'd come to love. Down the corridor came the click of high-heeled shoes. I turned to see the monster approaching me. I didn't hide my face. I stared at her with all my surliness, as if it could make her disappear in a puff of smoke. She regarded me diffidently and made it clear I wasn't a concern to her.

Miss Hoffman brushed by me. Her gray jacket swept my hand, but she didn't excuse herself. She walked precisely but rapidly, leaving a trail of cold air that sent a chill down my back.

She paused at the door and looked me over again.

"Are you here for someone?" she said, her tone flat.

"Yes... I'm waiting for someone."

"May I ask who?" Her nose twitched as if smelling carrion.

"My daughter. She's down the hall."

Miss Hoffman gazed at me, then nodded. "Please remember that visitors must obtain permission from the office before entering school grounds." Then she walked into the music room and closed the door. The piano playing paused for a moment, and then restarted.

I took a deep breath. It wasn't until then that I realized what a remarkable thing it was that the woman had spoken to me. She'd seen me, and I'd felt her cold presence. I was here, in the flesh, and able to feel the touch of others. My only previous thoughts of that woman had involved my hands around her throat. Now my skin tingled where she brushed against me, and I savored the sensation. I was here and I was real. I had it in my power to make things right.

The same janitor I'd seen the last time appeared around the corner, humming what sounded like "Cupid" by Sam Cooke. As he glanced at me, I checked my watch and shook my head irritably. "Where can she be?" I said, feigning irritation. The janitor shrugged. Another father waiting to pick up his kid – nothing to worry about. People were a lot more relaxed about this kind of thing in the 1980s.

The music stopped again. When the janitor disappeared inside a classroom, I moved to the music room door and put my ear against the metal. I heard muffled voices, one vibrant, the other clipped. I silently cracked open the door. Melissa sat at the piano, just as she had before. Miss Hoffman was rubbing her shoulders.

I rapped loudly. "Excuse me."

Melissa turned and looked up at me. Her teacher's look could have frozen steam. Her cheeks were flushed, and she took a deep breath.

"May I help you?" she said icily. There was something in her eyes and I could see that she was trying to place where she'd seen me before.

"Yes, I have a question for you. It's about... teaching music to young people. I wonder if you could step into the hall."

"This is not a good time. Can you not see I am instructing a student?"

Melissa shifted her gaze to her sheet music.

"This will only take a moment."

"It will have to wait."

"I don't think you want me to say what I have to say in front of a student."

Miss Hoffman's sigh had a slight hitch to it, as though she anticipated trouble. "Carry on, Melissa. I will return in a moment." Her hard gray heels thudded softly into the carpet as she followed me into the hallway.

"Yes?" she said curtly. The color in her cheeks had mellowed slightly, but she was still clearly exercised.

Her foot tapped the floor once, twice. I hated her more every second I was in her presence.

I couldn't restrain myself any longer. I slammed her against the wall. Her bony shoulders squirmed in my grip and her face registered shock.

"Let me go or I will scream," she said in a fierce whisper.

"Go ahead and scream. Go ahead and call the police. You know what they'll do to someone like you? Tell me how many girls you've hurt, Miss Hoffman. Give me a number."

Surprise loosened her clenched jaw. The color fled from her cheeks entirely, leaving behind flesh as gray as her jacket. "I do not know what you are talking about. Who are you? If you release me this instant, I will not go to the police. I will forget this ever happened."

For a moment, I stood transfixed by my own power. A thousand fantasies of killing this woman in exquisitely painful ways crossed my mind. I could destroy her now with my bare hands and disappear into another universe. How could they prosecute a man who was never really here?

I squeezed her shoulders until she let out a thin whimper. That she was utterly terrified did nothing to lessen my rage.

"Listen to me very carefully," I said. "I know what you were planning to do. If you touch that girl in there – if you touch any child ever again – I will make you feel a level of anguish you could never have imagined."

"I do not know you," she said weakly. "Who are you? Are you the father of one of my students?"

"Who I am isn't relevant. The only thing that is relevant is what I can do to you if you don't take me very, very seriously."

The woman's breath came in great gasps as if her own lungs couldn't bear to live inside her. "You have no proof. No one will believe you. I am a respected member of this community. What are you but vulgar trash?"

"You don't think I can find proof? Do you think Melissa and the other girls would lie to protect you?" I was guessing about the other girls, but based on her reaction, it appeared my guess had hit the mark. "I hope you look good in an orange jumpsuit, Miss Hoffman."

"Why are you doing this? I have done nothing to harm you. Is it money you want? I have some savings. You may have it all if you keep silent."

"This isn't about money. You were about to hurt someone I care for. You were about to destroy the promising career of a girl who trusts you as a mentor. Right now, I could snap your stiff neck like a wishbone, but I am going to give you a break. I am going to show you the mercy that you never gave anyone else."

I could see the relief in her eyes. "What do you want me to do?"

"You are going back in that room to tell Melissa that you are no longer her piano teacher. You will make clear that this is not because of anything she did, but because of a scheduling problem you have. You will then inform her that she will be getting a new teacher, which you will arrange as soon as you leave. You will then resign your position with the school and never cross Melissa's path again. Do you understand what I am telling you?"

Her teeth were bared like a cornered rat. She made a guttural sound.

"I trust that meant yes."

Her coldness flared into a glare that could have melted steel. "Very well. I will do as you say." Her voice was subdued but her eyes were not.

I released her shoulders, my fingers leaving dents in her jacket. She hissed through her teeth and spun on her heel.

"Miss Hoffman."

She stiffened, then turned around.

"Remember that I know what you have done and what you are capable of doing. Just as I know what you did before. I will know if you ever do it again. One false step, one hint that you are even thinking of doing something like this again, and you will rot in jail for the rest of your life."

Her lips opened, but no words came out. She reentered the room and closed the door behind her. I pressed my ear to the door, but all I could hear were faint voices. A minute later she strode out of the room, glared at me one last time, and marched away. Her anger told me just how frightened she was. She wouldn't bother anyone again. Of that much, I was absolutely sure.

A door opened down the hall, and the janitor emerged pushing his squeaky sidekick. His white-thatched head swiveled as the piano teacher stomped past him. Then it swiveled toward me. I shrugged. He shrugged. Then he whistled something that sounded like "Strangers in the Night" as he clanged into another classroom.

It was time to go. My brain warned me not to linger by the door, but my body had other plans. I froze as Melissa stepped out, a book bag over her shoulder. Her neck was red where her teacher's fingers had rubbed her. She seemed confused by everything that had happened in the last few minutes, but this confusion would be gone quickly, maybe even before she left the school. She stared at me for a second. Then she smiled shyly and walked away. She strode confidently down the hall, and I watched her admiringly until she turned a corner.

Gray and apple-green dissolved into red fog and when it lifted, Stephon stood in front of me wearing a blue suit. I tilted my head.

"When did you change clothes? You were dressed in a turtleneck before." The wall clock still read 12:34. A nice trick – the physics of this process must be fascinating.

A blue suit? With a red tie? I glanced around the shop. There seemed to be more silver and less gold than I remembered. Behind the counter, a samovar bubbled. Samovars made tea. When had Stephon given up cappuccino?

It looked like an antique samovar. That kind of samovar must have come from... oh, no. I couldn't have caused that. Suddenly the science fiction stories I'd read when I was a kid came back to me. My brow dampened as I tried to remember my college language classes.

"Gov-or-itz-iya Pah-ruskee?" I said in butchered Russian. I knew my pronunciation was as bad as my professors had always told me, but I hoped it was clear enough.

Stephon's eyebrows twitched, and then he laughed. "Yes, Mr. Timian, I do speak a little Russian, though I have not had reason to use it in many years."

"I... I saw the samovar. I know they come from Russia."

"Yes, I picked it up some years ago on a trip to Siberia. Allegedly it belonged to the Tsar, though if the

Romanovs owned every item that was offered to me, even the Winter Palace in Saint Petersburg would have been too small. However, it does make excellent tea. Would you like a glass?"

"No. No, thank you."

Stephon walked behind the counter and poured tea into a tall glass. I continued to look around the store, finding new things in every display. Even Stephon's inventory didn't turn over this quickly.

"If I understand your implication," Stephon said, taking a brief sip, "you are wondering if your adventure in the past has caused the Soviet Union to conquer America. No, the Soviet Union is still gone and America still won the Cold War. Though you might think otherwise from much of the rhetoric you hear in this city. In any event, this is still Washington, D.C., in the United States of America. The nation and world are essentially the same as the ones you left behind."

"Nothing has changed?"

Stephon put a cube of sugar in his mouth and then took another sip, a quaint Russian custom.

"I didn't say that."

"Don't play games, Stephon. I'm more than a little nervous now that I'm back here. Are things different or not?"

He put his glass down on the counter. "You will recall that I warned you that if you changed events, there could be consequences. Fortunately, you did not assassinate a world leader or something equally cataclysmic. The world as you know it has not fundamentally changed. That doesn't mean there haven't been any changes at all. As far as your personal life is concerned, I have no way of knowing."

"No way?"

"I'm not omniscient, Mr. Timian."

I felt a little lightheaded. "Someday maybe you can tell me how all of this works."

He smiled patiently. "I really can't."

The glint of a passing car drew my attention outside. Melissa was outside. Out there where the rest of my future was waiting. I suddenly felt an overwhelming need to hold her in my arms.

I turned back to Stephon. "I have to go."

"Yes, you do." He reached for his teacup again.

I had a little trouble getting my legs to work. I wondered if it was a byproduct of being shunted to an alternate world or if it was something else entirely. "Can I come by again if I have any questions?"

Stephon nodded. "I'm here, Mr. Timian."

"Please call me Ken."

"If you'd like."

"And only you and I know what happened?"

"To the best of my knowledge."

I shook my head. I had a feeling I wouldn't fully comprehend the strangeness of this episode for some time. I made my way toward the door. I turned to say something more to Stephon.

But he had already disappeared into the back room.

Chapter 9

Not the Boundaries of Space or Time or Circumstance

I stepped out into a strange new world. Only it wasn't strange and it wasn't new. Taxis dipped in and out of traffic as cars maneuvered to avoid buses picking up passengers. Drivers honked as they zoomed in death races to capture parking spots.

The uneasy feeling I'd had since returning to Stephon's had began to subside. I hadn't done irreparable damage to the time-space continuum. There were no antigravity cars here or pedestrians zooming through the air with jetpacks. Dolphins hadn't become the new master race. This looked and smelled and sounded just like the Washington I knew.

I looked up at a White House helicopter overhead, so I didn't see the rollerblader until he banged off my arm. The gawky teenager went into a split-legged landing like a fledgling ballet dancer. His pimply face twisted into a feral snarl. "Why don't you look where you're going, dude?" he said sharply.

"Why don't you rollerblade in a park? And don't call me dude, dude." If he had been halfway polite, I would have helped him up. Instead I left him wallowing in a pool of his own obscenity as he struggled to stand. There was someplace else I needed to be.

For further assurance, I reached my hand into my pocket and pulled out my wallet, flipping through the compartments. My Platinum Visa and American Express cards were there. My name and address were the same on my Virginia driver's license. So was my photo – I refused to contemplate the implications if *that* had changed. I definitely seemed to be the same Ken Timian who walked into Stephon's shop some indeterminable time ago. I relaxed a little bit more.

I really wanted to hear Melissa's voice. I could be home soon enough, but at that very moment, the thing that was most important to me was checking in with her, just to hear what she sounded like. I wondered if her voice would be a little different coming from a body that hadn't had to carry a huge secret around for the past eighteen years.

I pulled out my phone and my number. One ring (so it hasn't been disconnected). Two rings (a stranger hasn't answered). Three. Four. Then a loud click. "Hi, this is Ken. I can't take your call now. Leave your name, number, and a brief message and I'll get back to you as soon as I can."

I assumed Melissa was out running errands. We certainly had enough of them to do this close to the wedding. I took a deep breath and held the phone against my forehead.

My Audi was where I'd parked it, and when I reached the car, I discovered yet another indication that the world was very much the same. The supernatural powers of the Washington parking cops were still as strong as ever. The red EXPIRED tab had flared only three minutes before, yet already a ticket lay under my windshield wiper. This was a $25 tariff that I wouldn't even think of complaining about.

Traffic on the way to Arlington was light for a late spring Saturday. I lowered the power windows as I crossed Memorial Bridge, smiling at the joggers and bi-cyclists on both sidewalks. The farther I got from Ste-phon's the more real everything felt to me.

Jeez, I pulled this off. I kicked that horrible woman's ass and I'll still have plenty of time to make Melissa a great dinner. I hope she still likes Fettuccine Alfredo.

As I turned into the parking lot, luck blessed me again as a packed minivan backed out of a space near the apartment house door. I waved at the boisterous tots in the back of the van and they waved back. I didn't even think twice about whether the doorman would rec-ognize me, and his friendly nod underscored that I had nothing to worry about.

The mailman was just leaving as I entered the build-ing. My mailbox key fit perfectly, revealing the usual flyers for pizza and oil changes, a couple of bills, and as-sorted solicitations. As I closed the mailbox door, my eye went to the white address label stuck to the front. KEN TIMIAN – APT. 12D. It would say, "Ken and Melissa Timian" soon. I was a little surprised that Melissa want-ed to take my last name after we got married, but almost any guy will acknowledge that this is what he hopes for.

I glanced through the envelopes in my hand. I sighed longingly at the notion of changing history to eliminate whoever invented junk mail. Then the light bulb finally went on in my head.

KEN TIMIAN – APT. 12D.

Our mailbox said KEN TIMIAN AND MELISSA ARGENT.

The phone machine said, "Hi, this is Ken."

Our answering machine said, "Hi, this is Ken and Melissa."

Oh, my god.

I ran toward the elevator. With a sidestep worthy of an NFL wide receiver, I evaded the maintenance man coming out of the opening doors. He screamed at me in Spanish as I slammed the button for the twelfth floor.

At the seventh floor, the car stopped. Doors rattled open, revealing a curly haired woman in a short skirt. *Get in,* I willed her. *Get in or get out of my way. I need to get to my apartment. I need to know that Melissa is still here.*

Two more stops and we were finally on the twelfth floor. A left from the elevator, a right down the next corridor, and I was at Apartment 12D.

The plastic sticker on the door bore my name only. It was getting a little hard to pretend.

Maybe we didn't move in together yet. Maybe the new Melissa is more independent than the old one was – if that's humanly possible. Maybe she didn't want to move in with me until we were married. Maybe we've already found that great house that we're going to live in together.

I didn't want to go inside. Inside was the answer to the most important question I had ever asked. I rested my forehead against the door for several seconds. My heart beat a Morse code. Finally, I stuck the key into the lock. It had been a while since I last prayed, but I asked for a few things and promised many more.

The lock turned smoothly and the door swung inward, the bottom hinge greeting me with its familiar squawk. I stepped over the threshold very, very tentatively.

This was not the place I shared with Melissa, but I knew it all the same.

I checked the kitchen first. There were the familiar red-and-white boxes stacked in a Leaning Tower of Pizza. Beer cans were piled in the recycling bin while dishes waited patiently in the sink for a trip to the dishwasher. I hadn't been this sloppy in two years.

I went into the living room and examined the furniture. Everything was where it had once been. The leather-and-chrome sofa lay against the wall, clashing with the brown recliner and the mahogany table. I was once proud of my living room decor, and paid good money for it, too. That was before Melissa came along to point out that the furnishings blended as tastefully as a blue pinstripe jacket with plaid pants.

This was my place and my place only. *But it could still be that Melissa and I just didn't move in together.* Maybe she'd just decided this apartment was beyond repair. There had to be a trace of her somewhere in here. Maybe a photograph, or a postcard, or just a yellow sticky note with neat handwriting resembling calligraphy. What about Sierra Club magazines and tourist guides for the Amazon jungle? Tofu and bok choy in the fridge?

But there wasn't a single indication that she'd ever stepped foot in this apartment. That she'd ever walked into my life.

I collapsed into the recliner, grateful for the support of its plush, narrow arms. Something crunched underneath me. I looked down and saw a crushed Cheese Doodle that left an orange blotch on my pants.

"This can't be happening," I shouted to walls that did not answer. "This isn't the way it was meant to be."

I heard a sound.

"Melissa?"

Yellow eyes regarded me curiously from the foot of the chair. The cat jumped up into my lap, then just as quickly jumped out again.

"So I lose Melissa but I still have you, Wizard. Tell me life is fair."

Wizard licked his paws. Then he meowed and rubbed against my leg in the universal feline signal that it was feeding time. Absently, I got up, took a can of cat food from the cupboard, and fed him. At least one of us would have what he wanted. This Wizard was a little chunkier than the cat I'd seen this morning. I used to share my takeout lasagna or Kung Pao chicken with him before Melissa convinced me that it was terribly unhealthy to feed him this kind of food.

I reached down to pet the cat, but he slipped away from my fingers. We were back to uneasy coexistence. I sat on the floor and stared off at this familiar/foreign apartment. Then I noticed the red light blinking on the answering machine. The digital counter indicated that I had two messages. I hit the play button. First came the sound of traffic. I forgot that I was being recorded when I called from the street.

Next came a woman's voice. "Hi, Ken," she said, and my heart skipped a beat. But the voice was higher-pitched and bubblier than Melissa's, with a Southern accent and the bright and friendly tone of an airline reservation clerk. "This is Lori. Your friend Paul said you might like to get together. Someone I work with has two tickets to the Kennedy Center that he can't use Wednesday night. Let me know if you want to go. It should be fun."

I'm a logical man, magical trips to someone else's past notwithstanding. As an attorney (at least I assumed I was still an attorney), I was trained to assess facts, not speculate. Now the facts assembled themselves in front of me in all their heartless glory:

Fact: There was no sign that Melissa lived with me.

Fact: A woman named Lori left a message asking me out on a date that my friend Paul set up.

Fact: That Paul was setting me up with women meant that he believed I was dating and not getting married next weekend.

Fact: I had managed to make an incomprehensibly huge mess of my life.

Take a deep breath. Get your bearings. Take stock of your resources.

That's a good drill to follow when you're in trouble. Of course, if I followed it in the first place, maybe I wouldn't have ended up in this temporal trap. I could have questioned Stephon more closely about the potential consequences of my actions. Maybe he would have mentioned that Melissa's life might not only change, but that she might also vanish from my sight. If I had known that this could happen, I would have brought more information with me.

I scoured my apartment for clues about who I was. The good news was that most of my life seemed to be the same. Sifting through the jungle of my home office, I found that I was still an attorney with Warwick and Gray. My credit card bills were higher than before, and my checking account lower, but that was no surprise. Until Melissa took over the finances, I earned a lot and spent almost as much.

A glance through the *Washington Post* revealed that the world was the same one I left. The night before my journey, when I lay awake watching Melissa's chest undulate in the rhythm of restless sleep, I wondered briefly if what I did could make a difference. If I gave the world a happier Melissa, wouldn't the entire world be a better place? Yet the Middle East still smoldered, Democrats accused Republicans, and Republicans accused Democrats while Congress remained deadlocked over the federal budget.

I drummed my fingers on the dining room table and recalled a man who no longer existed. My life before Melissa seemed a blur of ambition, hard work, and frantic fun. It was as if someone else had rented my life and then handed back the keys. Yet if my apartment now looked as if it belonged to that man...

When I was four, I was afraid to open the closet door in my parents' bedroom for fear a monster would sprout arms and legs in my father's suit and then eat me. That dread came over me as I gazed at the bottom door of the stereo cabinet. My old nemeses were there, I had no doubt. I opened the door and confronted the enemy.

I could take comfort that in this life I was doing somewhat better; in the old world, there had once been fifteen or sixteen bottles lined up in perfect formation. This cabinet contained three bottles of good Russian vodka, two of tequila, two of scotch, and one of gin. Their ranks were joined by bottles of grappa and ouzo. Grappa and ouzo? Evidently I had expanded my alcoholic horizons.

One by one, I poured the contents of the liquor bottles down the drain, tossing each into the recycling bin. I had no idea what life I was leading now, but I certainly wasn't going to lead a party life again. Something told me that under the circumstances, one stiff drink would lead very quickly to several dozen others. That wasn't an option. It wasn't what Melissa would want me to do. It was not what the man I became with Melissa wanted either.

In this world, I never met Melissa Argent. I knew that, because if we ever met, we would be together now. But she was out there. And I would find her.

There was nothing – not the boundaries of space or time or circumstance – that could keep me from this mission. Not when I knew how desperately I needed her.

Chapter 10

A Life I Would Have Easily Wished for Her

I tried calling Melissa's old apartment and got a dry cleaner. I tried her office number and got the voice box of a guy named Chad. I tried her parents' house and the phone just rang endlessly. This approach wasn't proving useful at all.

I felt the desperate need to be in motion, to physically *do* something, even if I had no clear plan. I grabbed my car keys and headed for the front door. The cat looked up at me disinterestedly as I passed. I always made a habit of letting Melissa know my itinerary whenever I went out. But the cat could not have cared less.

It was only when I started driving that I realized I was headed for McLean. Melissa's parents loved that house; there was an excellent chance they still lived there, even if they hadn't bothered to get an answering machine. It should have taken twenty minutes to get to their place on Mockingbird Lane, but I was rippling with energy now, spurred on by the belief that I was taking an important first step to bringing Melissa back into my life. I made it in fifteen.

The houses looked the same as they had during all of those roast beef dinners in what seemed like an eternity ago. Even the tree stump in front of the Argent house was there.

The house was not the same, though. The only way Mr. Argent's house could have been red was if he'd set it afire. And whatever color he painted it, he would have done so long before the siding peeled like whiskers.

The garden was the second clue. Where roses and tulips had bloomed, gardenias now spread blue and purple pom-poms over a lawn where the formerly crew-cut grass sprouted ankle-high. I paused for a moment to read the walking billboard that was the rear fender of the old Volvo resting in the driveway. A Volvo? Bumper stickers urging the world to "Save the Dolphins" and "Abolish Nuclear Weapons Now?" Unless Melissa had used her replenished store of karmic energy to turn her father into a member of Greenpeace, there was little to no chance that the Argents still lived here.

A high-pitched yip greeted me as I walked up the front steps, nearly hitting my head on the turtle-shaped wind chimes. The doorbell didn't work, so I rapped loudly on the door. It opened a minute later, revealing the curly white paws of an overeager poodle and the curly brown hair of the woman I assumed to be the dog's owner.

"Get down, Francine," the woman said, trying in vain to prevent the animal from jumping against the screen while issuing a sound that was only barely audible to the human ear.

I smiled at Francine nervously. Small dogs made me jittery, and I was pretty damned jittery already. I looked up at the woman.

"I wonder if you can help me. I'm looking for the Argent family. They used to live in this house."

Francine yipped again, banging her narrow snout against the door.

"It's okay, darling," the woman said, bending to the dog and resting her cheek against the top of Francine's head. She turned to me. "She doesn't like strangers. The Argents, you said? I don't remember the name."

"It was a family of four. The father was a Marine colonel. They had a daughter named Melissa."

"Hmmm." She scratched her head with a hand laden with rings on every finger. "Let's see. Francine, how long have we been in this house?" The poodle yipped twice. "I think you're right. It has to be ten years. The family I bought it from was named Lorenzo, if I remember correctly."

They'd left more than ten years ago? I wondered why. The woman stood up again, which got the dog barking animatedly. For some reason, I felt like Francine was taunting me. I took a deep breath, looked around the property for a moment. Then I turned back to the woman. "Thanks for your help. I'll try to find them some other way."

"Sorry I don't have more information for you. I might have the contact information for the previous owners somewhere, if you'd like."

That seemed like the longest of long shots, but I wasn't in the position to reject any details. Even though the poodle was now yipping manically, the sound cutting sharply into my addled brain. "If you have that, it could be a big help."

"Come on in for a few minutes while I look," she said. "You seem safe enough, and Francine seems to have taken a liking to you."

I smiled as politely as I could and said, "I think I'll just wait out here, if you don't mind."

"Be my guest. I'm pretty sure I know where the file is."

She went off to find the information and fortunately the dog followed her. I sat on the stoop and looked out toward the street. Melissa and I had sat here the day of our engagement party, taking a break from the revelry of friends and relatives. I felt her head on my shoulder and heard the soft music of her chuckle as a kid from down the block stood on his bike and proclaimed that he was "King of the World." I remember kissing her hair and the expression on her face when she looked over at me – the one that said she believed we were taking a glimpse into our own futures.

The woman returned a short while later. For whatever reason, Francine wasn't with her. I stood up and she stepped out onto the porch with me. "I remembered correctly. Their name was Lorenzo. Their forwarding address was a D.C. post office box, but I have the number of their real estate lawyer as well. I don't know if this will do you any good. Maybe the lawyer handled their closing when they bought the house as well."

She handed me a piece of paper with the details, though I was certain there was nothing I could do with them. "Thanks."

"I remembered this as well. It's been sitting on my bookshelf since I found it in the attic about a year after

I moved in." She handed me a notebook with the words "My Dream Book" written on the cover. The handwriting was unmistakably Melissa's. I felt tears come to my eyes. This was the first hard evidence I had that she even existed.

"Maybe it's from one of the children?" she said.

"I think it is." I ran my fingers over the cover and opened a page. There was a short essay entitled, "101 pets." I flipped to another page and found one titled, "When I Come Back Here to Teach," and then another called, "My Opening Night at Carnegie Hall." I read the first paragraph. It spoke in grandiose terms about Melissa's debut on the biggest of musical stages. There was no Miss Hoffman here to sully this dream. Reluctantly, I closed the book and handed it back to the woman.

"Thanks."

She waved it away. "Why don't you keep it? For some reason I've thought of it as a good luck charm for me, but I always thought the girl who wrote these 'dreams' might like to have it back some day. Maybe if you find her, you can give it to her."

I smiled and felt myself getting choked up again. "I'd really like to do that."

She patted me on the hand. "Take it. Maybe it'll be *your* good luck charm now too."

I nodded.

"Well," she said, "you take care of yourself. You'll have to excuse me, but it's time for Francine to take me for another walk."

I didn't go home right away. I stopped the car at a nearby park and read some more of Melissa's dreams. There were stories about friends and boys and ambitions. There was so much optimism here, so much unfettered joy for life. I'd seen this Melissa, got to know her for all too brief a period on my first journey from Stephon's store. Here Melissa talked about being a junior in high school, which meant that she'd managed to maintain her wide-eyed view of the world beyond the point when I intervened.

When I got back to the apartment – I was still having trouble considering it only my apartment – the first thing I checked was the answering machine. The light glowed a steady red. No messages. I tried to convince myself that I wasn't expecting any, but I knew I was waiting for Melissa to call, to tell me that things weren't anywhere near as dire as they seemed to me.

I stood in the middle of the living room for several seconds, maybe even several minutes. I wanted desperately to find Melissa, to bring her back into my life, but every move I made seem to take me further and further away from her. Finally I pulled myself out of neutral and went into my office to boot up the computer.

I checked my e-mail first, though I'm not sure why. Maybe my new ISP allowed access to parallel universes and I could reach Melissa that way. All I got for that effort was spam and a message saying that my order for hot sauce had shipped. When did I start buying hot sauce on the Internet?

I went to an online telephone directory whose database supposedly contained the most phone numbers in the United States. It was a handy tool for locating someone whose city or state you didn't know. I typed MELISSA ARGENT in the search box and clicked the GO button. Melissa's name appeared, with her address and phone number underneath. There was even a button I could click to send her flowers using my credit card. The only problem was that my credit card would have maxed out, because there were ninety-eight Melissa Argents, living everywhere from Alabama to Wyoming, though not a single one anywhere near Washington, D.C. I could call each of these women, but what would I say? *Hi, I've just arrived from another timeline, and I'm looking for my fiancée. I'd like to take you out to dinner, but first, can you tell whether you play the piano?* Even better, I could butter them up by sending flowers before I called. It would be weeks before the police arrested me.

I set that notion aside, at least for the time being.

I searched for the name Harold Argent and found one hundred and sixty-two hits. None were particularly close to Washington. Not that I had any idea how I would approach the Colonel. When Melissa brought me home to meet her parents, her father quietly told me that he expected his daughter's boyfriends to treat her like a lady. Then he showed me his gun collection. I could just imagine what he would do if I contacted him from out of nowhere and told him why I was looking for Melissa. I would be lucky if he only set the dog off after me.

I decided to Google Melissa, hoping to perhaps find some mention of her in an alumni newsletter or something. I was stunned to come up with nearly a million hits. Of course they could have been for any one of the ninety-eight Melissa Argents living in the United States or the many others around the world. I figured I'd start at the top with the "Official Melissa Argent website. I clicked on it – and suddenly found myself staring at a nearly full-screen image of the smiling, bright-eyed woman I adored.

Melissa had always been photogenic, but this shot was remarkable. It was inviting and appealing and my heart broke just looking at it. For several moments, all I could do was stare, until my brain finally considered the notion of finding out *why* there was an "Official Melissa Argent website" and how it could get me back to her as quickly as humanly possible.

One click took me to her bio page and another stunning photograph. There I learned that Melissa had indeed followed her dream of becoming an accomplished pianist. She studied at Juilliard and the London Conservatory of Music, and, while she was in Europe, began developing a style that bridged classical, jazz, New Age, minimalist, rock, and pop, and embarked on a career that gained her considerable notoriety within serious music circles.

My heart swelled with pride as I read on. Melissa was on the leading edge of a movement called "New Fusion," and she was in the process of becoming something of a pop star. She'd released three albums and had appeared on numerous others. She'd toured on four continents, performed at the White House, and appeared on the "Today" show. I moved to a link titled "Photo Gallery" and found a slideshow of Melissa performing, talking to fans, reading to children in West Virginia, and posing with dignitaries.

And in each of the photos her eyes shone brilliantly blue. The last time I saw those eyes, they were puffy and red. Last night before I left – had it really been last night? – Melissa could barely contain her sorrow. But here she was beaming. Her smile belonged to someone at the top of her form and the top of her life. There was so much more to learn about this Melissa, but nothing would be as essential as the radiant smile on my screen.

I had accomplished my mission.

This should have made me unreservedly happy, and certainly I was very glad that my prevention of Ms. Hoffman's horrible acts led to Melissa fulfilling one of her most important dreams. But seeing this website, with its reviews from major periodicals and its pictures of her with international figures, made Melissa seem impossibly far away from me. I realized now that, while there might be ninety-eight Melissa Argents I could send flowers to with a single click, not one of them was going to be the Melissa Argent I loved. She wouldn't have a publicly listed telephone number. I wouldn't be able to friend her on Facebook (though, as I would soon learn, I could become one of the tens of thousands of people connected to her through her fan page). She would have a manager and a team of handlers and an entire retinue of people whose job it was to keep guys like me from getting too close to her.

I went back to the home page of the website and stared at the picture there for a very long time.

I really am glad for you, Melissa, I thought. *Incredibly glad. But we're supposed to be together. How is that going to happen now?*

Stephon was right. This was my new life. There were no more clever temporal tricks available to me – what I saw was what I had.

All at once, I felt terribly tired. I had no idea what my next step should be and no strength to take that next step. I needed to lay down, to recharge. Maybe something would come to me after some sleep – if sleep was even a possibility.

I went into my bedroom for the first time since I'd come back from Stephon's. The blankets on the bed were yet another reminder that in this world I'd spent the previous night alone. As I undressed, I noticed an empty space on the nightstand. Once there had been a snapshot of Melissa and me that a helpful tourist had taken while we stood on the precipice of the Grand Canyon. Our love always seemed as permanent as that eternal, awe-inspiring gorge.

Now it was gone. As far as the brilliant, beautiful and beloved Melissa Argent knew, Ken Timian didn't even exist. And he didn't matter. I'd erased the trauma from her life, but I erased something else as well – the knowledge of what we were like together, of the singular magic we created when we held each other. She had no knowledge of this and therefore couldn't possibly mourn its loss. That was left to me alone.

What was I supposed to do now? Could I just forget Melissa? Could I simply get on with my life? Stephon would almost certainly recommend that. And much as it pained me to believe it, he would probably be right. Where just a short while ago, I was convinced that I could cross any barrier to reach Melissa, I now felt overwhelmed by the odds. She had a fabulous life, a life I would have easily wished for her. It didn't include me, though.

I had erased her from my world. Not from my memory. Never that. Still, she was gone all the same.

Today was Saturday. Tomorrow I would figure out how to rejoin the world. I would drive to the supermarket and buy food. I would live my life with the recollection of everything Melissa had taught me, everything she brought to me. I wouldn't go back to being the person I was before I met her, but I couldn't be the person I was with her either. I would need to become someone else yet again.

I got into bed and looked across at a pillow Melissa had never slept on and imagined her there.

She would always be with me.

Even if I was never again with her.

Chapter 11

Consolation Prize

I didn't intend to sleep away most of Sunday. I couldn't recall the last time I'd stayed in bed until the middle of the afternoon. When Melissa and I were together, we often lingered under the sheets on weekends, embracing, kissing, sometimes making love, but we always had something to do and those plans would ultimately roust us, get the coffee brewing. A more perceptive man would have seen my languor as a sign of depression. My first thought was that time travel had knocked me out physically.

I eventually ran a number of errands and spent a little more time reconciling myself with the person I was in this world. I straightened out the apartment, wondering if the guy who cleaned it still came on Tuesdays. That night, I spent several more hours reading about Melissa and downloading her albums.

Monday morning I got into the Audi and drove to work. Before I started dating Melissa, I took the train in, but afterward I didn't want to share her with the rest of the commuters at the beginning of the day and it felt so much more intimate to have the extra time alone together, listening to NPR and briefing each other on our agendas. Maybe I'd go back to taking the train again, because the car felt very empty today, even with Melissa's music filling some of the spaces.

The offices of Warwick and Gray were deserted when I arrived. It was before seven, and I wanted to scope out my work situation before everyone else showed up. My electronic key opened the lock with a reassuring buzz, and I stood by the receptionist's desk straining to hear any noise. All was quiet other than the hum of the air conditioning in the subdued glow of overhead lights turned down for the night.

This was an Old Money firm and it looked the part. It was all polished wood and brass, like a robber baron's office in 1898. Harrison Warwick – or Harrison Warwick III, as he preferred to be known – said the decor added dignity and solemnity to the office. The rumor was that Harrison's father made his son swear not to change the furnishings in any way and III didn't have the backbone to challenge him. Harrison's father was known as Warwick the Great; his son was known as Warwick the Lesser.

Several younger married attorneys swore their spouses could smell the mustiness in their clothes when they got home. Yet for all of its adherence to timeworn tradition, the firm's systems were fully up to date. Warwick the Lesser's agreement with his father obviously didn't prevent him from making Warwick and Gray the most wired firm inside the Beltway.

This place was intimidating when I first interviewed for my job here. The Timians were no barons – my father owned a hardware store outside Philadelphia and made an adequate living until a big chain drove him out of business and into retirement. They were proud that their son made good, but I was the first member of my entire extended family to crack the six-figure salary barrier. I simply didn't know from trappings like these. Still, they quickly became part of the backdrop – except on days like these (had there ever been a day like this one?) when I reexamined everything I saw.

Down thickly padded corridors I crept, under the gaze of portraits of the firm's Founding Fathers. A former Secretary of State hung his shingle here, as did two ambassadors, a Congressional special prosecutor, and a White House Counsel. Power and influence hummed through this place like an electrical grid. Warwick and Gray didn't advertise its connections. That would be vulgar and pointless. The rates we charged made it abundantly clear that we were very highly esteemed in this town.

I found my name on the door of my office on the west side of the building, overlooking K Street. It wasn't a corner office – you only got one of those if the previous owner left feet-first – but my window gave me a nice view of the street. As my hand grasped the doorknob, I reflected that Melissa and my job had made up nine-tenths of my previous life. Now Melissa was gone, but my work was still there. It wasn't much of a consolation prize.

I quietly opened the door and entered. My head spun just as it did when I first entered my apartment. My office was the same and it was different. There were still the shelves of dun-colored law books that always seemed to intimidate clients. Folders lay stacked on my

desk, tabbed in red, blue, and yellow for quick reference. My law degree still hung from the wall in all its
Gothic-lettered glory. The one concession to decoration
was a watercolor of a blue-and-brown seascape depict-
ing no beach I'd ever seen.

The majesty of law spread its imposing wings over
this room. Dignity clung to it like the smell of polished
hardwood. Yet where was the warmth? The signs that
a unique, distinctive individual occupied this space?
Things were missing, as I knew they would be. One was
the photo of Melissa that should have graced the corner
of my desk, replaced by a gray plastic file tray. Other
personal touches were gone as well – the Redskins coffee mug, the handmade paper clip holder we got at a
street fair, the titanium clock we got from a craft store
– reminding me that I was more than satisfied with standard issue until Melissa taught me better.

And Mr. Smith had left Washington.

The day Melissa brought him to my office was etched
in my mind. He was four feet tall, black-and-white like
the pandas at the zoo, and he wore a Sherlock Holmes
hat. She sat him in the corner beside a filing cabinet and
looked up at me with a sly smile.

"A teddy bear in a law office?" I said. The assistants
swore they could hear my voice on the other side of the
building.

"It's good for your image," Melissa said. "I've already named him for you. He's Mr. Smith – like Jimmy
Stewart in the movie."

"Is there a message there?"

"I'll leave it for you to figure out."

She sat in a chair opposite my desk, looking gorgeous as always. I was a little flummoxed, but it was hard to stay flummoxed when Melissa was in the room.

"How, exactly, is this good for my image?"

"It makes you seem more approachable."

"I think I can hear the partners approaching now with my severance check."

"Don't be ridiculous. Trust me on this."

Of course she was right. The next day, I saw a prospective client. She was a senior executive with a Fortune 500 company. Her attire was Corporate Clone, down to the gray jacket, perfect hair, and humorless expression. She sat down, noticed the teddy bear and stared. Before I could stammer out an explanation – let alone throw a blanket over the thing – she smiled sadly. She told me that business had made her miss her daughter's third birthday party the day before, and to make it up, she'd bought her a huge stuffed dog. She told me that she admired a person who could "be himself" in a corporate setting. The meeting took off from there. When Harrison Warwick came to congratulate me on picking up the case, he looked at the bear, shook his head, and walked away. He never looked at the thing directly again, but he certainly never suggested I find it a new home.

But Mr. Smith never resided in the corner of this office. Instead, he took his place in some little kid's bedroom or warmed up the workplace of some other woman's boyfriend. Maybe Melissa had found the bear in a store on her way to perform at the White House and bought it for another man. There was a thought I couldn't even begin to contemplate.

I took stock of my current caseload. On my desk was the same case I was working on in my other life. It was a trade dispute pitting a big American multinational against a shopping mall masquerading as a Southeast Asian nation. I'd put in so many late nights and weekends researching that case. It was a huge undertaking, one that forced me to get up ridiculously early to phone Asia, regularly waking up Melissa who was a notoriously light sleeper.

I looked through some of the other files. There were fewer cases on my desk in this universe. I'd complained recently to Melissa that things were really starting to pile up and, in one of my least romantic moments ever, even suggested to her that the honeymoon was going to set me back months. There's that old line about people on their deathbeds never saying they wished they'd spent more time at the office. An obvious corollary came to mind now.

My musings were interrupted by a knock on the door as my assistant, Sharon, entered.

"You're in early, Mr. Timian," she said cheerfully. Sharon was always cheerful, no matter how hectic work was or how stressed I became. That she could do so in the middle of a divorce was all the more remarkable. One of the truisms in this field is that behind every good lawyer there is a good legal assistant, and I had drawn the best. A plump peroxide blond with a cherubic face and a cheerful smile, Sharon didn't have the polished look of the younger assistants. When she was first assigned to me a few years ago, I even groused to the office manager about the choice. But a certain glint in her hazel eyes led me to suspect that she had a sharp mind, and in the intervening time, I learned she had so much more than that. I looked at Sharon fresh-faced at eight in the morning and I felt reassured that there were still some good things left in my life.

"I had a lot of work to catch up on. I'm making headway." I smiled. "Everything good with you?"

She seemed mildly surprised by the question. "I'm fine. Thank you for asking."

Thank you for asking. I wondered what made her say that.

"The kids are okay?"

Her eyes narrowed a little. "They're fine, thanks."

It seemed that I was making Sharon uncomfortable with this innocuous exchange of pleasantries. Things moved quickly around the office and we often communicated in shorthand, but she had to know that I was always available. For more than a year now, we carved out some time in every week – either a lunch or just some coffee behind my closed office door – to catch up with one another. Ostensibly, it was to review the week's agenda, but we always diverted onto personal topics. As it became clearer to her that she and her husband were heading toward a split, she confided in me her concerns, especially regarding her two sons.

Maybe that was gone along with Melissa and Mr. Smith. Maybe in this world, I focused only on my headlong rush toward a partnership. That sounded vaguely like someone I used to know.

"That's good. Say hi to them for me." I took a quick glance at my desk calendar. Sharon was definitely not on it. "Listen, can you schedule some time for us this week?"

"You and me?"

"Yes. Move something if you need to."

Sharon seemed very nervous. "Can I ask why?"

I tried to give her a disarming smile. "I just think it would be a good idea to go over some stuff."

She glanced off to the side for a moment and when she looked back at me, she seemed on the verge of tears. "Mr. Timian, if you're going to fire me…"

"Fire you? Why would you say that? I'm doing the *opposite* of firing you."

"The opposite?"

"Well, not the opposite exactly, but, jeez, the thought of firing you never even entered my mind. I just think it's a mistake that we don't set aside time to catch up. It's bad for the team."

"The team?"

I pointed between us. "*This* team. You and me. How can we do our best if we don't have team meetings every now and then?"

Sharon nodded. She still seemed very uncertain. I tried to think back on what our relationship had been like earlier. I went through a fair number of assistants early in my career, but I thought Sharon and I had always clicked.

"I'll put something on your schedule, Mr. Timian."

"Thanks."

"Remember that you have a ten o'clock conference call with Tim Golden."

Golden's file was on my desk. "Got it."

"Would you like your coffee now?"

"That would be great." I tried to remember if I liked my coffee differently pre-Melissa. As far as I could recall, that hadn't changed, but anything was possible.

Sharon started to back out of my doorway.

"Oh, one more thing," I said. "By any chance, has anyone named Melissa called for me recently?"

She thought a moment and shook her head. "Not that I can recall."

If Sharon couldn't recall it, it hadn't happened. "If anyone by that name does call, put her through immediately, please. Regardless of what I'm doing."

Sharon seemed utterly perplexed now. "I'll do just that."

"Thanks."

Sharon nodded and started to leave again.

"Hey, Sharon?"

"Mr. Timian?"

"Sorry if I made you nervous earlier. I had a weird weekend."

"That's okay, Mr. Timian. Let me go get that coffee."

I smiled and she walked off. I picked up the Golden file and tried to focus on it, making sure that I was as up to date on it as possible to avoid any embarrassments during our ten o'clock call. My mind kept wandering back to my exchange with Sharon, though. She seemed truly confused by my friendliness. Had I really been that much of a jerk to her? Was that what I was like without Melissa? Had I gotten *worse* in the last couple of years because Melissa hadn't been there to round me out?

For the hundredth time in the last few days I promised myself never to forget what Melissa meant to me and what she did for me. No matter what people thought of the Ken Timian who existed in this world, they were only going to get the new, improved version in the future.

Chapter 12

The Most Important Thing In the World

A bead of water dripped down my glass and I followed its journey all the way to the tablecloth. It made me think of the sweat of passion. It made me think of tears over loved ones lost. It made me think about nearly anything other than the ugly psychodrama that was taking place across the table from me. Paul and Angela Taylor were tearing each other apart.

"Isn't your birthday coming up, Ken?" Angela said, pulling herself away from their joust momentarily. Her voice was as deep and brassy as her red hair.

"At the end of August. Thanks for reminding me. I would have forgotten it."

"Yeah, don't worry about it," she said. I'm sure she thought I was being sarcastic, though there was a very real chance I would have forgotten my birthday given how my world had turned upside down. "Did you know that Paul forgot our anniversary? It's only the *second* time he's done it."

Paul snorted into his wineglass. "Five years of marital bliss. How could it slip my mind?"

You never should have gotten to your fifth anniversary, Paul. In another world you and Angela split up, you met another woman, and you were married – and insanely happy – within six months. Do you know why you're still with Angela? I do, but if I tell you, you'll think I've lost my mind. I kept silent and hunkered down in my chair, ducking the crossfire and smiling at the occasional ricochet.

Paul and I went back a half dozen years. We'd been thrown together in a foursome on a golf course in Fairfax, had a few beers together after the round, and stayed in regular contact ever since. Melissa loved him, and she really loved Jeannie, his second wife who was unfortunately as absent from this scenario as my fiancée. I was thankful that Paul and I were still friends in this world. I needed him more than ever and I contacted him right away. When I suggested we meet at the Neapolitan, an Italian restaurant that we both frequented, he replied that, "We would love to come."

I expected to see Jeannie, though I shouldn't have. When I saw Angela, I knew this dinner was going to be very different from the one I'd planned. Paul always held the door for Jeannie. He let it close on Angela. Paul pulled out Jeannie's chair. He let Angela do it herself. I remembered Angela with a petite figure when she and Paul split. Now she had a figure like a fire hydrant. Paul had changed, too, from a tall, wiry man with gym-thickened arms. This Paul had an arid face and hair streaked with gray. Stress and emotional emptiness will do that to a person. I wondered how long it would take for it to affect me.

"We haven't seen you in a while," Angela said casually. The music wasn't loud, but her voice was just a decibel below a shout. She swore that being a supervisor in a customer service center gave her lungs of iron. I think she just liked to make herself heard. "You should come by our house more often."

I never got the sense that Angela liked me, and I was sure it was no different now. She had another agenda here, though I couldn't be certain what it was. I didn't really want to know. It was hard not to blame their marital problems on her. It's natural to take your friend's side in these kinds of situations. It went beyond that in this case. I knew what Paul really wanted out of a marriage. I knew how content and fulfilled he could be. It was physically painful to watch him being eaten alive by this toxic relationship.

And it hurt to realize that I had a lot to do with it. This Paul never met Melissa, so we never had the conversation one chilly night when he told me that seeing what I had with the woman I loved had convinced him to end the charade with Angela, to try to find the same thing for himself. He told me then that the two of us had completely changed his mind about what a relationship could be. I wished – for both of us – that I could show him again.

I realized both of them were watching me. I'd never responded to the last thing Angela had said. Truthfully, the silence was a relief. I shook my head. "Sorry, I got distracted there for a second."

"Eye caught a young beauty at the bar?" Paul said with a bit of vicarious thrill in his voice. Angela threw him a sharp look.

"No," I said, shaking my head again. "Something reminded me of an old case."

"Count on Paul to have his mind in the gutter," Angela said darkly. "Speaking of women, Ken, when are you going to settle down? You shouldn't be single. It's time."

"Why do you always get on this topic, Angela?"

"Am I talking to you, Paul? He's a good-looking man and a lawyer to boot. He makes more money in a day than you make in a week. I think any girl would be glad to grab him up."

Angela looked scornfully at Paul. I never kept up with her after the two of them split. Maybe she'd needed the change as much as he did. Maybe she even found contentment with someone else.

"I'm still looking," I said softly. "I guess I haven't found the right person yet. Or maybe she just hasn't found me."

"Or maybe the whole idea of a 'right person' is as much of a myth as the Loch Ness Monster," Paul said cynically. I actually thought I saw a little hurt in Angela's eyes before she sneered at him. It was hard to think of something to say after that, though I didn't want another awkward silence.

"This pasta is delicious," I said, much too brightly. "Yours good?"

"Yum, just like home," Paul said sarcastically.

Angela put her fork down. "Excuse me," she said. "I have to make a phone call."

I started to feel a little sorry for her. This is what happens when wounds are allowed to fester.

When she left, Paul rubbed his temples. "Sorry about that," he said with the gravity of an undertaker.

"We usually save it for home. Lately we've brought the Paul-and-Angela Show on the road. You don't need to see this."

"No apologies necessary. All couples fight. Even me and Melissa..."

"Who?"

"Just somebody I once knew. Hard to believe I never mentioned her to you. Anyway, it's good having dinner with you two."

"Yeah, we can brighten anyone's day." He ate another forkful of pasta, but the food seemed to disagree with him. He drank some more wine and his mood brightened. "Hey, did you ever hear from Lori?"

I nodded. "She left a message a couple of days ago. What's she like?"

"She seems great. Blonde, cute, friendly. A real Georgia peach. You know, just like Angela." He said that last sentence with a snarl, though he hardly needed to underscore his sarcasm.

"How did you meet her?"

"She's a friend of my sister's. I see her sometimes at Maureen's parties, and she mentioned she wasn't seeing anyone at the moment. I told her a few lies about how great you were. She was interested, so I gave her your number. You don't mind when I do that, do you?"

I remembered that Paul had tried to fix me up with a number of women before I met Melissa. They were all perfectly pleasant, and most of them were beautiful, but I always got the impression that they fit his ideal rather than what he thought mine was.

"I appreciate the effort, but I've been kind of busy at the office lately. Ridiculous hours. I'm not sure I'll have time to see someone right now."

"Since when does one have anything to do with the other? You were always able to slide 'em in before." He paused and studied me for a moment. He was a project manager for the Department of Transportation, and he claimed he could size up a person in less than two seconds. "You look different, Ken. Is everything okay?"

I really wanted to tell him. Right then before Angela got back. I wanted to throw everything that happened since Friday out on the table and have him tell me that he understood, that I wasn't crazy for feeling what I was feeling, and that he would figure out some way to get me back to Melissa. But I had no idea how to have the conversation, let alone have it *quickly*.

"I'm fine. Just a lot of things going on. Nothing I can talk about right now." I took a big gulp of ginger ale.

Paul shrugged. I didn't think he'd accepted what I said at face value, but he didn't push it. "So what's with drinking soda?" he said.

"I had a checkup. The doctor told me to cut down on alcohol."

"You? I'll believe you can do that when fish stop breathing water."

"At some point you have to realize when you're hurting yourself. Speaking of which, how are you really doing?"

"The same. The job is still there. I make sure states get their pork-barrel road projects and politicians get reelected. Occasionally, we build a road that goes somewhere."

Paul had never been that jaded about his job. He liked to say that he helped keep America moving. This was obviously another indication he'd been worn down. "I meant you and Angela."

"You need to ask?"

"It seems to have kicked up to a new level."

Paul snorted and gulped his wine. "It's been the same for a while, really. It's kind of amazing that you couldn't see it. How does this shit happen? I mean I really thought we were right for each other when we got together. But now..." He drained his glass and quickly signaled the waiter for another. "You can see for yourself. We went to visit a marriage counselor – a hundred bucks an hour to have some touchy-feely fool tell us we had a communications problem. Hell, our dog could have told us the same thing. On second thought, don't call Lori back. If you got saddled with one of these long-term, I'd never be able to forgive myself. You have no idea how lucky you are not to be burdened with this crap."

"I don't feel very lucky, to tell you the truth. I've been thinking a lot lately about settling down. I'd love to find a wife and have a family. Buy a house with a big backyard and a garden."

"You?" Paul looked at me as though I'd just told him the Redskins' quarterback was switching to professional badminton. "You'll settle down about two days after the Ice Capades play Hell. Don't get all romantic on me, Ken. Some of us need to live our lives through you."

"Trust me; bachelor living isn't all it's cracked up to be. And marriage doesn't have to be a trap. To tell you the truth, I feel empty without a significant person in my life."

Paul simply stared at me for what must have been thirty seconds. Then he said, "Ignore your doctor, Ken. Really, I mean it. If this is how you see the world when you aren't drinking, I'd suggest taking several stiff ones right now."

"Do you think you could be just a little more cynical? Your rosy-eyed optimism is a little naïve."

The waiter brought Paul's new drink, and he took a long sip before raising the glass in my direction. "Exactly my point, buddy. Look, I'm sure there are people in the world whose marriages turned out a whole lot better than mine. That doesn't mean the institution still doesn't suck."

I was getting frustrated. Not only wasn't this the conversation I'd intended to have with Paul, but I didn't like this version of Paul very much. "So why don't you do something about it?" I said. "Why don't you make some effort to get out of the rut you're in?"

"I couldn't climb out of my rut with a grappling hook," he said miserably.

"You're going to die a bitter old man if you keep up this attitude."

He regarded me angrily. "Are you telling me to dump my wife?"

"I'm not telling you anything. Other than if your life is as awful as it seems, you kinda have to do something about it."

He laughed humorlessly, and when he made eye contact with me again, there was something more conciliatory in his eyes as well as something a little more hopeful. "I never told you this for reasons that will become obvious, but a while ago I thought about leaving Angela. We were fighting. As you said, everybody fights, but ours started turning really ugly. The kind of brawl where each of you scrounges under the carpet for every bit you can pick up and hurl at the other person."

"So what happened?" The other Paul told me a story of a fight so nasty that he went to a lawyer and filed divorce papers the next day.

"I talked to a lawyer. I took off work and went to a divorce attorney who someone recommended. I really had to pull strings to see him so quickly; there are an awful lot of people divorcing out there, you know."

"I could have gotten someone at the firm to help you."

"You're out of my league. Besides, I didn't want to get into this with any of my friends until I had a few details. I went to see this guy and he told me what my options were and how to begin the process. A few nights later Angela and I were going at it tooth and nail again – I think I forgot to take out the garbage or something – and I started dividing up the furniture in my head. I got the television. She got the couch. As long as I got the TV, I would have given her just about anything else she wanted." Paul drained his glass and signaled to the waiter.

"Are you driving?" I said. "You might want to slow down a little."

"What's the point? Anyway, I was all set to walk out and even had the scenario set up in my head. At breakfast I would march into the kitchen with suitcase in hand and say, 'I'm out of here.' In my fantasies, I even had visions of Angela begging me to stay, holding on to my leg and everything. But the next morning I wimped out. I couldn't do it."

"Why not? From what I can see here, it sounds like it would have been a good move."

Paul's head sagged. He looked utterly defeated. "The truth, my good friend, is that there just didn't seem to be any real reason to do it. The divorce process would have been a nightmare, and in the end, I'd just be alone for a while until I hooked up with some other woman to have a little bit of fun before *that* all turned to shit. It just didn't seem worth the energy."

"You're wrong."

"I don't think so."

"I know so."

Paul laughed indignantly. "Really? Are you gonna tell me you have a crystal ball in the car."

"I'm just telling you that I can imagine you – imagine you very vividly – with an attractive, intelligent woman who adores you. She thinks you're smart and funny and handsome. This woman – let's call her Joanie – and you will be so in love that within a few months you will be married and planning babies and picket fences and all of that stuff."

For a moment, I could see that the image fascinated Paul, as though he got a glimpse of Jeannie/Joanie and saw his future in her eyes. Then he shivered and shook his head.

"I think you've been working too hard, Ken. Your brain is going soft, and you're starting to sound like a bad greeting card."

"You need to listen to me. You can meet the woman of your dreams and fall in love. This is not the best life has to offer."

Paul threw up his hands. "Thanks for the pep talk, buddy, but you live your life and I'll live mine, okay?"

I wasn't going to give up. For some reason, getting this message across to Paul was hugely important to me. As I leaned in to give it another try, though, I saw Angela approach the table. Her expression was stony, as though she'd spent the last several minutes draining herself of any emotion. She sat down without saying anything, offering me a look that I interpreted as recrimination, though I know she couldn't have heard our conversation.

I glanced over at Paul. His latest drink had arrived, and right now it seemed like the most important thing in the world to him.

Chapter 13

A Different Magic Trick

I felt very alone in this world. Paul was different. The people in my office saw me as someone I hadn't been for a long time. Even the cat's attitude wasn't the same. Meanwhile, Melissa was impossibly far away, seated behind her grand piano practicing in some rehearsal hall or perhaps the glass-enclosed great room of a magnificent villa out west (her online bio was no more specific than that). I needed to connect with someone who knew me, someone who knew who I really was.

I went to see Stephon.

"I was wrong," he said with a patient smile when I stepped into the store. "I guessed you'd be here yesterday."

"I was too stupefied to come in here yesterday."

He dipped his head and nodded. Stephon seemed a little different too – different beyond his businesslike clothing. Had I somehow changed him as well? Did it have something to do with the jewelry I didn't buy for Melissa, that bauble he went out of his way to get for me and then I ignored altogether? Or was it something else entirely, something about the trip he'd sent me on?

"Tell me what you've found," he said softly.

"You really don't know?"

"I really don't know."

I approached the counter slowly. I don't think I'd ever walked this far into the store without my eye landing on some remarkable item or other. Today, the only thing I noticed was the carpet.

"She's gone," I said. "Completely gone. We never met, she doesn't live in Washington, and she has a completely different, completely fabulous life without me."

Stephon seemed touched by the news. "You knew this could happen."

"To tell you the truth, I had no idea this could happen. I mean, after seeing Melissa and Hoffman, I didn't think about much of anything other than destroying that horrible woman."

"You did save Melissa from her, didn't you?"

I shook my head sadly. "I did."

"And you say she has a great life now."

"She certainly seems to. She's a professional musician. I never knew it, but this is what she always wanted."

"Then you did a great thing for her."

I closed my eyes and took a deep breath. "Yes, I did."

"But?"

"But I did a terrible thing for me. Not to mention what's happened to my friend Paul, or that my assistant thinks she works for an unfeeling jerk, or that my cleaning person needs to wear a HazMat suit every time he comes to my apartment."

"I tried to explain to you that there could be unfortunate consequences to your actions."

I threw my arms up in the air. "I know you did. I mean, I heard you say it, though I didn't really comprehend it. There has to be something I can do. There has to be something *you* can do. Don't I get a third wish or something?"

Stephon smiled dimly. "That's a different magic trick, and not one I'm capable of performing, I'm afraid."

"You can send me back again, can't you? There has to be a way to set this up. I'll give it a huge amount of thought this time before I go. I'll arrange a way for me to meet Melissa just before she gets her big break. I'll set up signposts."

Stephon held up a hand to stop me. I hadn't intended to do this when I came here, but I couldn't help myself. "I don't think you realize what this cost me," he said gravely. "I can't send you back again. It's impossible."

I felt physically heavier with those words. "You really can't?"

"I'll never be able to do that for you again."

I rubbed my face with my hand. "I can't believe how totally I've screwed up my life. Why didn't I anticipate this?"

Stephon leaned forward and touched me on the shoulder. It was a surprisingly intimate act. "What would you have done if you *had* anticipated it?"

The unexpected physical gesture shook me. "What do you mean?"

"What would you have done if you knew things were going to turn out exactly the way they turned out? If you knew that your alternatives were allowing Melissa to carry a terrible scar the rest of her life or freeing her at the cost of losing her, would you have chosen not to go back that second time?"

He took his hand from my shoulder and I held his gaze for several long seconds before I answered. "I would have gone back," I said, absolutely convinced of the fact.

He nodded sadly. "I know you would have. That's why I did what I had to do to get you there."

"So what happens now?"

"Now you have to live with your decision and do what you can to make the most out of your life."

"You mean I should forget about Melissa?"

"I never said that."

"I can't. I won't. Ever."

"Nor should you."

"But I have no idea what to do without her. I've never felt lost before. But I feel completely lost now."

"What do you think Melissa would want you to do?"

I knew the answer to that question. I just never thought for a second that I would ever put that knowledge to use.

⌇

Melissa looked like a soldier when she stepped out of the bedroom. Her appearance was so martial that I snapped to attention and gave her a stiff salute worthy of the Marine guards at the White House. Melissa responded with two fingers to her forehead and laughed.

"I think you have me mistaken for my father," she said with a chuckle.

She was dressed in a khaki jacket and pants with enough pockets to supply an entire platoon for a week. Her brow was hidden under a wide-brimmed bush hat that looked like a leftover from a safari documentary.

The owner at the camping equipment store could have bought a yacht with the profits he made from selling her all that outdoor gear. Her equipment was supposed to be appropriate for environmentalists spending two weeks in the Amazon.

"I think your inner Colonel is coming out," I said. "Why do I have the sudden desire to call you 'sir?'"

"Do it once and you'll regret it the rest of your life, Mister." She looked down at her duds and then up at me quizzically. "It's pretty awful, isn't it? Not to mention that these new jungle boots are killing my feet."

I smiled. "You look great. You really do. You should have gotten this outfit months ago. Promise me you'll wear it for me again when you get back."

"Is *everything* a turn-on to you?"

"*You* are always a turn-on to me. Even when you're dressed like G.I. Jane."

She rolled her eyes, smiled, and looked up at the ceiling. When she looked back down, though, her expression was different. She pulled a folded paper from her jacket pocket. "Ken, I have to be at Dulles in an hour. I want to talk to you about something before the car service gets here. You know the place where I'm going has some problems."

"I've tried to avoid thinking about that." That wasn't true. I'd thought about little else since Melissa told me about this insane mission of hers. Where she was going was full of Marxist guerrillas killing capitalists, rightwing paramilitaries killing guerrillas, and cocaine growers killing anyone who stumbled on their jungle operations. It was one of those areas where the good guys and the bad guys were often the same, and travel agents crossed themselves before accepting your reservation. I tried to convince her not to go, but a crisis drew her like a moth to a flame. Extinction was threatening some rare species of rodent with a long Latin name that looked like a furry baseball with teeth. I certainly didn't want the animal to disappear off the face of the earth – but I wanted Melissa put in harm's way a whole lot less.

"You have to think about it."

"What if I don't want to? What if I choose not to understand why you're going to one of the most dangerous places on the planet to save a rat?"

"Don't be that way, Ken. You know how important this is to me. This is why I do what I do. Do you have any idea how frustrating it is seeing my efforts undermined by special interests day in and day out?"

"We've had a few conversations about it, yes." There were days when Melissa could barely speak at night because of her pent-up frustrations.

"Well, I'm tired of sitting in Washington and arguing with stupid politicians and arrogant bureaucrats all day. Sometimes even I forget that what I'm doing isn't about pushing papers or making speeches, but saving the ecology of our planet. For the first time in ages, I have a chance to go out in the field and make an active difference. I have to do this."

"Melissa, I know how important these things are to you and I'm very proud of you for doing them. But I just don't think this is worth risking your life for. People get hurt out there. Seriously hurt. Every day."

"I'm a big girl."

"There are a lot of *bigger* men over there."

"I can't live my life in a bubble, Ken. I have to be willing to act on my beliefs. Once this species is wiped out in the Amazon, that's it. There will be nowhere else on earth where it can be found, and it will be gone for-ever. And the whole planet will die just a little bit more."

"There's a tremendous chance that this species is go-ing to die off regardless of your intervention, you know. You can't stand guard down there forever."

"You may be right, but if I don't try, I won't be able to live with myself." Her shoulders relaxed and she walked closer to me. "Let's not fight like this before I go." She sat down next to me and handed me the folded sheet. "They told us to give these to our families. It's a list of names and phone numbers for you to call if something happens."

I took the sheet from her and grimaced. I knew the "something" she was talking about.

"The people on the list know what to do if those situ-ations occur," she said. "They will know how to get us out."

"Melissa, I read the newspapers. I've also handled cases for multinational companies who operate in that region. They take out special insurance polices to pay the five million dollars those kidnappers out there charge. I also know what the kidnappers do if they don't get their money right away."

She wrapped an arm around my shoulders. "That's not going to happen. This is just a precaution. Ameri-cans go in and out of that region all the time." She kissed me on the cheek. It was hard to feel her body through all the gear. "Besides, who would be dumb enough to think that anyone would pay five million dollars for me?"

"I'd pay every penny I made for the rest of my life."

She squeezed me and tried a smile. "I'd better be careful then. I mean, what's the point of coming home if we're going to be broke?"

Her attempt at humor didn't work on me.

"Listen," she said. "I know everything is going to be all right. Our people on the ground there know how to keep us safe. If something does happen, though, just remember that I love you and I want you to live the rest of your life the best way you can."

"Is the fact that you feel the need to make this speech supposed to make me feel better?"

"Hey, maybe I'm doing it because it makes *me* feel better. Here's the rest of it: I know you will wait a while, but don't wait forever. Find a nice girl and bring as much joy and laughter into her life as you have brought into mine. Promise me you will do that."

"I'm not making any promises."

"You have to. You can't send me out there without this promise."

"Can I be really miserable and just screw around a lot?"

Melissa squeezed me harder and put her face right up against mine. I could feel her breath in my ear and I ached for her to stay right here beside me. "Promise," she said forcefully.

I closed my eyes. "I promise."

She pushed me away from her. "Really? You would just forget about me like that?"

"You know how unfair this is, right?"

She moved into my lap and kissed me. "I'm serious. I always want you to be happy. Even if it can't be with me."

Chapter 14

Mind Eraser

"I promise," I said as I sat in my recliner shrouded in solitude and darkness. The lights were off, except for the red bead of the answering machine and the liquid green glow of the clock on the cable box. It was nearly ten o'clock.

Melissa wanted me to make the most of my life. Stephon wanted me to make the most of my life. How, exactly, did one go about doing that? I hadn't been looking for a total life transformation when I met Melissa. I wasn't expecting to gain entry to a whole level of existence so much richer and more satisfying than I knew possible. But now that I was aware it was out there, I also knew how many things had to go exactly right to attain it. Trying to recapture it without Melissa seemed about as possible as a Cinderella team winning a world championship two years in a row, or catching a glimpse of the Aurora Borealis by just walking outside.

What was "the most of my life" without Melissa?

The rest of the night and all the next day I played Melissa's albums and wallowed. No, this wasn't moving forward, but I frankly didn't care.

On Monday, Harrison Warwick knocked on my office door. As usual, he had a Cuban cigar in his mouth – unlit because of city laws – and he bore the well-fed look of a man treated generously by life. His hair was the silver of a shiny quarter, his paunch spilled comfortably over his belt buckle, and the cost of his suit exceeded the gross national product of several nations. He was a dandy and a boor. He was also a world-class lawyer, born to power and well-trained in using it.

"I have noticed how you have been spending your time," he said once he closed the door behind him.

"Excuse me?"

"It's obvious that you have been working very hard the last few months. You know I'm not big on back-patting, but I wanted to let you know that your zeal has not gone unnoticed."

He should have seen me yesterday morning. "I'm just putting my nose to the grindstone, that's all."

"It's impressive when someone with your talents decides to turn up the intensity. I just wanted you to know that the partners and I are aware of this. We have some decisions to make around here. You're making at least one of them easy."

"Thank you, sir."

"No reason to thank me, Ken. Just keep producing."

I gestured toward the brief on my desk. "Doing just that, Mr. Warwick."

Warwick nodded. "I won't take any more of your time."

He left the office, closing the door behind him. My eyes stayed on the door for a minute after he left. Obviously, I knew what Warwick was talking about. The decisions he referred to regarded fifth-year associates. My goal from the time I'd left law school was to make partner in my early thirties. Now my boss was suggesting I was on track. Under different circumstances, a conversation like this would have been cause for me to pick up the phone and crow for a little while, but I had no one to crow to. There was no one in my life who really cared whether I made partner or not. And if it happened, there would be people to celebrate with, but no one who really understood how much this meant to me.

My intercom sounded.

"Mr. Timian, Marty Gaynor is in the reception area. You don't have an appointment with him. Would you like to see him?"

Marty Gaynor? It had been a long time. I looked down at my calendar and saw that I had a few minutes before my next appointment. "Sure, Sharon, bring him in."

Marty knocked on the door and bounded into the room. He was built like a fullback, with thick brows overshadowing dark, darting eyes. He had a sharp legal mind and he was also clever enough to use his thuggish features to disarm and intimidate his opponents. We'd met years ago, going toe-to-toe on a case: We bloodied each other and then became friends over several dozen drinks when the trial was over.

"Hey, Ken," he said in his booming voice.

"Hey, Marty. This is a surprise. What are you doing here?"

"Had to stop by to confer with one of your colleagues. Thought I'd come see how you were doing."

"Yeah, thanks. It's been a while." Melissa had taken an instant dislike to Marty. It probably had something to do with the way he leered at her when they met. Or maybe the way he ridiculed her chosen profession. Or perhaps his eating habits. Or the fact that he instructed the waiter to "keep the drinks coming" when we sat down. She never explained and she didn't have to. I hadn't seen him socially since, dodging a few invitations until he got the message.

"Yeah, well that bitch ball and chain was a real problem."

I nearly sprung out of my seat to pummel him until I realized that he couldn't have meant Melissa. "What are you talking about?"

"I finally dumped Lynn. I thought I'd stop by personally to give you the good news. I can't believe I let her drag me around for the past few months. She even had me convinced that I needed to spend less time hanging out with people like you. As of yesterday afternoon, she's history."

I nodded, trying to comprehend all of this.

"So now I need to make up for lost time," he said coarsely. "Friday, the Shamrock Saloon, seven o'clock. A little jailbreak party for me. I assume you'll join in the celebration."

The idea made me a little queasy. My memories of nights at the Shamrock with Marty were hazy for good reason. "Gee, Marty, I'm not sure I can get away on Friday. Warwick was just in here hassling me about improving my level of production. I'm probably going to be working straight through the weekend."

Marty hurried to the window and peered through the blinds. "That's funny, the sun hasn't gone nova, but Ken Timian is passing up a night on the town. Maybe I should call Lynn and ask her if hell has frozen over. She'd know – she gets the news firsthand from her mother."

"I'm afraid it's a matter of priorities, Marty. If Warwick the Lesser tells you to put your nose to the grindstone – especially when you're in your fifth year – you grind away."

"Hey, I know a little something about hard work. I've been in four cities over the last two weeks. My mind is on Zurich time and my body thinks it's in Korea. But do you see me stiffing my friends? We're both entitled to let off some steam after hours. Hey, go back to the office afterward. It wouldn't be the first time – assuming you don't get a better offer from one of the ladies. I mean, what would these festivities be without you? Everyone will ask where you are. I don't want to have to tell them that The King of Friday Night has turned into a wimp."

The King of Friday Night? Even in the wildest of my pre-Melissa days, I had not acquired that moniker. What, exactly, *had* I been up to?

"I have not turned into a wimp. Maybe I've just grown up. Have you checked your birth certificate lately?"

Marty regarded me strangely for a minute. Then he broke into a smile. "I get it. You're giving me shit because I didn't go out much when I was with Lynn. Temporary insanity, buddy. Very temporary and very insane. Seriously over now."

"That's not it."

"Let me make it up to you. I'll pay for the Mind Eraser."

The Mind Eraser. Yet another thing I hadn't thought about in a couple of years. The very memory of the drink made me queasy.

"Was that meant to persuade me?"

"Okay, I know you make a lot more than I do, but hey, a free drink is still a free drink. Especially when it's a pint of shots."

I really felt I was going to lose that morning's granola. I hadn't had a single drink since I stepped into this universe. What would something like the Mind Eraser do to me? I started to take another tack in avoiding going out with Marty and "our" friends when another thought came to mind. Friday would have been the eve of my wedding. I knew it was going to be a tough weekend. Maybe impossibly tough. Perhaps a little *erasure* wouldn't be the worst thing.

"All right, you wore me down," I said. "If I don't make partner, I'm holding you personally accountable, but I'll be there."

Marty thudded me on the back. "Just made my day, Ken. I'll see you at the Shamrock."

He started to head toward the door when he stopped and turned back toward me. "You know I was kidding about paying for the drinks, right?"

"It's okay, Marty. I can handle it."

〰〰

I never made a conscious decision to curtail my drinking. None was necessary. Never in my adult life did I fear that I was becoming an alcoholic even though I drank a great deal, because there had been stretches when I was working so hard that I didn't even think of getting a drink. Once Melissa and I got together, my interest in getting drunk naturally dissipated. What was the point of achieving an altered state when my current state felt so good? Over time, the notion of drinking to get drunk became increasingly unpleasant, the way one might feel about a return trip to Mexico after a bout with Montezuma's Revenge.

Friday was tough, though. For months, I'd had this day planned out. I would serve Melissa breakfast in bed. Afterward, a reiki specialist would come to the apartment to give her a massage, and then we would return to bed until the late afternoon. That night, we'd have an intimate dinner party at Galileo for family and friends and then come home for some slow dancing in the living room before getting to sleep early for the big day that followed.

Instead, I woke up early Friday morning, grabbed a bagel, took the train to the office, and sat through an endless series of droning meetings. With each minute that passed, I felt just a little emptier, a little more like the best part of my life had passed me by. If Friday had been this bad, Saturday was going to be a nightmare.

By the time the evening rolled around, the idea of an altered state was no longer repellant. A last-minute phone call from a nervous client detained me in the office, so I was running late as I headed toward the Georgetown bar. That was okay. The King of Friday Night had the right to show up after everyone else, didn't he?

As I climbed out of my car, I glanced up at the sky. A storm was due, and the first tendrils were already creeping overhead. I made my way along sidewalks crowded with chattering college students until I reached the bar. The Shamrock was an Irish pub where students raised in the Midwest pretended to be Irish waiters and waitresses. It was all pretense and more than a little silly, but it was a setting that worked for the numerous evenings of debauchery I once enjoyed.

"Good day to you, Mr. Timian," an olive-skinned hostess said in an accent more Chicago than Dublin.

I smiled nervously. Being recognized by the first staff member who saw me made me uncomfortable. "Hello."

"Your party is in the back room."

The Shamrock was filled with cigarette smoke, loud music, the smell of fried food, and overheated conversation. Getting to the back required weaving through numerous other tables, filled with people who seemed to have started their nights much earlier. One guy backed into me and spun around in confrontation. I threw up my hands and he calmed down. Melissa and I had never been here together and I realized as I continued my journey that I'd never wanted her to see this place, let alone know that I once frequented it. Melissa knew I drank a great deal before we got together. She just didn't need such a vivid picture of it painted for her.

"Good evening, Mr. Timian," a waiter staggering under a big tray of nachos shouted. His green shirt matched the cardboard shamrocks dangling from the ceiling. I could barely hear him over the piped-in sounds of an Irish jig played by a California band. Theme bars always had the subtlety of sledgehammers and the authenticity of international pavilions at amusement parks.

"Hey, Ken." Marty waved a half-empty beer stein in my direction. "You made it. For a few minutes there, I thought you might actually have been serious about having too much work." Marty was sitting at the foot of three tables pulled together. There were at least fifteen people sitting there with him, all of whom looked like they'd been drinking for a while.

"It was touch and go for a second there," I said, "but I couldn't miss out on this, now, could I?"

Chairs scraped the floor as everyone made room for me in the middle of a table. As I settled in my seat, I took stock of my companions. I only knew a few of them. But the business-formal or expensive-casual clothes on the rest were the sign of young Washington professionals. Without asking, I knew that most of them worked for law firms, the government, think tanks, or the myriad places that drew the bright and ambitious to this town.

As a dozen hands reached out to shake mine, my eyes traversed their fingers. Most of them weren't wearing wedding rings, except for a ponytailed man who wore a plain gold band. I was sure that the lucky woman who it was pledged to was not the giggling blonde currently draping her arm around his shoulders.

A waiter appeared. "What are you starting with tonight, Mr. Timian?"

"Just a club soda," I said automatically. The waiter seemed confused. I caught Marty's surprised expression out of the corner of my eye. I'm sure I was imagining it, but I could swear the conversation level dropped while people stared at me. "And a double Bushmills, of course," I said with a huge smile. The waiter laughed and I saw Marty shake his head.

A leggy brunette sitting beside me smiled with her dark red lips and introduced herself as Andrea. "I'm a friend of Jean," she said. "She's told me wonderful things about you."

"That was nice of her," I said tentatively. I had no idea who Jean was, and I didn't want to think too hard about the "wonderful things."

On the other side of me was a slender man in a blue pinstriped shirt who introduced himself as Burton. Across from him was the ponytailed man with the blonde accessory. The two men were arguing politics while the woman looked bored and sipped aggressively at her drink.

I glanced at Andrea, who also looked bored and maybe a little tipsy. She smiled at me again. Her teeth were just a little irregular – not the picture-perfect smiles of so many people I knew. It was refreshingly attractive.

"So what do you do, Ken?" Obviously Jean hadn't told her that. Of course, she could have simply been making conversation. It was the first thing everybody asked around here. This was a town that defined you not by who you were but by how you made your living.

"I'm a lawyer. How about yourself?"

She laughed shyly and cast her eyes down.

"Nothing so exciting, I have to say. I'm an office administrator for Wilco Systems. You know, the guys who get those half-billion dollar contracts to run the government's computers? Sometimes I think we run the government, but that's another story. Anyway, I make sure we have enough coffee and printer cartridges."

My whiskey came and I took a careful sip. The sensation was a little disorienting and I reminded myself to go slowly since my body had little tolerance for alcohol at this point. I took another sip. I had to admit that I loved the taste of Bushmills and maybe even missed it a little.

"Let me guess, Andrea. You come from California."

"Santa Barbara, as a matter of fact. How did you know?

"You have no regional accent. California natives never do."

"You have a slight one. New Jersey?

"Close enough. Just outside Philadelphia."

A couple more sips and I started to feel comfortable. The music, the noise, the heat of bodies crowded together, and of course the whiskey, were all a bit of a cocoon. I could do this for a while. I could probably even enjoy it if I lowered my standards.

"Being a lawyer sounds interesting," Andrea said. She had very nice legs under her black mini. They were hard to miss, since she'd angled her chair around to face me more directly.

"It has its moments." I smiled. "But nothing like running the government."

She laughed and touched me on the arm, allowing her hand to linger there a little bit. Like the whiskey, there was something familiar and both mildly disquieting and mildly fascinating about this exchange. Like most single, well-off guys in this town, I'd had dozens of encounters like this. I had no idea if Andrea was seeing me as a dalliance or a potential catch, but she *definitely* saw me as game to be hunted. That was clear within thirty seconds.

Marty tapped a spoon against his glass. He rose and moved over behind me, clasping my shoulder.

"For those of you who haven't attended one of our little outings before, you are looking at a local legend. I refer to Ken Timian, the gentleman before me. Care to say a few words, Ken?"

I felt instantly uncomfortable, the soothing nature of the Bushmills quickly forgotten. "That's okay, Marty. I'll leave the speeches to you."

"If you insist. In a moment, our waitperson will bring a special drink for Mr. Timian. It is known as the Mind Eraser, for reasons that will be obvious as soon as you see it. I cannot divulge the recipe for national security reasons, lest the enemy mount it on their missiles. Though as far as weapons of mass destruction are concerned, this would be a much more pleasant way to die than most. Are you feeling fit tonight, Ken?"

"A little early in the evening, Marty," I said nervously. In spite of his mentioning the drink earlier in the week, I hadn't expected to have to deal with it unless I chose to order one myself.

"Nonsense. You're a little behind the rest of us. This will get you up to speed."

"Maybe you and I could split one."

"I don't think so, Ken. I haven't prepared my will yet." Everyone laughed, which did nothing to make me feel more comfortable.

I looked around and noticed that Andrea was regarding me with fascination. She leaned forward and squeezed my leg. "Jean told me you have a superhuman ability to hold your liquor. I can't wait to see you in action."

What is it about a woman's describing you as "superhuman" – even regarding an idiotic activity – that makes men preen ridiculously? Suddenly, I felt emboldened, inspired. Andrea smiled and squeezed my leg again.

"Ladies and gentlemen," Marty said like a ringmaster at the circus, "I give you the Mind Eraser." While everyone applauded, a waitress approached the table bearing a pint mug filled with scarlet liquid. I couldn't remember everything that went into one of these, but I knew it was all more than a hundred proof.

The waitress deposited the drink in front of me. The bartender had put a long pink eraser attached to a toothpick at the rim of the mug. I noticed several waiters and waitresses clustered around and that everyone else at the table stared at me.

I smiled politely and took a tiny sip.

Marty thumped me hard on the back and laughed loudly. "Very funny, Ken. Don't worry, your boss is nowhere in sight. It's showtime."

I stared at the mug and imagined Melissa watching me. What would she think if she saw me in this situation? *Not exactly the '96 Barolo I was planning to order at Galileo, is it?*

Then the thought came to me: what difference did it make? Melissa wasn't watching me. We weren't getting married tomorrow. If word ever got back to her about Ken Timian and the Mind Eraser, her response would be, "Who's Ken Timian?" There was a woman in a short dress practically sitting in my lap, exhorting me on – and a whole lot of oblivion waiting on the other side. I reached for the mug.

"Ken. Ken. Ken."

The rhythmic chant of the crowd inspired me. I brought the mug to my lips. It smelled sweet and pungent. I closed my eyes and took a huge pull. There was no chance I was going to drink the entire thing in one chug. I don't think I'd ever done that, and I wasn't sure it was humanly possible. Still, I downed the equivalent of at least five shots at once.

I gasped for breath and reached for my club soda. Applause replaced the chanting. Marty pounded me on the shoulders, exclaiming, "My man's still got it." Andrea squeezed my leg again and kissed me on the temple.

I reached for the mug....

≈

I opened my eyes to see the ceiling leaning like a weeping willow. Watery light slipped past the blinds, floating like the dust motes they silhouetted. I moved my head – and paid the price. Nausea splashed through my stomach. My head felt squeezed by giant pliers.

A quick glance told me I was in my bedroom. I lay fully dressed on top of my bed. How had I gotten here?

I was parched and aching. I felt like I had the flu, but I knew the disease that caused this "infection" was psychological, not viral.

The last thing I remembered was laughing at some joke Marty told. Now it was the next day – at least I assumed only one day had gone by. The dresser clock said it was almost noon.

I got up gingerly and made my way into the bathroom. I was sure I was going to throw up and even more certain that I wanted to. Nothing happened, though. I stood upright, caught glimpse of myself in the mirror and quickly averted my eyes. I splashed cold water on my face and went back into the bedroom. I thought about laying down again, but that seemed too pathetic for words.

I decided to change my clothes. As I took off my pants, a yellow sticky note fell to the rug. Though I

wasn't sure my head could handle it, I bent down to pick
it up.

> Ken,

> You were in no condition to drive home last
> night, so I drove your car over and Andrea
> gave me a ride back. Incidentally, I wouldn't
> call Andrea for a while. Passing out on her
> chest wasn't the smoothest move. She said
> she thought you were a nice guy, but just a
> little too wild. What does she know?

> Anyway, sleep it off, buddy. Like I prom-
> ised, we had fun.

> Marty

I sat on the bed and put my head in my hands. I'd
passed out on Andrea's chest? What did that mean exactly? This might have been the most embarrassing night
in my life. Then again, since I had no idea what I was
like in this world, maybe it wasn't even in the top five.

Today, in the world I destroyed, was my wedding
day. I suppose in some segments of our society waking
up with a Size 10 hangover the day you get married is
standard practice. But having the wedding cancelled
because the bride didn't know who you were definitely
wasn't. The hangover would go away several excruciating hours from now, but the reason for the hangover
wouldn't be cured by time.

I'd tried on the notion of "moving on." It didn't fit.
There was nothing I could or would do to make it fit. I

didn't want to live in a world without Melissa. I didn't want to go back to being the old me, and I was equally certain that I didn't want to set off on a new life, finding a woman who might make me feel the way Melissa had made me feel.

I wanted one thing and one thing only. There was no substitute for Melissa and no replacement for the life we shared. I had to get back to her. She might be cloaked in celebrity and surrounded by an entourage, but I would find a way to get to her.

If I didn't, life wasn't worth living.

Chapter 15

Coming upon an Oasis

> HELLO PIANOMAN555. THIS IS
> MELISSALOVER.

The words flashed from my computer at the speed of light. Where did they go? To Los Angeles? Around the world to Australia? The apartment next door?

I waited impatiently as seconds ticked by. Then words appeared across my computer screen.

> HI MELISSALUV. WHAT CAN I DO FOR
> YOU?

> I WANT TO SEE MELISSA PLAY. DO
> YOU KNOW WHERE HER NEXT
> CONCERT IS?

Who was Pianoman555? Was he indeed a man, or was he a woman who liked the Billy Joel song? My searching around the Internet for information about

Melissa landed me in this chat forum for piano aficiona-
dos. The people who participated in it seemed to have no
social lives outside of this world, but it became obvious
very quickly that they knew a ton about Melissa. And
among them PIANOMAN555 was unquestionably the
most knowledgeable.

NOT ON TOUR NOW.

I LEARNED THAT FROM HER SITE. I
WAS HOPING THERE MIGHT BE SOME
NEWLY ANNOUNCED DATES NOT
POSTED YET.

THERE'S THE BENEFIT SHOW, OF
COURSE.

BENEFIT SHOW?

AT BENAROYA HALL IN SEATTLE
TOMORROW NIGHT. BIG CHILDREN
FIRST BENEFIT. SEEMS SHE CAN'T SAY
NO TO THESE THINGS.

THINK I CAN GET TICKETS?

DONT KNOW. HER TICKETS ARE
VERY HOT, ESPECIALLY WHEN IT'S A
ONE-OFF SHOW. CALL BOX OFFICE.

IF NOTHING THERE, LET US KNOW.
SOMETIMES PEOPLE HERE CAN HELP

THANKS A LOT PIANOMAN.

ANYTIME.

I felt a thrill of excitement as I left the chat room and picked up the phone. I was going to be able to see Melissa in the flesh soon.

I called the box office, but the woman there smugly told me that the show had been sold out for more than a month. I tried sweet-talking her, hoping there might be something on reserve, but that was useless.

I went to an online reseller next. $325 later, I had a good seat.

Next I needed to buy a ticket to Seattle. Having made several next-day plane trips in my life, I expected to be hit hard on this price as well. Amazingly, there was a deal on last-minute fares. I considered it a good omen.

I called Sharon at home to let her know that I wouldn't be in tomorrow. She seemed stunned to hear this and even a little worried. Though our relationship was in the process of improving, I think she still had some inkling that my change in personality was the result of an emotional breakdown. I eased her mind to the best of my ability.

When I got off the phone with Sharon, I started packing. I was a pro at this sort of thing and had been known to pack for a sudden business trip in less than five minutes. However, I'd never taken a business trip with the intention of introducing myself to my future wife. This was going to require more than simply grabbing a suit or two out of the closet.

Melissa liked me in blue. *It makes your eyes come alive,* she'd told me. So I threw a blue suit and blue shirt into a garment bag and a blue tie into my carry-on. I even threw a blue polo shirt into the bag in case Melissa and I wound up spending some time walking around the city the next day.

I completed the rest of my preparations, including calling the car service to deliver me to the airport a full two hours before my flight. I wasn't going to allow a traffic jam to prevent me from getting back to Melissa.

Of course I didn't sleep. I probably could have used a drink to calm me down, but I was very much off drinking again. Instead, I tried thinking about cases, I tried counting backward from a thousand, and I even tried remembering one of Melissa's concertos to soothe me. At 5:00, I finally just got out of bed. If I was lucky, I'd sleep on the plane. If not, I had more than enough adrenaline coursing through my veins to get me through the day.

~~~

The first surprise was that the flight arrived on time, despite leaving more than a half hour late. I saw this as another positive sign. If our pilot could overcome adversity and reach his goal, so could I.

We descended through lazy gray clouds and taxied through a patter of fat raindrops. The pilot announced the weather in the same matter-of-fact tone he might use to announce a sunny day in Phoenix. I hadn't thought to pack rain gear, but not even rain could dampen my sense of anticipation.

Through my cab's rain-spattered windows, SeaTac Airport slid by. "Business or pleasure?" the driver said. His reflection in the rearview mirror showed a bearded young man wearing a headband.

"I'm here for the Melissa Argent concert."

"The piano player? Yeah, I saw something about her on TV not so long ago. She still dating the lead singer in Act?"

"They split," I said tersely. As I learned through various fan sites, Melissa had been romantically linked for a while with someone from a popular British rock band. The celebrity media responded to this the way they always did: by glamorizing it and then overanalyzing it and finally reporting on it endlessly when it was over. While I didn't like to think about Melissa being romantically linked with anyone, I considered the breakup to be an indication that she was still searching for the right man.

That search would end today.

It was three o'clock by the time I arrived at the hotel. Pressurized air had squeezed my sinuses, while my legs still groaned from being confined for so long. In spite of the rain, I decided to take a walk to clear my mind and ease my body.

I went downhill to the harbor where the breeze off the gray water was moist and refreshing. I bought a cup of delicious red fish chowder from a waterfront shack. My stomach protested the light fare that barely made up for the tasteless sandwich I'd bought on the flight, but I didn't want to be bloated and logy during the concert. I wanted to be fully attentive for every minute of it.

As I walked back uphill, I passed a men's clothing store with an ad showing a gray-suited corporate clone transformed into a ponytailed dude wearing jeans and a leather jacket. I had last been to Seattle more than four years earlier, not long after I joined Warwick & Gray. The pace of this place was so quiet compared to the nation's capital, though I remember finding myself a little charmed by it. While dropping out of the fast lane was the last thing on my mind at the time, I could see the appeal of the pace of this city.

The sun came out while I walked and I perused the city for an hour and a half. Finally I returned to my room to shower and shave, even though I still had plenty of time. I tried to occupy myself with work, but I couldn't concentrate. I wound up watching television absently and checking the clock every three minutes. Finally, I got dressed. I considered my reflection in the mirror. Would Melissa like what she saw? I convinced myself that she would.

The home to the Seattle Symphony, Benaroya Hall was an elegant and beautifully maintained building. Milling in the glass-framed lobby were old money retirees in conservative formal wear and sleek young computer executives in stylish casuals. My ears picked up relaxed West Coast voices, the more clipped cadences of people from back East, and some soft-spoken Canadians likely down from Vancouver. Melissa's fans crossed continents and borders.

They even crossed time.

The doors to the auditorium opened and the crowd filed through like children in a school assembly. I moved quickly to get to my seat, as though doing so would hasten Melissa's arrival. Patrons buzzed in anticipation as I kept my eyes focused on the darkened stage. I imagined Melissa backstage, battling the butterflies she always got in her stomach before she spoke in public. They say great performers never get past that sense of anticipation just before they take the stage, no matter how prepared or confident they are. As the moment grew near, I felt my own butterflies. It had only been two-and-a-half weeks since I last saw Melissa, but at that instant, it felt like centuries.

Then a spotlight lit up the piano at the center of the stage and the crowd applauded enthusiastically. It arced stage left until it illuminated a figure entering calmly from the wing.

It was Melissa – and it wasn't. She was the same, and the sight sent my heart pounding so loudly that it drowned out the applause. Yet she also seemed different. It seemed to me like one of those science-fiction movies where the hero dimly perceives that a look-alike has been substituted for his wife. Her hair was the same raven-black, maybe blacker, coiffed perfectly in rings on top of her head. But she wasn't wearing a power suit here. Instead, she wore a gown of shimmering blue like pastel fog under the lights.

My Melissa and the Melissa who bowed to the audience both had an air of competence, the calm, controlled demeanor of a person who is good at what she does. This Melissa radiated confidence at every step as she walked to the piano, the unhurried tread of someone accustomed to success. The applause grew louder and Melissa seemed to grow bigger, as if someone had stuffed fresh batteries into a child's doll.

I clapped until my hands hurt. I was the last to stop clapping, earning a glare from a balding man in front of me. *Go ahead and stare at me like I'm a fool,* I thought. *That's my fiancée up there. You think you know her because you know her music. But I know what it's like to be loved by her.* A hush settled over the theater as Melissa nodded slightly toward the audience and flexed her fingers over the piano, pausing as if waiting for some internal cue to begin.

Then she played. The music on her albums was beautiful, but a recording to live music is like soy beef to steak. Some musicians are technicians who perform with cool efficiency, like attorneys who master case law but not the art of swaying a jury. Melissa was something else entirely. She coaxed the piano to play for her, as though she had formed some intimate compact with it. The result was passionate, personal, and deeply moving. She played with a style that stretched the range of her instrument, infusing classical pieces with influences of rock and jazz.

I could feel the audience warm to her enthusiasm, her zest, her love for what she did. Yes, she was a great pianist and the piano is a magnificent instrument. Melissa could have played a harmonica tonight and the audience would have been moved deeply by it.

She spoke very little during the performance. Thanking the audience for coming after her first piece and introducing a few original compositions. Every time she spoke, though, I felt transported. Hearing her voice was like coming upon an oasis. It sent me back to our apartment, to the warmth of our bed and the comfort of her arms. It made me realize more than ever how terribly I missed her.

A few times I rose halfway out of my seat, hoping Melissa would see me, but she kept her eyes focused on the instrument, only turning her head from time to time to look at the audience. After she played her last piece, she rose and bowed graciously at the standing ovation. Her face was totally relaxed now and her smile was broad. She knew she was great tonight. She knew she'd made us happy.

"Tonight's performance was for the benefit of Children First, a foundation very dear to my heart. With the purchase of your tickets, you have all donated generously already, but if you have it in you to give more, please visit the booths set up in the lobby."

That was classic Melissa, reminding those who had the means to give that they should give as much as they possibly could. Then, after making her pitch, she smiled and sat down at the piano again. Eschewing the tenets of classical music altogether, she performed a heart-melting version of the Beatles' "In My Life" before coming to the edge of the stage to bow one last time.

At that moment, I knew I had done the right thing for Melissa. I'd given her a chance to find her true destiny. She could help people, much more than she could in Washington. She could inspire people, as she had inspired all of us tonight. And, as was undeniably apparent from the smile on her face, she could enjoy every second of it.

That smile was all I needed to see, but I got more. Melissa took a final bow and her eyes fixed on mine. They penetrated into my very being with the familiarity of a soulmate. She held my gaze and I was certain she recognized me. I waved to her enthusiastically. *Yes, it's me. We've found each other.*

Her gaze traversed to my left, sweeping the wing seats. My eyes stayed locked on her, waiting for her to return to me, looking for some kind of gesture that would tell me to come backstage. She glanced up to the upper tiers and spread her arms wide.

Then she waved and walked off the stage.

༄

Drizzle gently massaged my scalp, keeping me alert as I waited in the shadows of a parking lot across the street from the stage entrance. The concert had ended an hour ago and I was essentially alone. On the other side of the lot, some college students were playing Melissa's "crossover" album, *Charting the Path*, and talking loudly. She played two selections from the album tonight, and as I waited here, the memory of those performances filled my heart with Melissa's presence.

What if Melissa wound up leaving from some other exit? What if a limousine swung around to whisk her away? Somehow that didn't seem right for her. After all, in another world, she'd felt a little guilty even riding in my Audi. I took deep, moist breaths and pushed any negative thoughts from my mind. There was only one of me to cover one exit and I was feeling lucky. Things had gone my way all day.

I held a bouquet of roses close to my body, shielding them from the rain. I'd bought them on impulse after the show, feeling that I needed something to present her, something to mark the occasion.

The dull black door opened for a moment, and then it didn't. Objects always seem to move when it's late and you're straining your eyes. Especially if you wish with every fiber of your being that the door will open and the one person who means everything to you will walk through it. The entrance lay at the top of a short flight of metal stairs. A single yellow lamp stood lonely watch over it.

I checked my phone for the time yet again. It was just after midnight. Whatever performers were still in there would certainly leave soon. I leaned against the ridges of the rough concrete wall that jabbed my spine and kept my eyes fixed on that doorway. My foot tapped the asphalt to one of the songs coming from the students' car, a piece that sounded like seventies folk-rock reinterpreted for the piano.

Suddenly, something blocked my view.

"Help the homeless," muttered a man in a tattered black coat with a baseball cap tucked over his forehead. I tried to look around him at the door, but he shifted position to stand in front of me. "It's good luck to help the needy."

He jumped slightly when I laughed. I handed him a five and said, "I can use all the good luck I can get."

"Bless you, sir," he said as he receded. He tipped his cap in my direction.

I began to feel very tired. It was past 3:00 EST. As my wait continued, I began to notice the lack of sleep and the wear on my body. I should have eaten more today. That would have helped. For some reason, I found myself craving a milkshake.

Then the door really opened. In a microsecond my brain grasped that the person moving down the steps could not be Melissa, unless in this universe she had grown six inches and switched genders. The tall young man jumped the last couple of steps to the ground, his shoulder bag thudding against his body.

His footsteps quickly faded away. Sirens groaned in the distance. Down the street, puddles gleamed green and red in the wink of a traffic light. Something small and fast skittered across the sidewalk and behind a bag of trash someone had dumped on the curb. Then something bigger crept down the street. It paused and looked at me with darkly glowing eyes.

"Hello," I said. "Did Wizard send you?"

That was unlikely – Wizard didn't get along with other cats. This one was scrawny, tiger-striped, and very wary. It hunched motionless in front of me, uncertain of its prey, fearful of the bigger predator looming before it. Then a blur raced from behind the garbage bag, and the cat squealed and took off in pursuit.

I looked back at the door. Suddenly a crack of light appeared. Hollow laughter echoing off walls drifted out of the entrance. The crack of light grew into a rectangle that traversed the sidewalk as the door swung open all the way. Several umbrellas opened in unison and twirled like windmills as the group made its way down the slippery stairs.

I tried to untangle the voices that blended into the continuous buzz of a group of friends hitting the town. Once everyone descended to the sidewalk, the group re-formed around someone whose umbrella glowed translucent green in the lamplight. This was unmistakably Melissa. I heard her voice, though I couldn't make out the words. It was rich and animated, and it made her companions laugh. My heart leaped at this. I was separated from her by only a few hundred yards.

Melissa stopped for a moment to adjust her umbrella. As she did, she turned in my direction. She seemed to look right at me, though there was no indication that she'd seen me. Then the crowd moved her forward with tidal force.

I slapped the bouquet against my palm, sending a rose petal on a death dive to the asphalt. If Melissa had been alone, I would have approached her. Even if she was with one or two companions I could have presented her with the bouquet and hoped that she would be flattered enough to talk with me. But there was at least a dozen people in her group, and I couldn't possibly get her undivided attention, even if I was allowed through the circle of her protectors.

They continued down the street. I was going to have to follow her, wait for a moment when she was alone. It was going to be a long night. I began walking, careful to keep an eye on the traveling pack.

"Waiting for someone?" My feet almost left the ground as I felt a hand on my shoulder and heard a voice deep, congested, and grouchy. They belonged to a police officer in a rain slicker. His frown announced what he thought about foot patrol on a night like this.

"I want to give flowers to one of the performers," I said casually, hoping he wouldn't mistake my rain-induced shivering for something else.

"Lousy night to wait outside." His gaze focused on my shoes and methodically rose to my face. "Would you mind standing over there, sir?" He nodded toward a more brightly lit patch of sidewalk. His radio crackled, and he muttered something into the shoulder transmitter under his cape.

I tossed a quick glance behind me, trying to make the gesture look relaxed. Down the street, a green dot receded like phosphorescent algae carried away by the tide. Hastily I moved into the spot the officer designated. If I got this over with quickly, I could catch up with her.

"Can I see some ID?" The voice had the calm authority of someone accustomed to being obeyed.

"Did I do something wrong, officer?"

"I didn't say that, sir. It's just that sometimes people who hang around theaters after shows don't have the best intentions." He shone his flashlight on my driver's license for a minute or longer. "You're from out of state, Mr. Timian?"

"I'm visiting from Washington, D.C."

"Who are you waiting for?"

"Her name is Melissa Argent," I said, a little too promptly. "She's a pianist. She gave a concert here tonight."

His shrug said the name meant nothing to him. "You're waiting in the rain at midnight to see a piano player?"

"She's a pianist."

"Sure." He took a notebook out from under his cape and jotted something down. I risked another glance behind me. The green dot shrank to a colorless pinpoint almost lost in the distance. "I think everyone's left the theater by now. Why don't you head on back to your hotel? Maybe you'd be better off writing her a fan letter. Performers tend to like a little distance from their admirers." He handed back my license and walked away.

At that moment, the drizzle swelled into a downpour. I waited a moment, then looked backward. Melissa's umbrella was gone. I walked in her direction until I reached the next corner. I turned and saw that the police officer had disappeared. My lungs sucked air and rain as I ran down the street, straining to see a flash of green or hear the tinkle of voices. The city lay quiet, a landscape inhabited by ghostly lights and the mutter of traffic.

Melissa was nowhere to be found. I was so close to her, but again she was impossibly far away from me.

Chapter 16

Brush with Greatness

Brick and mortar trembled under the sound of 2,500 clapping hands. Chandeliers shuddered as the audience cheered the woman on the stage. Melissa shimmered like a fountain in her silver gown as she bowed before the storm of adoration.

"Ladies and gentlemen." Her voice soared to the top of the vaulted ceiling, regal, yet tinged with eagerness. "There's someone I would like you to meet. In the audience tonight is someone special. Someone who has traveled a great distance to show his love for me. It took me too long to feel this man's love, to understand the enormous sacrifice he made, but now that I have it, I'll never, ever, let it go. I would like to introduce you to my new husband. Please welcome my one and only love, Ken Timian."

A wave of warmth engulfed me as the spotlight shone in my eyes. Through the silver corona, I dimly saw Melissa wave me on. I rose and groped my way toward the stage. As I tried to mount it, a hand took mine, soft but strong. Melissa lifted me and raised my arms and hers over our heads. I turned toward her and smiled at her radiance. *I love you*, she mouthed silently as applause washed over us. Then we both faced the audience and bowed. Her hand reached across my shoulder, her hand on my neck....

I fought to stay in the daydream, to have that precious moment last forever. But it ended as they all did, with Melissa's arms replaced by the arms of the recliner. I soared high every time, only to crash at the realization that I was dreaming.

I arrived from Seattle exhausted, unshaven, and depressed. A neighbor I had never spoken with stared at me as if I were a burglar. She was as suspicious as I was angry. Angry at myself for believing it could be so easy. Melissa had seen me – I know we locked eyes – and then moved on. Why wouldn't she? She had no reason to know who I was or what I'd meant to her. Melissa lived a charmed life, and if the absence of Ken Timian had left something lacking in that life, she was completely unaware of it.

I felt staggered, but not defeated. For me it was simple. I had no desire for life without Melissa. Therefore, I would do everything I could imagine to get her back and never be deterred from trying. Persistence was the key. Persistence had sustained me through those long nights studying law. If I could endure something that arduous for the sake of my career, what did it matter what I endured to return to the woman I loved? I have always believed that if you want something badly enough, you can get it. I definitely wanted Melissa badly enough.

Yet I was stymied over what my next move should be. I couldn't do this alone, but how could I ask for help in a world where I was a stranger among friends? The people who knew me would help me if I were sick or needed money, but they would have committed me if I told them the story of how I'd changed history. If that Seattle cop regarded me with suspicion, what would Paul, Marty, Sharon, and everyone else think of my babbling about alternate realities?

Something black slid quickly across the kitchen floor. "Wizard," I said as I jumped from my chair, "my address book is not a toy." He retreated to a corner and cheerfully licked his coat. Playtime wasn't fun unless I got mad.

I picked up the black book that he'd knocked off the kitchen table. Wizard was playing kitty soccer with it, and I was lucky he hadn't scored a goal in the narrow gap under the refrigerator. The address book was flopped open to the J's. There were no names penciled in under that letter. I guess in this world, I didn't know anyone whose last name began with J. The only acquaintance I could recall whose last name began with J was Kate Jordan.

Wizard scuttled away as I slammed the address book on the table.

"Come back," I said to his quickly retreating form. "I'm not angry." I went to the refrigerator and took out a small chunk of cheese. I brought it to the cat, who was watching me cautiously. I placed it on the floor and he studied it for several long seconds before jumping down and nibbling at it.

"Enjoy," I said as I walked away. "For once, you've earned your keep."

I went to the computer and called up a phone directory. Did Kate live at the same address? Yes, there she was in Georgetown. It was fairly late, but I dialed the number anyway.

"Hello?" a woman answered after two rings. Her voice was deep and sharp with annoyance.

"Is this Kate Jordan?"

"Yes, it is."

"Kate, it's Ken Timian."

"Ken?"

"Yes, hi." It was good that she'd used my first name. It meant that we knew each other in this world. Were we friends? "How are you doing?"

"Fine. My God, it's been a long time. We haven't seen each other since my going-away dinner when I left Warwick & Gray."

"I know; it's been a while." I'd seen Kate less than a month ago. We had dinner together after Melissa's bridal shower. "I was wondering if maybe we could get together. Maybe meet for a drink somewhere."

Thunder boomed over the Potomac, crackling the line with static.

"Sure, I guess. I can use a few laughs."

"Great. Let's meet tomorrow night. If you're free, that is."

"Let me check my busy social calendar. No, I'm not dining at the White House until next week. The Vice President is bringing the pizza, and I'm bringing the beer. Yes, I can fit you in tomorrow. How about Donovan's on M Street?"

"Donovan's is perfect. I'll see you then."

"That's it? You call completely out of the blue, make a quick drinks date, and then jump off the phone? I'm not that easy. What the hell have you been up to?"

"A lot of things. I'll give you all the nasty details tomorrow."

"Hmm, sounds interesting."

"Not *that* interesting. For some reason, I found myself thinking of you. It seemed a shame that we lost touch."

"That's funny; I was thinking of you only a couple of months ago after I ran into someone else from the firm. You were one of the few people I liked there." Certainly she wasn't the president of the Harrison Warwick Fan Club. People still talked about their final (though certainly not their *only*) argument. Certain words were used that hadn't been uttered in those hallowed halls before or since.

"It hasn't been the same since you left. The place is one hundred percent stodgy now."

"Present company excluded of course."

"Of course. Hey, you know Melissa Argent, right?"

"*Knew* would be more accurate. I haven't seen her since high school. Except in magazines and on television and even on stage once. Why do you ask?"

I needed to handle this delicately. "I saw something on PBS about her recently. You mentioned that you used to be friends with her, so you're my brush with greatness. I use it to get tables in restaurants."

Kate laughed deeply. Her laughter was always good to hear. "Yeah, I should have thought of that myself. After all, how many other people have a friendship bracelet in their attics handmade by the acclaimed Melissa Argent?"

"You just gave me goose bumps," I said with a laugh, though the image did cause a little shiver.

"Yeah, I'm sure I did."

"I've recently gotten into her music. I bought all the albums."

"You? Don't you normally listen to Metallica and Def Leppard?"

"Never Def Leppard."

"And never people like Melissa Argent, if I remember correctly."

"Hey, you get older and you grow."

"You'll have to tell me all about it tomorrow night. I'm looking forward to it. Bye."

I held the phone in my hand for several seconds after Kate hung up. I felt intensely warmed by our conversation. It felt like the first real connection I'd made in this new world. Kate not only sounded like herself, but we quickly fell into the banter that had marked our relationship. It would be nice to feel natural around *someone*.

Of course, there was much more than that making me feel optimistic tonight. Kate was an honest-to-goodness connection to Melissa. Even if they hadn't seen each other in more than a decade, she was closer to Melissa than anyone else I knew. If I handled things the right way, she might be able to lead me to her.

〜〜

"I told him that he misunderstood," Warwick said as he bounded into my office.

"I'm sorry?" I said. I had been studying a case file, which these days took more concentration than ever before.

"I told Peter Darlington that he misunderstood. He *did* misunderstand, right?"

Peter Darlington was a potential client I'd spoken with on the phone earlier. "What did he understand?"

Warwick chewed on his cigar for a moment and then pulled it out of his mouth. "Somehow he got it into his mind that you were turning him down."

I should have expected this conversation. "Then he didn't misunderstand."

Warwick glared at me, then regarded the damp cigar in his hand. There was little question which he found more appealing just then. "What exactly is the problem here?"

"There's no problem, Harrison. I just don't think I should take this case."

Warwick the Lesser nodded slowly. "Let me see if I understand this. A client asks specifically to retain you after another client recommends your services. This is an important potential client who could generate a great deal of business for this firm. Yet you turn him down. When did you go insane, Timian?"

I refused to get riled up along with Warwick. "I am not insane. I simply choose not to accept this case. The client wants to retain our services to facilitate a deal that will involve the destruction of some twenty thousand acres of Amazonian rainforest. This number is the client's own estimate, which means that the true figure will be much, much greater." I looked down at my desk and gathered myself. "The Amazon is a precious natural resource – a barrier against global warming and the home of many unique species of plants and animals. I don't want to be involved with this project, nor do I believe it to be in the best interests of this firm to be associated with it in any way."

Warwick looked at me as though I'd just force-fed him castor oil. "Not in the best interests of this firm? Who made your our corporate conscience? When did you become a tree hugger, Timian? You never had any qualms about ravaging the environment before."

"I took a careful look at the circumstances around this case and they're appalling." This had been a touchy subject between Melissa and me. Her passion was impossible to ignore and it was equally impossible to be unmoved by it. At the same time, the reality of my professional life put her ideals (ideals that were increasingly becoming mine) at odds. I subtly refrained from taking on the most egregious sinners as clients, but it was never nearly enough for her. We'd debated this as recently as a month ago. This all came back to me when I was reviewing the plans Darlington had sent over from his logging corporation yesterday. All I saw was pillage camouflaged by neat diagrams and spreadsheets. What was especially disheartening was that the client specifically asked for me to handle the deal. Warwick thought it was a compliment; to me it was a mark of shame. There had been far too many Peter Darlingtons in my past.

Warwick put his small hands on the edge of my desk, as if he were going to topple it over me. He still wore his Harvard graduation ring, along with a gold wedding band that was surprisingly plain. "Tell me, Timian; are you aware of a shortage of lawyers in this town? Because I am not, and I can assure you that this client will find a firm to represent him in the time it takes to dial a phone. Are you telling me that you suddenly had a revelation that our clients are not always the good guys? You must be joking. We have represented the Chinese and we have represented dictators. Hell, I was pretty sure that one of our clients was supplying the Taliban, though I will deny ever saying that. Either way, they are entitled to legal counsel, and it is not our job to make moral judgments. And before you mount your high horse, let me remind you that the Southeast Asian deal you so ably handled was not clean. I play golf with an undersecretary at the State Department. If you knew what your client was really doing – what you helped facilitate – your hair would turn white. So let's drop this foolishness, okay?"

I couldn't do anything to correct what I'd done for the firm in the past, but I was determined not to make my record any uglier. "It is not foolish to protect the environment we live in. I am simply not going to take this case."

Harrison Warwick, esteemed lawyer, gave me a lecher's grin. "There's a woman involved in this, isn't there? You met some graduate student at American University who is majoring in saving whales. Your new social awareness is coming to you from pillow talk, isn't it?"

I looked Warwick straight in the eye. He was truly a miserable excuse for a human being. "My personal life has nothing to do with this."

"It appears that your personal life has very much to do with this. I'll have to keep that in mind." He turned toward the door. "I have to get back to Darlington. I'm sure Marks will handle the case. I know he has ambitions. And he won't let anything get in the way of them."

Warwick sent me one more smoldering glare and then left.

Sharon came in a moment later and closed the door behind her.

"I'm surprised he said all of that with the door open. I could hear everything from my desk." She looked at me as if a stranger were sitting in my chair. "That was quite a stand you just took there. I can't believe you did that. Warwick is accustomed to getting his way."

She stared at me until I began to feel uncomfortable. "Come on, Sharon. It isn't like I dyed my hair purple or came to the office naked."

She covered her mouth and coughed. "It's a little like that, actually." She looked at me with a bemused smile on her face.

"What?" I said, feeling like she was toying with me.

"*Are* you dating a graduate student from American University?"

"Why does that have to be the reason?"

"It doesn't." She smirked. "People change personalities overnight all the time."

I had a tough time retaining eye contact with her. "Maybe this does have a little to do with a woman I used to know. Someone I'd like to get to know again."

Sharon moved forward and patted my desk. "I hope you do. Looks like she's good for you."

We never would have had a conversation that personal a couple of weeks ago in this new world. I suppose that was progress of sorts. Maybe she'd even come to work for me again after Warwick fired me.

Chapter 17

Gravity and Sobriety

No matter what your taste in music, you had to feel accosted by the sound system at Donovan's. Hip-hop and metal stood toe-to-toe in a high decibel battle of the bands that took no prisoners. You didn't as much groove to the rhythms here as you succumbed to them. Compared to the gorgeous sounds that had filled Benaroya Hall just a few nights earlier, it was the aural equivalent of a mugging.

Then again, sports bars weren't known for their quiet ambiance. At least three dozen HDTV screens were displaying baseball games from various spots around the country. Enormous signs announced the bar's allegiance to the Orioles and the Redskins, while others indicated that they bowed at the altar of Budweiser and Cuervo Gold. Even when I used to frequent bars almost nightly I tended to stay away from places this loud because I found them a little hard to take. Now it was simply sensory overload.

The bar was a beehive of people drinking, talking, and laughing. Everyone moved at a frantic pace, as if their energy propped up the building, and a moment's rest would collapse the ceiling. Someone tapped my shoulder. I turned and saw Kate. She spoke, but her words bounced off the barrier of noise. I pointed at a table farthest from the bar. She nodded and followed me.

As we sat down, she leaned over the table and shouted, "Did you bring your earplugs?"

"Forgot. Thanks for recommending this quiet little place for a chat."

Like other things in this world, this Kate looked the same – just a little different. Her hair was short instead of shoulder-length. Her navy business suit was more tailored. It was Melissa who had convinced Kate to let her hair grow long and loosen up with her clothing. It made a huge difference in her appearance, warming her up. She was still very attractive, but she seemed harder somehow. Then again, maybe that wasn't the hair. Who knew what life without Melissa had done to her?

After a few minutes, our ears adjusted until the music became white noise. "What will you have?" I said, gesturing toward the bar.

"Any German beer is fine."

I elbowed my way through the crowd and returned with a beer and a ginger ale.

Kate took a healthy gulp and smiled, regarding me. "Ken Timian. It's been a long time since I've seen your face."

"You mean you missed me?"

"I didn't think so, but now that I see you, I think I just might have."

I raised my glass to her, choosing to ignore what it meant that Kate "didn't think" she missed me and focusing on the compliment instead. "Well I missed you, too."

She smiled. It was amazing what happened to her face when she smiled. The vulnerability that she worked very hard to hide slid through, making her so much more appealing. "So you're still working for Warwick the Loser, huh?"

"At least until partnerships are announced. I might be working for legal aid after that."

"You're a lock for a partnership, aren't you?"

"I've ruffled some feathers lately. Nothing is guaranteed at that firm."

"Don't I know it? Hey, if they do make you a partner, do you have to throw out all of your colored shirts?"

"The only thing I'm required to dispose of is my personality. I get to keep all of my clothing. I just can't wear anything but gray and white to the office."

She laughed and studied the room for a minute. She looked back at me, but didn't say anything right away. To fill the void, I said, "I've been really getting into Melissa Argent's music lately."

Kate nodded and rolled her eyes. I had no idea what the gesture meant. "She's pretty hot these days, about as hot as a concert pianist can get. You'd never know she once got a B in chorus when we were in middle school."

"See, there's something you could sell to one of the tabloids."

"Yeah. That would probably qualify as dirt in Melissa's case."

"So what's she like?"

Kate tilted her head and studied me for a moment. It almost seemed as though she was going to ignore the

question, but then she sat back in her seat. "You'd probably be better off asking someone from the tabloids. We
were best friends, but that was in school. If you had
ever been a high school girl, you would know what that
means."

I had no idea what she was talking about. "What was
she like back then? I mean you can read her bio on the
Internet. but what was she really like?"

"You have a serious little crush going here, don't
you? You want to me to describe Melissa? What can
I tell you? You remember those perfect kids you went
to school with? The ones who got straight A's in all the
important classes, edited the school newspaper, put together the yearbook. That was Melissa. I was a decent
student, but I did my share of partying. Not Melissa.
She didn't have time. Melissa was always involved with
something, whether it was school work or some after-
school project. It was like she was a robot programmed
to keep moving."

"She wasn't a robot," I said defensively.

Kate offered me another confused look. Again, she
stared off toward the front of the bar. She shrugged.
"No, she wasn't, actually. If you want to know the truth,
she was a very, very good friend. We were in the Girl
Scouts together, she helped me with my homework, and
I helped her meet her first boyfriend."

"Really? What was *he* like?"

Kate gazed off dreamily. "Steven Santori. What a
babe. He was vice president of the junior class, and he
was...why am I telling you this? Men always have to
know what other men get, like it's a competition. Let's
just say he was a good catch and for a while it looked
like they might become serious. Until he dumped her

for a cheerleader who two months later dumped him. So maybe I didn't do her any favors." She threw her hands up in a questioning gesture. "But she did plenty for me. Helped me through some pretty rough patches in those years. I'm certain I would have done the same for her. The only thing was she didn't have any. Not that I saw, anyway, and I think I saw *everything*. Melissa was just one of those people who got it right."

Kate hadn't seen everything, as I well knew. But perhaps in this world she had. "So what happened between you? It sounds like you were pretty close."

"Nothing. Not a fight or anything like that, anyway. We just went our separate ways, that's all. She was into music, and I was on a pre-law track. We went to different colleges and both studied very intently. Neither of us made it back to D.C. very often, and when we did, we didn't have much time to see each other. After she went to Europe, we totally lost contact."

"That's sad. Good friends shouldn't lose each other like that."

Kate cupped her chin on her palms. "You seem different, Ken. It isn't just that we haven't seen each other in a while. You seem to have more – I don't know – *gravity* now."

"Is that bad?"

Her smile lit the dimness. "No, not at all. It's kind of nice, actually. When I knew you at the firm, you were a smart guy who was definitely up and coming, but you were also a little immature – a bit of a frat boy. You look like you finally figured out that the world is a serious place."

"Yeah," I said softly, perhaps too softly for her to hear. "Maybe I have."

Kate's eyes twinkled and she leaned forward in her chair. "Except, of course, for this fascination you have with Melissa Argent. If you were going to fixate on a celebrity, shouldn't you have chosen one who was a little more mainstream? Or at least one who wore shorter dresses?"

"I have a great imagination," I said, smiling.

"I'm sure you do."

I rolled my eyes and Kate did the same. We laughed. "Anyway, you've had absolutely no contact with Melissa since high school?"

"Not one bit. She's making a name for herself, so she's probably forgotten all about the little people." Kate paused and tilted her head. "Really, Ken, why all this interest in Melissa? You didn't really call to get together just so we could talk about her, did you?"

"No, no, of course not," I said quickly. "You and I never should have lost touch. I guess Melissa just provided me with an easy excuse to call you."

"That has always cracked me up."

"What has?"

"The way people talk about public figures using their first names. Like, you know, you listen to her music in your underwear so that means you're intimate."

I found the comment insulting, but I didn't want to respond forcefully. I simply said, "Sorry."

Kate reached over and patted my hand. "I'm just having some fun at your expense. Trust me, I do it, too. I spent the whole weekend with my soulmate Johnny – Depp, that is – and a bunch of his DVDs about a month ago."

I'm sure I sounded just like that to Kate. I sought a way to back out of it. I needed to make the connection to

Melissa carefully or risk losing it entirely. "So what have you been up to since you left the firm?"

Kate gave me another one of those indecipherable nods and sat back again. "Thanks for asking. I'm doing great. Still running the legal rat race, which you certainly know about. I'm doing back flips for a partnership, too. I was almost engaged – emphasis on 'almost.' To an accountant I was seeing until a couple of weeks ago. Turned out we couldn't reconcile our balance sheets." She laughed cynically and took a big swig of beer.

"You're not seeing anyone now?"

"Nope. I'm out on the free agent market again." She laughed loudly. "Bidders are knocking down my door, of course."

"Of course," I said with a smile.

Kate drained her beer and held it toward me. "I need another."

I stood. My ginger ale was still half full. "I'll get it."

She put a hand out to stop me. "My turn." She looked down at my drink. "What is that, anyway?"

"Ginger ale."

"Any particular reason?"

I shrugged. "I like ginger ale."

"I like hot chocolate, but I wouldn't drink it in a bar."

"I'm cutting back on the alcohol."

"Wow, I'm impressed. Want another?"

"I'm fine."

Kate twirled and entered the scrum to get another drink. Why would she be impressed that I was cutting back on alcohol? Was that something to be impressed by?

When she returned to our table, she clinked her bottle against my glass and then took a long drink. The she put the bottle down and watched me. "Gravity *and* sobriety. It's the new, improved Ken Timian."

"I'm working on it."

"With a particular person in mind?"

"Maybe."

Kate smiled, though I wasn't sure what she was smiling about.

"Did you hear that Melissa broke up recently with that guitarist?" I said.

Kate sighed. She seemed supremely disappointed. "We're back on *that* topic?"

"From everything I've heard, he's kind of a jerk. I wonder why she started dating him in the first place. He's definitely not good enough for her."

Kate glared at me. "You know what? This is getting a little creepy. Creepy and boring. You may be sober, and you may have more gravity, Ken, but you've also got some weird shit going on."

"I'm not some obsessive fan," I said quickly. "I just keep talking about her in front of you because I know you know her."

"*Knew* her, Ken. Knew her. I haven't seen her in more than a decade. I get the impression, though, that you see her in your dreams every night. That's more than a little bizarre."

"It's not what you think."

"I think it's *exactly* what I think." Kate stood up and I stood with her. She put a hand out to halt me.

"Where are you going?" I said.

"This has been a real blast, Ken. Call me if you ever find all of your marbles."

Chapter 18

The Realest Thing in This World

The silver arrow was motionless and yet it soared over us.

"It flew into outer space," I said, feeling the awe I always felt when I was here.

"It's pretty incredible, isn't it?" Paul said, his voice filled with wonder. We craned our necks to get a better view of the X-15 rocket plane suspended from the ceiling. With its razor-sharp wings and sleek nose, it looked ready to slip its restraints and blast a hole through the museum wall.

The Melissa who wore my ring relaxed by going to art museums. Her fiancé preferred the National Air and Space Museum. She called it "The Hall of Flying Gadgets," and always felt the need to remind me that these planes and missiles diverted precious resources from human needs. I could never make her understand that these machines helped us to dream. There was power behind these latticed walls; power and achievement that one could almost reach out and touch. It was one of the areas upon which we agreed to disagree.

The day after my fiasco with Kate, I asked Paul if he wanted to meet for lunch. He suggested Chinatown, but I felt a need for something more elevated, something that might make me wonder again. We decided to meet at the Air and Space Museum cafe, a hectic room busily dispensing hot dogs to throngs of tourists who would eat the carpet if you put enough mustard on it.

We took a quick stroll through the museum before we ate. Though he probably knew most of this, I explained the histories of the various planes and rockets. I knew them all. The Spitfire and the Messerschmitt in the World War II section, like predators in their camouflage colors. The little Mercury capsules that first took Americans into orbit, dwarfed by the huge Skylab and the spidery Lunar Module that landed on the moon. There was something about each one of these vehicles that captured my imagination, and when I stood among them, everything seemed a little more possible.

I remembered the first time Melissa and I came here, after an afternoon looking at sculpture. Her arm was wrapped around my waist as we jostled through the perpetual crowds. After seeing the warplanes, we visited the solar system exhibit. Jupiter was shimmering in its multi-hued immensity, Saturn was basking in the glory of its rings, and Io's red volcanic skin made me hungry for pizza.

"This is the one part of the museum I really like," Melissa said with a satisfied sigh. "Look how magnificent nature is, Ken. What can compare to Saturn's rings or the colors of those moons? All this technology here seems so insignificant compared to the glory of nature."

"You think so? I'll show you something that isn't insignificant." I took her to the Apollo hall, where spacesuits and space memorabilia of man's greatest achievement lay behind glass cases. I pointed to a Saturn V rocket engine as wide as our kitchen. "This is the ultimate. Look at those rocket engines. Man made the inconceivable a reality with the help of these."

Melissa shook her head. "You're right, Ken, it's all very impressive. But how could this possibly compare to the majesty of nature and creation?"

"You're not blown away by this?"

"It's awesome, you're right. But is it necessary? Is it really essential for us to overwhelm the forces of nature for the sake of conquest?"

I thought about overwhelming the forces of nature now as I stood before the same rocket with Paul.

"It's just so amazing when you think about it," he said.

"It is, isn't it?"

"Too bad you can't book passage on these things. I'd get my ticket tomorrow."

He smiled as though he was a little embarrassed that he'd said that, and then he shrugged. I smiled back to let him know that I got what he was talking about.

"I'm starving," I said. "Let's get lunch."

We grabbed a couple of overpriced hot dogs and sodas – Paul called it our contribution to erasing the budget deficit – and sat down at the only available table. The tourists were out in throngs today. I covered a gooey pile of ketchup on the table with a napkin.

"How's it going?" I said. "You look tired."

"I slept on the couch last night. I'm too wasted to even remember what we argued about. Something to do with money, I think. It might have been sex – no, that was the night before. After a while, all the fights just blend. It's like a boxing match where the bell never rings."

"Maybe you should try counseling again."

"Are you kidding? We talked about it once, but we couldn't agree on which counselor to go to." Paul bit into his hot dog and made a face. "Maybe we should have done Chinese after all. I'll get to sleep in the bed tonight. We've been through this dozens of times." Paul wiped a dab of mustard from his lips. "Although – and I know this is going to sound weird – lately I've had this strange feeling that all this is wrong."

"What do you mean?"

"I mean I have this feeling that my life should be different. That maybe I'm meant to do something else with it. That probably sounds ridiculous."

"That doesn't sound weird." I felt some excitement creeping into my voice. Was it possible that some of Paul's other life was "bleeding through?" "I believe there are different paths in our lives. I mean, who's to say that there aren't multiple universes with multiple copies of ourselves?"

I removed the napkin from the ketchup spot and used a plastic knife to etch two circles. "Suppose you had two universes. Let's say they are parallel universes like on 'Star Trek.'" I tapped the left circle with my knife. "Let's say there is a Paul in one universe. He has a wife he fights with. Maybe he's not the happiest guy in the world, but in the other universe, there is another Paul who made different decisions. Perhaps he isn't married, or perhaps he's divorced. Even better, maybe this Paul found a woman who he truly loves. His life is content.

Remember, this is the same Paul – he looks the same, had the same childhood, works the same job, but he turned left instead of right at a certain fork in the road. And why stop at two universes? Why couldn't there be ten or a million? Every one with a Paul or a Ken whose life might be just a little different."

Paul stared at me with his mouth open slightly. "Where did all of this come from? All I meant was that I thought I should be doing something more constructive with my life. Like going back to school, earning a teaching certificate, and becoming a high school history teacher."

"You would be a great teacher, Paul," I said quickly, caught up in this. "In another universe, you could be in a classroom right now, telling students about George Washington and Napoleon Bonaparte."

Paul put his hot dog down and looked at me as though I'd ruined his appetite. "What is it with you? Parallel universes. Multiple copies of me running around." Paul's voice rose with exasperation. "Did your head come in contact with a blunt instrument recently?" He looked around the room as if he were plotting escape routes. "What's going on?"

I should tell him, I thought. *Of anybody on this planet, he has earned a right to know.*

"Don't have a stroke. I haven't lost my mind. It's just something that I wonder about sometimes. I guess I like thinking that our lives can be different. It certainly sounds like you want *your* life to be different. Why not make the move? Why not follow up on this notion of becoming a teacher?"

Paul's shoulders sagged. "Because I can't afford to indulge in fantasies. I'm too busy just trying to survive in *this* world. Angela wants a bigger house. That means more money, and I couldn't afford to do it on a rookie teacher's salary. I'm just blowing smoke, Ken. I'm not going to throw away everything I have and start over."

"Sometimes you have to take big chances to make things the way they should be."

"That's a myth, Ken. The reality is that you just have to step as carefully as possible and try to avoid the land mines. Angela and I will probably have sex tonight. We usually do after the really big blowouts. I take what I can get."

〰〰

I called Kate's office that afternoon. When she didn't return the call, I tried her at home that night.

"Let me guess, Ken; you want to know about the time Melissa and I went shopping for our first bras together. Or maybe you want me to tell you some behind-the-scenes stories about the third-grade play."

"I deserved that, I'm sure. I didn't call to talk about Melissa."

"That's what you say now. But something tells me her name will come up in the next thirty seconds."

"It won't. I swear."

"Then why did you call?"

"I called to say I'm sorry. I don't know what got into me."

I could hear Kate expel a long breath on the other end of the line. "Trust me, Ken, I've had plenty of weird drinks dates in my life. But it was creepy how many times you brought Melissa up. It was like you really wanted to know her. It reminded me of the guy who killed John Lennon."

"I'm over it. I promise. It was a little episode and it's done."

"If you mean it, then you're forgiven. You know, when you weren't being a psycho, you were kind of fun to be with."

"Thanks. That's the other reason I called. I wanted to see if I could make it up to you by taking you to dinner tomorrow night."

"It's gonna have to be someplace fabulous."

"I know a few of those."

She chuckled. "I guess you would. Where and when?"

The thought came to mind that pursuing a friendship with Kate was disingenuous; that I was only doing it to get her to introduce me to Melissa, regardless of what I was saying here. Certainly, that was part of it. I would have felt guilty about it if not for the fact that I had another need that was nearly as pressing: I really wanted a friend. Other than Paul, who saddened me, all the people I hung out with in this world were overgrown children, work hard/play hard types who were no more interested in what was going on in my heart than they were in a quiet evening at home. Though I'd managed to freak her out, I got the sense from Kate that she wasn't the same as these people. She might have liked loud bars, but she was more interested in talking there than drinking. I really wanted someone I could talk to.

We met at a stylish New American place. Kate wanted fabulous and this was the most fabulous place I knew. The chef was a regular guest on the Food Network, and his creations spawned imitators all over the country.

Kate was twenty minutes late, which I guessed had more to do with our drinks date than with a holdup at the office. I stood to greet her as she walked toward me. She was wearing a sleeveless knee-length black dress that made her look both formidable and sexy.

"Nice choice of restaurant," she said as she sat down. "I've been meaning to come here. Who did you have to pay off to get a table on a day's notice?"

"Some of us just know the right strings to pull," I said smugly. "Actually, the owner is a client of the firm."

"I should have guessed that."

The waiter came by with menus and a wine list. I was still a little repelled by the notion of drinking, but a fine wine in this setting seemed about as far away from the Shamrock as possible. I chose a Jordan Cabernet, and we made small talk while we decided what to eat. As our appetizers came, Kate shifted into another mode.

"Do you ever think about the fact that with every day that passes you become more of the person you will always be?"

This was quite a switch from talk about new movies. It took me a second to adjust. "What does that mean to you?"

"I guess that would depend on the day. On some of them, I feel pretty satisfied. On most, though, I think about all the things that I planned to do with my life that I know now I'll never do."

"Kate, you're in your early thirties. Unless you have a terminal disease, you have plenty of time to do everything you ever wanted to do."

"That's not true, though. Not really, anyway. I mean, when I was a teenager, I had such huge dreams. I was going to act. I was going to invent something. I was going to play professional basketball. But as time passes, I realize that those dreams are not only gone, but they're essentially unattainable."

"Are you saying you're unhappy with your life?"

"No, I'm not saying that. That's the thing. I like my life. I like that I'm fast-tracking through my career and that I live in a great city and do lots of great things. But, you know, you make all these tradeoffs along the way, and every now and then I feel like I've let too many things go."

I nodded slowly. "Trust me, I know what you mean."

"Do you? I mean, you sort of got me thinking this way with that stuff about Melissa."

"I promised I wouldn't mention her name."

"I know you did, and you're being a very good boy about it. But I started to think about all the stuff we used to do together. We really were great friends, and yet it was the most natural thing in the world to just let it slip away. Our lives weren't meant to stay in synch with one another. But the person I was back then didn't expect to be the person I've become. Like my friendship with Melissa, I let a lot of ambitions dissipate naturally over the years."

"At some point you have to choose a path."

"Of course you do, and like I said, my path is very nicely paved, but sometimes I wish I could go off-road for a while."

I took a sip of my wine and watched Kate. The Kate I knew was never this contemplative in front of me – even in the wake of the numerous breakups she'd endured while Melissa and I were together.

"Tell me one of your dreams from when you were a teenager."

She laughed softly and lowered her eyes. "I wanted to be an astronaut."

"Wow, really?"

She wrinkled her nose. "I really did. I would watch those transmissions from the space shuttle and imagine myself up there performing experiments, launching satellites, walking out into the blackness to make some essential repair. It seemed unbelievably appealing to me."

"Why didn't you do it?"

She tossed her hands out to the side and then looked down at her meal. "Reality just took over for me. I knew I had the talent to be a good lawyer and the odds of making it seemed to be a whole lot better. I mean, how many people ever get to go into space?"

"It would've been fun to try, though."

"Yeah, I suppose. But that's what I was talking about before. That's something that I really wanted and now it's something that I'll never be. It doesn't make my life emptier because of it, but one of the things that defines me is *not an astronaut*."

I took some time to ponder this. How had I been defined by the chances that passed me by? Was Melissa one of those chances? I refused to believe so.

"A lot of guys would have laughed or made a joke about that," Kate said.

"About the astronaut thing?"

"Yeah, that."

"No, I think it's a great dream. I was just at the Air and Space Museum yesterday."

"I love that place."

"Me, too. We should go sometime."

Kate nodded slowly. "I'd like that."

We changed courses and the conversation changed course. We talked some more about work and then I remembered that Kate was a huge women's basketball fan. Though I didn't know nearly as much about the Washington Mystics as I did about the other local teams, I could keep up my end of the conversation and let Kate wax effusive. I suppose she would have given me equal consideration if I wanted to talk about the O's, but I decided not to find out.

We finished the bottle of wine and then had an after-dinner port and then another. I knew there was no truth to the notion that finer liquor gave you a more refined buzz, but I didn't feel drunk at all. Just comfortable. For really the first time since I'd arrived in this world, I felt at ease.

I didn't even notice that the restaurant had emptied out. Eventually, we were the only diners still seated, and from the expressions of the waitstaff, we weren't nearly as welcome as we had been a few hours earlier. I asked the waiter for our check.

"We can split this if you'd like," Kate said when I got the bill.

"No chance. This was an apology dinner, remember?"

Kate smiled. "Actually, I forgot."

That was good to hear. "My treat."

I walked her back to her car, a red Lexus. The temperature had dropped and Kate was probably a little chilly without sleeves. I thought about giving her my suit jacket to wear and then decided against it. When we got to the car, she turned to face me.

"This was really nice," she said.

"It was. Thank you."

"Turns out you haven't turned into a craven maniac."

"Or I'm just really good at hiding it."

She laughed and dropped her gaze. "Maybe that." She looked up at me and our eyes locked. It was a remarkably intimate act. "Want to come back for a nightcap?"

The fact is I really wanted to. At that moment, Kate was the realest thing in this world and I was desperate for something real. She moved a little closer to me and I felt myself drawn to her.

All at once, I pulled back. It probably looked hilarious, though Kate wasn't laughing.

"Is something wrong?" she said.

"I can't do this. I'm not ready."

"I thought we had a good time tonight."

"We did. A great time. You have no idea how much I appreciate it."

"But..."

"There's someone else."

Her eyes dropped. "Oh."

I felt the need to explain. "We're not together now, but I'm not ready to start something, and I don't think things would be casual between you and me."

Kate chuckled sadly. "Just once I want to find a man at the right time."

I took her hand, careful not to suggest too much with the gesture. "If things were different, I would beg you to be with me. But I need to work this thing out, whichever way it goes."

She squeezed my hand. "Then do it."

"I'm trying. I can't begin to tell you how glad I am that you're back in my life, though." I grinned at her. "You *are* back in my life, right?"

She squeezed my hand again and then kissed it. "I'll see if I can make room for you."

I reached across and kissed her on the cheek. Even this simple contact made me long for what I'd had with Melissa. My body ached for her touch. For her unimaginably soft skin. For the gentle sighs she breathed when we exchanged tender gestures.

Kate squeezed my hand one more time, then got into her car and drove off. I stood in the parking lot until she was gone. This night had been both fulfilling and disquieting. It was great to have Kate as a friend. Maybe she would even lead me in some way back to Melissa.

However, the thought of what might have happened between us made me miss Melissa more than ever.

Chapter 19

Resources

Melissa bowed as the audience gave her a standing ovation for yet another brilliant performance. I jumped from my aisle seat and clapped until my hands ached. I never grew tired of hearing her play.

Melissa's beaming face swept the crowd, her yellow chiffon gown sunshine in the spotlights. I looked around me, feeling prouder by the second as the audience saluted her. No one was left unmoved by what she gave them.

But one man in another aisle seat three rows down was not applauding. His face was steely and tight. He had stringy blond hair and a cadaver's face ghostly in the reflected glare of the stage lights. He reached into his pocket and made his move toward the stage.

Time slowed for me. Melissa was still standing on the stage. *Why was she still there? She never stayed on stage this long at the end of a show.* She was completely oblivious to what was coming. The man pulled a gun from his pocket, holding it in two hands. He bore down on

Melissa's chest. His lips moved as his left hand cocked the weapon.

I leaped at him like an NFL free safety trying to prevent a game-breaking score. I flung him down on to the floor as the audience gasped. He fought like an animal, trying to point the gun at my head. I wrestled his arm down and drove my fist into his jaw once, twice, until he moaned and lay still.

A crowd gathered around me as the theater exploded in frenzy. I grabbed the gun from his limp hand as the man moaned again. "Melissa, I love you," he said crazily. "I can't live without you. If I can't have you, nobody will."

A police officer approached, his own gun drawn. He took out his handcuffs and bent over the assailant.

"Good work, sir," he said to me solemnly. "You might have just saved Melissa Argent's life."

Melissa reached down and lifted my hand tenderly. Gently she pulled me to my feet as the spotlight bathed us. "Thank you," she said softly as she kissed my cheek.

My arm drew around her waist as I whispered in her ear. "It's over. You'll never have anything to fear ever again."

She touched me lightly on the shoulder. I moved into her caress and was surprised when she started shaking me.

"Sir? Sir?"

Sometimes the dreams were so vivid that it was physically painful to come out of them. Even as I realized what was going on, my subconscious fought in vain to send me back under.

I opened my eyes to find a flight attendant gazing down at me with concern on her face. "Sir, are you all right? You seemed to be very upset. Can I get you something?"

I shook my head and ran a hand over my face. "No, I'm fine. I'm sorry if I caused a disturbance. When will we be landing?"

The woman smiled at me, seemingly relieved that I wasn't having a psychotic episode. "The captain estimates we will be getting into Chicago in about two hours. We've run into a little bit of a headwind. You'll still have plenty of time to make your connection to Washington."

"Thanks."

"Are you sure you're okay now?"

"I'm fine, really."

She continued her way down the aisle. Two days after my dinner with Kate, I needed to make an emergency trip to Los Angeles. The nonstop meetings of the last forty-eight hours had been draining, and I was definitely running on empty. The intensity of the dream had taken what little energy I had left in me.

I leaned my head against the tiny double-paned window. Beneath us, the Rocky Mountains stood triumphantly, seeming huge even from this distance. Off to the right – close enough to be seen but too far to be dangerous – another airliner was flying in the opposite direction. Its navigation lights winked as it slowly lost altitude.

I stretched out my arms, grateful that the seat beside me was empty. It was good to have a little breathing room for once. Attorneys at Warwick & Gray used to fly business class until the firm decided to cut expenses. It was hard to consider business class a necessity, but when you're more than six feet tall, it borders on that.

I tried stretching my legs, but that only made me feel more cramped.

"That was quite a performance," the man in the aisle seat next to me said.

I turned in surprise to my row mate. His belly was bulging through his yellow golf shirt, and thinning gray hair covered his suntanned scalp. Yet his arms were as thick as telephone poles, and he had the look of someone who could do pushups until the day he died.

"Excuse me?"

He smiled, displaying jagged teeth with a gold cap glittering in the corner. "You were jumping around your seat like you had a snake in your pants." The way he cut off his syllables said he was from the New York area.

"I was just stretching."

"Looked like you were doing a full cardio workout in your sleep. Guess that's one way to make the most of your time."

I offered a half-smile; enough to stay polite while clearly indicating that I wasn't really interested in talking.

"Something troubling you?" The man said, oblivious to my signals.

It was going to be a very long flight. I glanced around. There were some empty seats to escape to if this became a problem. "Not really, but thanks for asking."

The man laughed and nodded sagely. He stuck out a tanned, hairy hand. "Name is Harry Goldberg."

I shook his hand and wondered if I could get up to go to the bathroom and simply never come back to my seat. "Ken Timian."

"Nice to meet you, Ken. So who's this woman you're all worked up about?"

"I'm not worked up, and what makes you think it's about a woman?"

"It usually is. It *could* be about money, but people don't usually wriggle around in their sleep over money. They just get really, really depressed. Seems to me that what you're going through is definitely a woman issue. Did she dump you or did you dump her?"

Who was this guy to think he had me pegged? On the other hand, he *did* have me pegged. Though my better instincts told me to exit this conversation immediately, I ignored them. "There's a woman I love. If she knew me, I think she might love me too, but she doesn't even know I exist and I can't think of any way to get her attention."

He shrugged as if what I told him was the most inconsequential thing imaginable. "Gotta do something about that."

"I've *tried* doing something about it. I flew clear across the country to see her. I brought her flowers. I couldn't even get her attention."

"Might as well give up, then," he said sarcastically.

His attitude was starting to annoy me. "I can't give up."

"No, I don't suppose you can." He turned toward the aisle and I assumed he'd said everything he planned to say. He barged into my life and then simply walked away. I felt frustrated and unsatisfied, but I wasn't going to chase after him.

"You know," the man said, still facing away from me, "before I retired to Arizona, I drove a bread truck in New York for thirty years. I started when I was fresh out of the Army. Drove a tank, I might add, and earned a Bronze Star. If I could drive a Sherman tank, why not drive a truck? It paid well and no one tried to blow them up. So every morning I delivered bread to all the little grocery stores." He turned back to face me. "One morning, I saw this young lady opening up her father's place. She was gorgeous – more beautiful than anyone I ever saw on a movie screen. And I think to myself, that's a girl I'd like to meet. So I timed my stop so I got there just as she opened. I always gave her the best loaves of bread I had."

The guy was fully immersed in his story at this point. We went through some turbulence and the plane rocked, but Harry just kept on going, his eyes fixed somewhere on the distant past.

"One day she said to me, 'the customers really like the bread you bring.' She told me her name was Sarah. I wondered if she wanted to get to know me, but that was all she said. I told myself that a classy girl like Sarah – a college graduate, I might add – wouldn't go near a guy like me. Her father hated me, I knew. He'd see me talking with his daughter and tell me to get on with my deliveries, like a truck driver wasn't good enough for his family. But something inside me told me not to give up. So I kept bringing her the bread and smiling at her and asking her how she was, all the while ignoring her father's evil eye."

Harry's wistful expression was starting to get to me. "Please tell me this has a happy ending."

"I think it would be safe to call forty-eight years of marriage a happy ending. Her father was a cantankerous bastard, but even he came around after a while."

He chuckled and I chuckled along with him. "That's a good story. But I'm really starting to believe that I missed my chance at having one of those."

"That's a load of crap," he said sharply before turning to face the flight attendant who'd come by with a drink cart. I took a Coke while Harry frowned at his tomato juice. "The doctor says I should drink this instead of beer." He sneered. "Yeah, tastes great ice-cold when you come in from the broiling Arizona sun." He took a swig and put down his cup. Then he turned back to me.

"Anyway, like I was saying, your whole thing about missing your chance is a load of crap. If this woman means as much to you as it sounds like she does, you gotta get off your ass and make something happen. You act like you're invisible and she'll treat you like you're invisible."

"It's not that easy," I said.

Harry leaned across his seat and pointed a finger three inches away from my nose. "No one said love was easy," he said sharply. He leaned back in his seat. "And if you think you can live without it, you're a fool."

This guy wasn't anything like what I'd expected. As though I needed to be told by this point that appearances could be deceiving. "Your wife is a lucky woman," I said with admiration. "Are you off to see her?"

"Not quite yet," he said with a sad smile. "She's in heaven now. I hope I'll be joining her some day." His sinewy fingers squeezed the cup, flipping a drop of tomato juice on the gold wedding band he still wore.

"I'm sorry." Why couldn't I think of anything better to say?

Harry's broad shoulders relaxed as he shrugged off memories. "That's life. It's hard to complain when I was blessed for so long." He coughed and looked down at his seat briefly. Then he turned to me again. "But I never would have been blessed at all if I had given up. Just remember that, Ken. Don't give up, or you'll regret for the rest of your life what you might have had."

"Yes, sir," I said with a smile and a tiny salute.

He saluted back and then returned to his drink. I would have bought him a beer if it wasn't against doctor's orders.

$$\approx$$

I still had no idea what my next step should be. Unfortunately, my situation was just a little harder than Harry's had been. It wasn't simply a matter of avoiding a surly dad, and I had no excuse to see Melissa, no delivery I could make to her. I needed to find a way to reach her, to get past her coterie, and to let her see what things could be like between us. The enormity of the distance between my desires and where I stood right now was daunting.

I went to see Stephon again. He was dressed in a blazer and open collar today, still more formal than he had been in the other world, but less so. An entire display case in his store was dedicated to intricately carved green crystals. I never saw him carry anything like this in the store before. Maybe his clientele was changing – though I still had absolutely no idea who that clientele was.

He was dusting a mirrored shelf when I came through the door. He glanced over at me and gave me a nod. "Good to see you, Ken. How are you faring?"

"I'm all over the place. Good days, bad days, hopeful days, desperate days."

"Sounds like most other people in the world."

"I guess. But not exactly for the same reason."

Stephon finished dusting and gestured me toward the counter. Without asking, and seemingly without any effort, he produced two steaming glasses of tea.

"Oh, I don't know," he said. "It seems to me that consternation over love is one of the universals in our world."

He was right of course. "I don't know what I should do next," I said, feeling the desperation creep into my voice as I spoke.

"What are you *trying* to do?"

"You know what I'm trying to do."

"So you've decided to try to reconnect with Melissa."

"There was never any other acceptable alternative."

"No, I suppose not. Have you found her?"

"Finding her isn't the issue. She's a public figure, as it turns out. *Getting to* her is the hard part."

Stephon took a sip of his tea and seemed to consider this. "I can see how that would be difficult."

He seemed even more obtuse than usual. He was like a therapist asking me how I felt about something when I really wanted *his* opinion. "Look, I know you can't send me back in time again, but is there anything you can do? Could you maybe send some kind of psychic message to Melissa, let her know that contacting me would be a good thing?"

Stephon laughed. "You want me to act as your cosmic matchmaker?"

"I'm really flailing around here."

He put his teacup down. "I'm sorry, Ken. I truly am. But I can't make someone fall in love with you. I can't even put the idea in her head. I'm afraid you're entirely on your own with this."

I leaned heavily against the display counter. I saw Stephon's eyes dart down to check for fingerprints. "What would you do if you were me? I'm asking you as a man, not a…magician."

"How did you meet her the first time?"

"A mutual friend introduced us at a party. The place was really noisy, but when we started talking there was suddenly no one else in the room. Things just took off from there."

"The two of you just 'clicked.'"

"Instantly."

"Then there's every reason to believe that it could happen again."

"I know that much. Even though she's a star now, I think the same thing could happen between us. If I could only get that far."

Stephon looked me squarely in the eyes. I don't think he'd ever done that before, and it was a little unnerving. Those eyes seemed to have been alive for centuries.

"You aren't using all of your resources," he said plainly.

"Is that the man or the magician speaking?"

"What difference does it make? Ken, use all of your resources."

〰
〰

Kate was a resource – even if she didn't know it – but I was reluctant to use her after our dinner together. Things had become so good between us, and while I couldn't get involved with her romantically, I really wanted to keep her as a friend. Whether I brought

Melissa back into my life or not, I wanted Kate to be a part of it.

Still, as distant as it was, Kate had the closest connection to Melissa of anyone I knew. There had to be some way for her to reach out to Melissa as an old friend, and I needed to ask her to do that for me. Regardless of the consequences.

That afternoon, I called Kate at her office.

"What are you doing for dinner?" I said.

"I was thinking Mexican."

"*With* someone?"

"Who knows? There are still a few hours until dinnertime."

"Let me take you to dinner. There's something I want to talk to you about."

"Is this something I'm going to want to hear?"

"Probably not, but I sort of need you to hear it."

Kate picked a Mexican restaurant near her office and I got there a little before 7:00. I had a Margarita waiting for her when she arrived.

"Getting a head start on me?" she said when she saw the two drinks. I hadn't touched mine, which was a challenge under the circumstances. I decided to dive right in.

"Listen, I haven't been entirely honest with you."

Kate took a drink and her eyes narrowed. "About what."

"About Melissa Argent."

Kate shook her head slowly. "Are we really going back there?"

"I need to meet her."

"So you can tell her how much you love her concertos?"

"Because we're supposed to be together."

Kate stared at me dumbfounded. "Please don't tell me this is the reason you refrained from kissing me the other night."

"I'm afraid it is."

Kate laughed so loudly that several people from other tables turned in our direction. "You really are out of your freaking mind. You know, you do a good job of hiding it for short periods."

I took a long sip from my margarita and delicately returned it to the table. While my emotions were raging at this moment, I wanted to show Kate that I was under control. "Look, I know this sounds insane. It even sounds insane to me – and I haven't told you the really crazy part. But there's a lot more to this than a fan's adulation or a fixation on her beautiful eyes. Much more. You have to trust me; Melissa and I are destined to be with one another."

"Why, exactly, do I have to trust you?"

"Because I'm not the kind of guy who does irrational things."

Kate smirked. "What part of this conversation illustrates that?"

I cradled my forehead in my right hand and then rubbed my face before speaking again. "Is there any way you could introduce the two of us?"

"No."

I was a little surprised by Kate's bluntness. "Just no?"

Kate laughed again. "Okay Ken, let's cover the logical reasons first." She used her fingers to tick them off. "I haven't seen Melissa in more than a decade. I don't know how to get in touch with her. There's an excellent chance that she doesn't have any real memory of me.

And even if she did, it's unlikely that she'd want to get together for coffee so I could fix her up on a date."

"You were her best friend for years. She remembers you."

"Maybe she does, but that brings us to the most important reason why I won't do it: because Melissa was once my best friend and best friends don't knowingly expose each other to CRAZY PEOPLE."

This was going so much worse than I'd anticipated. I assumed Kate would react skeptically. I even assumed that she would roll her eyes over the idea that Melissa and I were "meant to be together." But I didn't expect her to shut me down completely.

"Take some time to think about it," I said.

"I don't need to take some time. Do you really think I'd change my mind if I gave this some thought?"

I buried my head in my hands. "Kate, you're my best shot," I said. Even I realized how pathetic I sounded.

My head was still down when Kate stood next to me and put her hand on my shoulder. "Ken," she said, "I had a really good time the other night. A really good time. I thought it might even be the start of something, at the very least a nice friendship. But I'm not going to do this with you. I just simply won't."

I looked into her eyes and saw genuine sadness there. She was about to walk out on me again, and it pained her. "You can go if you want. I'll get the check."

She kissed me on top of the head. "Take care of yourself. I hope this passes." She patted me on the shoulder one more time and left.

I signaled to the waiter and ordered another Margarita.

Chapter 20

For a Fact

I was rudderless again. Harry might exhort me to never give up. Stephon could tell me to tap every available resource. But since I'd found myself in this situation, I had done everything I could think of and I'd come up totally empty.

In the days after Debacle Two with Kate, I tried to push Melissa to the edges of my mind. I submerged myself in work, so much so that Sharon asked if I could hire a temp to help her out. I went out drinking again with Marty and considered it progress that I was able to get myself home.

I thought about moving. Maybe that small town in Maine I mused about. Maybe New York or Los Angeles. The idea of going to a place where no one knew me and where there were no reminders of the life I once loved was very attractive. One thing was entirely certain: I couldn't stay where I was when everything brought another heartbreaking memory of Melissa.

I perused real estate websites for other cities. I found a four-bedroom, three-bath house thirty miles outside of Portland whose mortgage payments would be a little more than a third of the rent on my apartment. I found a one-bedroom place on the Upper West Side in Manhattan that cost about the same, and learned that I could live in a two-bedroom in Brooklyn Heights as long as I maintained the income I made now. Finding a job wouldn't be difficult. I had plenty of clients to recommend me, and even Harrison Warwick would probably give me a good reference in spite of our recent sparring. Maybe I'd start my own firm and get so caught up in it that I wouldn't have time for a life outside of the office. That would be merciful.

A week after I failed with Kate, I got a call from Paul asking if we could get together. We agreed to meet at the Angus Steakhouse in Arlington. It was in a strip mall off Wilson Boulevard, the sort of place that looked dark and smoky even though it was illegal to smoke there. I arrived a few minutes early, and found Paul waiting for me. He looked dreadful. He was dressed in a rumpled tan suit, and his tie was hanging loose from the opened button at his collar. In front of him was an empty glass, and the waiter brought him another scotch as I sat down. I didn't bother with pleasantries.

"You look like hell. What's going on?"

Paul lifted a glass and toasted me halfheartedly. "I left Angela last night." He took a drink and then looked at me as though he himself wasn't sure what to make of what he'd just said.

"I'm sorry," I said, though both of us knew I wasn't.

"Yeah, thanks. I had to do it, you know. I just couldn't keep going." Paul's voice was flat and emotionless. "We had a big fight last night. Right in the middle of the kitchen – the spaghetti sauce was burning on the stove the whole time. I can't even remember what we fought about. Maybe it was doing the laundry or unloading the dishwasher or something. When you have the same arguments over and over again, you do it on automatic pilot. She said something that got me especially riled up and I slammed the kitchen door and stomped into the living room. There was a mug on the coffee table. Angela's college roommate and her husband had given it to us years ago. It said TO OUR VERY SPECIAL FRIENDS. And I looked at the mug and it just got to me, you know? I realized that there was nothing special about us. We were just two people who'd learned to hate each other."

This was the longest speech I'd ever remembered Paul delivering, but I realized I needed to simply let him keep going.

"Angela came stomping into the room a few minutes later. She must have been working up another head of steam. Behind her was that big framed photo of us above the fireplace. The one we took about a year after we got married. Everyone always tells us how great we look in it. But you know what? At that moment, I remembered that I was pissed off at Angela that day, too. I couldn't remember the last time I *haven't been* pissed off at Angela.

"So before she could start another argument, I just put my hands on my hips and told her I was leaving. Just like that."

"What did she do?"

"Nothing. She didn't yell. She didn't cheer. She just looked at me like she didn't know me. Then she nodded and went back to the kitchen. I packed up some stuff

and headed out. I think she was more relieved than anything. I know I am."

"I can understand that."

"You really can't, buddy. You really can't unless
you've been through it. I mean I know I'll have a lot of
garbage to go through in the coming months, but it's a
huge weight off. A huge weight."

"So where did you go after you left?"

"I wound up in a second-rate motel in Prince
George's County. Not exactly luxury living, but the TV
works and the price is right."

"Do you want to stay with me until you find a place?"

"Thanks for the offer, but I think I'm going to enjoy
being by myself for a little while. I can't begin to tell
you how peaceful it felt in that place last night. Even
though the guy next door was on the phone until one in
the morning and I could hear every word."

"Maybe you can find a better hotel."

"Nah, I think I'll stick this out for as long as it takes.
It'll inspire me to move quickly to find an apartment. I'm
going out with a realtor tomorrow night."

Paul looked terrible, but he sounded okay. He
sounded resolute. He knew he'd made the right decision, even though it was a long time in coming.

"You had a lot to do with getting me off of my ass,"
he said, as though he'd heard my thoughts.

"Me?"

"The last couple of times we've been together, you've
come at me from a different angle. Believe me, I knew
you weren't the president of Angela's fan club, but you
always stayed out of it when we started clawing at each
other. Until recently."

"I've been thinking about a bunch of stuff myself."

"Well, it was good for me. Remember at dinner I told you that I'd been thinking about leaving Angela, but I didn't want to be alone? A few days ago, it dawned on me that you were perfectly happy being alone. Different girlfriends all the time. I don't know why I never looked at it that way before. Suddenly, it didn't seem so scary. I guess that prepared me for what came next."

"Don't give up so soon on finding the right woman and settling down."

"You don't need to give me a pep talk, Ken. I'm totally okay with the idea of going solo."

"Don't be. There's somebody out there for you. I know it for a fact. You just have to find her."

"You know it *for a fact*?"

"Just a turn of phrase. But I have good feeling about this."

"If you say so. Right now, I'm just gonna detox for a while. Can we order? I'm suddenly incredibly hungry."

〜〜〜

Melissa's website had put up some new photographs of her in a recording studio. There was also a review of the Seattle benefit concert. It didn't mention the moment at the end of the show where she locked eyes with the man she was destined to love forever, but maybe the reviewer didn't have a good enough seat.

I hadn't gone to the chat room since my latest dinner with Kate. I went there now, though, feeling the need to connect with *someone* about her. PIANOMAN555 was online, as always.

HEY MELISSALOVER. LONG TIME.

THINGS CAME UP. ANY NEWS?

FOUR TRACKS DOWN ON THE NEW
ALBUM. THERE'S TALK THAT SHE
MIGHT USE A GUEST VOCALIST ON AT
LEAST ONE OF THE PIECES.

CAN'T WAIT TO GET IT.

I wondered what Melissa's own singing voice was
like. I'd never heard her sing.

YOU LIVE IN D.C., DON'T YOU?

RIGHT OUTSIDE THE CITY. WHY?

ANY CHANCE YOU WERE ABLE
TO GET TICKETS TO THE KENNEDY
CENTER SHOW?

I felt the hackles rise on the back of my neck.

KENNEDY CENTER SHOW?

ANOTHER MAJOR BENEFIT
PERFORMANCE. TICKETS ARE
RIDICULOUSLY EXPENSIVE AND MOST
OF THEM WERE SOLD IN BLOCKS.

REST WERE SOLD BY LOTTERY
ON LOCAL CLASSICAL STATION.
THOUGHT MAYBE YOU WERE
LUCKY…OR CONNECTED.

NEITHER I'M AFRAID. WHEN IS IT?

NEXT MONDAY.

GOTTA BE THERE. THANKS FOR
LETTING ME KNOW.

GOOD LUCK. YR GONNA NEED IT.

≋

I phoned Kate. I considered it a good sign that she even took the call.

"Hey Ken, what's new?" she said, the sarcasm dripping from her voice.

"Kate, I know I sounded like I was ready for the loony bin the other night and I really want to apologize about that."

She hesitated on the line before she said softly, "That's okay."

"The thing is, I'm probably going to sound even crazier saying what I'm about to say. But if our friendship means anything to you – and I have no reason to believe it does given what I've put you through – you'll at least hear me out and understand that this is incredibly important to me."

"Tell me," Kate said, her voice heavy.

"Melissa is playing a benefit concert at the Kennedy Center on Monday. I need you to get us backstage."

"This is becoming physically painful, do you know that?"

"Please just do this for me. I need to get backstage. I need to meet her. I need her to see me and talk to me and for things to click into place."

"Click into place?"

"It's too hard to explain."

"As opposed to the rest of this, which has been really easy, right?"

"I need this, Kate. I promise you I won't do anything illegal or anything that will embarrass you. This will be the absolute last time I ask you for this. If this fails, I will never mention Melissa's name in front of you again."

Kate let out a long expulsion of air, as though she wanted to make the point of how deflating this conversation felt to her. "I haven't talked to her in more than ten years. What am I supposed to say? How do I explain why I'm getting in touch with her now?"

"Explain that you're an old friend who misses her high school pal. That's going to mean something to her. You know it will."

Kate hesitated again. "I do miss her. I've been thinking about her a lot since you dropped back into my life."

"So do something about it. Do it for yourself as much as for me."

"That was openly manipulative. I assume you're aware of that."

I chuckled. "Yes, I am."

"This thing is on Monday?"

"8:00 at the Kennedy Center."

"Thanks for all the lead time."

"Believe me, you've known about this nearly as long as I have."

There was a long silence on the other end. I began to think about what I would do if Kate said no. "I'm not making any promises, Ken. There's every chance this isn't going to work out. But I'll give it a try."

Chapter 21

Utterly Mystified

The next two days went by painfully slowly. The phone in my office rang constantly, but it was always someone other than Kate. I tried to keep a positive outlook, to distract myself with work and assume that things would turn out the way I hoped. But still Kate didn't call.

The message light on my answering machine was blinking when I returned home from a client dinner, and I approached it expectantly.

"I'm sorry," were the first words Kate left, and I leaned against the wall and closed my eyes. "I have tried several times to reach Melissa. I can't get anyone with any clout in her organization to talk to me. I'm afraid I've struck out, Ken. I'm really sorry. I know this was important to you and even though I think the whole thing is weird I feel bad that I couldn't help."

I thudded down into the recliner and stared off into space. The lights were off in the apartment and I made no effort to put them on. Wizard jumped into my lap and allowed me to pet him. That even the cat was offering me sympathy made me feel pathetic.

I had to get into the concert. I'd figure out how to get backstage after that. By this point, I knew that it was impossibly sold out and that even the ticket brokers had waiting lists. So few tickets had been made available to the general public for this benefit that even scalpers probably had a hard time getting their hands on them and they would be swarmed the night of the show.

I went to my computer and logged onto the chat room. For once, PIANOMAN555 wasn't around, but I knew a few others who were there. I asked if anyone had access to any tickets. No one in the room could provide any help other than to mention the brokers I already knew had nothing.

I watched the computer for nearly a half hour without participating as the conversation swirled from pianist to pianist. Finally, someone I'd never seen before with the screen name AVANT broke in.

> DID I HEAR SOMEONE WAS LOOKING
> FOR MELISSA ARGENT TIX?

I leaned forward in my seat and typed as quickly as my fingers would allow.

> YES, DESPERATELY. DO YOU KNOW
> WHERE I CAN GET ONE?

> U ARE IN LUCK, MELISSALUV. SISTER-
> IN-LAW SUDDENLY DECIDED TO FLY
> IN NIGHT OF CONCERT...WOULD
> RATHER HAVE MULTIPLE ROOT

CANAL THAN SPEND EVENING WITH
BELOVED RELATIVE. FOR SAKE OF
PEACE WILL SELL MY TWO TICKETS.
CAN'T BELIEVE I HAVE TO MISS THIS.

I was stunned at my good fortune. Not only did my Internet benefactor have two tickets that he was willing to sell *at cost*, but he lived just outside of town. I arranged to meet him in an hour in a bar off Wisconsin Avenue.

I wasn't surprised that the skies poured as I got into my car, nor did I care. Raindrops weren't going to deter me tonight. However, a three-car pileup on the Key Bridge delayed me, as did the lack of parking anywhere near the bar. Now twenty minutes late, I finally found a spot in a lot behind a restaurant. CUSTOMER PARKING ONLY, warned a red-and-white sign, but who would go out to check parking spaces on a night like this? Besides, I assumed I wouldn't be there long.

AVANT was not in the bar when I arrived. I waited an hour, hoping he hadn't chosen to go home when I failed to show up right away, and I drank three beers in the process. Then a young bartender with a ponytail leaned over and shouted over the din of music and chatter.

"Are you Ken?"

"Yes, I am."

"Somebody left a message for you. He said his wife freaked out when she heard he was going to sell you the tickets. Something about loving Melissa more than her sister, whatever that means. He said to tell you he's really sorry."

It was as though he'd just told me a loved one died. "Thanks," I said.

The bartender shrugged indifferently and moved to help other customers. I stared at the remains of my beer for several minutes and then stood slowly to walk outside.

I looked up at the sky and let the driving rain sting my face with needle jabs. I welcomed the discomfort, anything to draw my attention away from the fact that I had run out of options. I would go to the Kennedy Center early on Monday in hopes of turning my bank account over to a scalper, but the odds of success were even higher against me than the absurdly high odds I'd been fighting since I lost Melissa.

I got back to the parking lot just in time to see a tow truck drag my car away. I simply stared after it, and when it was gone, I leaned my head against a wall, getting soaked.

There was no Metro station where I was, and I hadn't even brought a raincoat. I thought about sliding down the wall and just sitting there until morning, but even a deluge wouldn't have washed away my heartache. I wiped the water from my eyes, found some cover, and pulled out my cellphone. It was after midnight, but I called the only person in this world I knew I could call.

Twenty minutes later, a Lexus pulled up in front of the bookstore doorway where I sought shelter. The passenger window descended with an electric whine.

"You look horrible," Kate said with little emotion in her voice.

I couldn't think of a thing to say.

She leaned across and opened the door.

"Get in."

Her short hair was neat in the front and disheveled in the back, as if a comb had been hastily run through it. I noticed that the shoelace on one of her sneakers was untied.

"Kate…thanks. I don't know what I would have done if you hadn't come."

"It's late, Ken, and I have to get up early tomorrow. We still have to retrieve your car. I hope you know where the towing yard is."

I climbed into the passenger seat, and sat uneasily, aware of what my wet clothes were doing to her leather upholstery. She reached into the back seat and pulled out a tan blanket. She draped it over me and I pulled it closer. I looked over at her and she barely met my eyes, shaking her head sadly.

"I know this is a huge inconvenience for you," I said. "I just want you to know that I really appreciate it."

Kate shook her head again. "This has got to stop, Ken."

"I realize this was an abuse of our friendship."

"That's not what I'm talking about and you know it. I'm talking about your whole obsession with Melissa. What the hell were you doing running around in the middle of the night trying to buy concert tickets from a stranger? Have you read *nothing* about the kind of crap that goes on through the Internet? You're lucky the guy only stood you up."

"I really needed the tickets."

"Do you hear yourself? Is there any part of your brain that understands how irrational your behavior is? I have left a dozen messages with Melissa's staff, and no one has gotten back to me. This is the end of the line. I know you want to meet her. I know you think there's something written in the stars about the two of you. But it's not going to happen."

"It can still happen. I'll find a scalper."

Kate grabbed my shoulder roughly. I turned to look at her and saw that she was seething. "Get over it, Ken. For God's sake! Get yourself some professional help for this ridiculous obsession. I'll do you the favor of giving you some names."

"The only favor I need is for you to keep trying to reach Melissa. Call another dozen times if you have to."

Kate seemed utterly mystified. She stared at me with an expression that spoke of frustration and even a little bit of hurt. "You have to tell me what is making you do this. I know there are fans who obsess about musicians, but I just can't convince myself that you're that kind of guy. There's something else making you do this. "

"You wouldn't understand."

"You're probably right. But I do understand this: you're hurting yourself. Badly, by all appearances. You look like you've been on a week-long bender."

She reached out for my hand and squeezed it. When I looked at her now, I could see she was genuinely concerned. I had no intention of upsetting her, but there didn't seem to be any way for me to avoid it.

"Thanks," I said. "You're being a lot nicer about this than I deserve."

"You bet your ass I am," she said with a half-smile. She looked out the windshield and I followed her eyes, tracking headlights and taillights as they passed us.

Again Kate turned to me. "I'm not going to pretend to know what is going on with you, but just because you wish for something doesn't mean it has a chance of coming true. It's time to put aside your fantasies, Ken. I'm sure Melissa Argent is perfectly happy with the life she has and gets all the adoration she needs already. You

have to face the fact that you're fixated on an image, not
a person. And you have to face the fact that that image
can't love you back."

I leaned my stiff neck against the headrest and closed
my eyes. There was a bitter taste in my mouth. Was it
really time to give up? Hadn't I tried every way I could
think of to bring Melissa back to me?

No. I could still pull it off. If I couldn't see Melissa
after this concert, then I'd catch the next one, and another one after that. She would almost certainly go out
on tour in support of her new album when it was ready.
I had enough money to buy theater and airline tickets,
and I would find some way to get time off from work.

"Can't give up yet," I heard myself say.

"What was that?"

I gave Kate a weak smile. "Nothing. I was just thinking out loud about what you told me."

Kate stared down at the dashboard. "Let's go get
your car."

☰

I went to the office late the next morning, getting a
few stares as I walked through the "hallowed halls." I
knew my erratic behavior had been the cause for some
consternation and more than a few whispers. I found it
difficult to care about this.

Mercifully, much of the day was filled with client
meetings and the completion of a document that had
to get out by late afternoon. It made the time pass and
made me think less about my awful night and what I was
going to do about Monday.

Around four o'clock Sharon buzzed me to say that Kate was on the line. I took a moment to pick up the phone, not sure I wanted to rehash our last conversation.

"Listen Kate," I said. "I'm really sorry about last night."

"Who cares? We have other things to talk about, like where you're taking me to dinner Monday night."

I felt a quick thrill of excitement. This could only mean one thing. "You reached Melissa?"

"I just spoke to her personal assistant. Some silly little twit named Jackeline who spells her name with a 'k.' I really would have expected the staff of a world-class musician to be a little less *Tiger Beat*, but maybe that's part of the whole Melissa Argent marketing strategy.

"Anyway, she had no intention of even giving me the time of day, but she was no match for my power of persuasion. You will, by the way, tell me repeatedly how brilliant I am for the rest of my life."

I laughed. "You're more than brilliant. You're brilliant and resourceful."

"And let's not forget gorgeous."

"And sumptuous."

"Sumptuous? Huh, I hadn't thought of that."

"You're definitely sumptuous."

"You think so?"

"Can we get back to the story?"

"No, I'm having too much fun drawing this out."

"If I have a stroke before Monday, you'll have to buy your own dinner."

"Point well taken. Anyway, I finally got her to take this to Melissa herself. I even got her to interrupt Melissa in the studio to convey my message. I was really rolling at that point. As it turns out, all of those years of doing homework, painting toenails, and fantasizing about boys together have accrued to your benefit. Melissa was delighted to hear from me – I hope you don't mind that I didn't mention you, but we were having too much fun dishing – and we've been comped for the show and invited to a reception backstage afterward. Are you as completely impressed as you should be?"

I was well past impressed. I was virtually euphoric. "I'm so impressed I'm practically speechless," I said, the words slightly choked as though to prove my point.

"I'm still thinking about how you're going to repay me."

"Anything you want will still be too little. You're priceless, Kate."

"The first man to tell me that, and he turns out to be a total lunatic. You promise that you aren't going to embarrass me or get our pictures in the *Post*, right?"

"I swear," I said, though I wasn't making any such promises to myself. Once I saw Melissa up close, I had no idea how I was going to react.

"As long as we have that straight, pick me up at six o'clock sharp. The dinner needs to be even more sumptuous than I am."

"Inconceivable."

"Give it the old college try. And make sure you wear your best suit."

She had no idea how little I needed that advice.

Chapter 22

Not Uncomfortable

Though it couldn't possibly compare to what I was feeling, Kate was obviously anxious or she wouldn't have been waiting on the sidewalk in front of her townhouse when I picked her up. I realized this evening had some real import for her as well. She was going to be reconnecting with a dear old friend after far too long.

Kate looked great. She wore a deep blue dress and her hair was fresh from the salon. What point was I missing about her romantic difficulties? Any man would be lucky to be with a woman this beautiful, this smart, this clever, and this caring. Any man, that is, who wasn't already in love with Melissa Argent. While playing matchmaker wasn't in my suite of skills, a surprising thought flashed through my mind.

As she climbed into the passenger seat, Kate looked me over.

"Not bad. You should have polished your shoes, but we'll forgive that."

"You, on the other hand, look perfect."

She smiled at the compliment. "I haven't been to the Kennedy Center in the company of a handsome man in a while. Besides, I needed to go to the hairdresser anyway. Bruno said he missed me." She gestured toward the bouquet that was sitting on the back seat. "I don't suppose those are for me, huh?"

"Sorry." I reached behind me and produced a single pink rose. "But this is."

She beamed when I handed the flower to her. "You may be a compulsive maniac, but at least you're a gentleman."

I took her to Marcel's where we ordered a white Burgundy and ate lobster pappardelle, *loup de mer* with beluga lentils, and bison strip loin. Melissa wouldn't have ordered any of this – at least she wouldn't have in our other world. I was so nervous about the evening to come that I could barely eat, but Kate had asked for a great meal and I wanted to deliver for her.

"Fabulous enough for you?" I said as we sipped coffee.

"You exceeded my expectations, Ken. That doesn't happen very often."

I smiled.

"Are you okay about tonight?" she said.

"I have a good feeling about it."

"Don't get crushed if nothing happens."

I nodded and took another sip of coffee. "I have a good feeling about it."

It was a quick walk to the Kennedy Center. The place was abuzz with finely attired patrons milling before the show. This was definitely an A-list crowd, and I recognized many faces from the worlds of politics and the arts. Few of them, however, had better seats than ours. Our comp tickets had put us in the orchestra, fourth row center.

The doors to the auditorium opened and the crowd began to make its way in. "Remember," Kate said. "Nothing embarrassing."

I smiled and hugged her arm as we walked into the theater. "I will be the model of comportment."

As we sat waiting for the concert to begin, I felt myself getting antsy. My good humor evaporated as the reality of what I was doing there caught up with me. This wasn't about seeing a show. Regardless of how brilliant it might be, it was merely preamble. I was on a mission – a mission that would begin in approximately two hours. Before midnight, my future would be defined.

The lights blinked and then darkened. Melissa strode onto the stage in a fluttery gown the orange of a Caribbean sunset. She began with the same piece she opened with in Seattle. Her second song, however, was something from the new album she was working on. Her performance was masterful, though I was too distracted to fully enjoy it. My hand reached into my jacket pocket to secure my backstage pass every five minutes, and I imagined repeatedly what would happen when our eyes met up close.

There was a huge ovation after Melissa's encore, but Kate and I barely participated. "Come on," I said over the din. I took her arm and pushed my way through our row, emerging into the aisle just before the crowd began to leave. We worked through this group and got to the backstage entrance. In spite of our haste, though, the reception line was already backed up and Melissa was nowhere in sight. We stood for an interminable period while more people lined up behind us. When was this thing going to start moving?

"You look a little insane," Kate said.

"What do you mean?"

"You seem just a tiny bit overanxious. Calm down. We might be waiting a while. Here." She walked over to a table laden with drinks and brought me a bottle of water. I sipped it and realized how dry my mouth was.

About ten minutes later, the line began to stir, slowly working its way into the next room. There must have been fifty people ahead of us, all of whom carried an air of self-importance. While these people might have admired her work, they would never have defined themselves as "fans." They were here for a meet-and-greet because it was an entitlement.

Twenty minutes later, we were making real progress. Though Melissa was still far away, I could occasionally glimpse flashes of deep orange.

"Any longer and these flowers will die," I said stiffly.

"Be patient. We're getting there."

Melissa really knew how to work this crowd of VIP's. She smiled graciously and endlessly as she shook hands and signed autographs. My Melissa was also a pro at schmoozing, though when she did it up on the Hill her aims were very different. This Melissa regularly stumped for any number of charities, so maybe her goals weren't that different at all.

Finally, after all the waiting, it was our turn.

Melissa stared through me for a moment. "Katie," she said enthusiastically, and she hugged my companion for a full minute. Melissa stepped back and smiled. "You look so great. You haven't changed a bit."

"Just a few pounds and a different hair color, that's all. You look fabulous. And you were wonderful up there tonight."

"Thanks. I was a little nervous about this show for some reason. I'm glad you liked it. It's *so* good to see you."

Melissa and Kate reminisced for what seemed like an eternity while I shifted my weight from foot to foot and prayed for them to hurry up. At one point, Melissa called for her personal assistant (the legendary Jackeline, I assumed) and asked her to take Kate's contact information. Finally, when I'd reached borderline frantic, Kate put her hand on my shoulder.

"Melissa, this is my friend Ken Timian. He's a ridiculously big fan of yours."

Melissa looked at me, and I swear that she recognized me. There was the same flicker of recall that I saw in her eyes when she came out of the music room after I scared away her piano teacher. Then she blinked, shook her head subtly, and stuck out her hand.

"Pleased to meet you, Ken."

I tried to give her the bouquet – and dropped it. I hastily bent down to pick up the roses.

"These are for you," I said, embarrassed.

"Thank you. That's very sweet." She accepted them and handed them over to her assistant. She shook my hand with a touch warm and familiar. "I wish I had more time to talk, but you will have to excuse me. There are so many people here tonight. These benefits are always harder *after* the show." I looked behind me and noticed for the first time just how many people had gathered there. I heard her say, "Katie, I'll call" and when I turned back, someone had taken my place in front of her. Melissa smiled as kindly to this man as she had to me.

As I stood helpless, another hand squeezed mine, firmer than Melissa's. "Not exactly what you were looking for, huh?" Kate said gently and much more sympathetically than I expected as she pulled me away. "She seemed to like talking with you even if it was only for a moment. Why don't I go see if I can bring her back after the line dies down? Just look around for a while. It's not every day you get a chance to be backstage at the Kennedy Center."

Kate headed back toward the reception line. As I glanced in that direction, I wondered how far the line extended into the other room. There was a very real chance that Melissa would be whisked away before it ended, even with all the movers and shakers in this crowd. It was hard to believe that I would get another personal audience with her.

It was also impossible to avoid the truth of what had happened here. I'd failed. I stood backstage, my mind a blank. The ghost of recognition in Melissa's eyes remained a ghost. Our love was like one of those false suns that never generated enough fire to become a blazing star.

Do something, my heart told me. But what could I do? I'd spoken with her. I'd touched her hand. Still, she was as gone now as she had ever been. She was no more than twenty feet away, yet the distance between us was an entire universe.

Kate joined me a few minutes later.

"Looks like it's going to be a while. And you look like someone just shot your dog. Cheer up, we'll figure something out."

"What?" I said hopelessly.

"*Something*. I still have no idea what you thought was going to happen. Not to mention that I have no idea why I'm trying to go out of my way now to *make* something happen."

"I feel empty."

"Go get a drink. It'll make you feel better. I'll do my best to retrieve Melissa once the crowd thins out. Meanwhile, I saw two guys from the State Department speaking earnestly over there. I'm gonna see if I can eavesdrop."

She kissed me on the cheek and walked away, glancing back at me with a smile that I tried in vain to return. Kate was enjoying herself, caught up in the moment. She was backstage at a celebrity event with half of Washington's luminaries. Why wouldn't she enjoy it?

I wandered aimlessly and found myself near the bar. I thought about taking Kate's advice and having a drink or two or three, but I couldn't even motivate myself to numbness. From this angle, I couldn't see Melissa at all. My life without her had truly begun.

Without realizing it, I'd made my way to the front of the drinks line. Feeling stupid, I ordered a Coke just to have something in my hands. I then moved toward an empty table and sat, watching the bustle around me as though it was through a glass partition.

From this point forward, I would need to set new goals, accept lower standards. I would achieve at work – either here or in L.A. or in Maine or in Nepal – and I would try to make some real and lasting friendships. Kate was a good start, and now that Paul was free of his terrible marriage maybe we could develop the kinship we'd had in my other life. And I would date again someday. The idea seemed preposterous to me at the moment, but at some point I would most likely date again. Once I came to accept those lower standards.

I could live without Melissa. I so completely didn't want to, but I could do it. I would always have the knowledge that I helped her, and the memory of our last touch just minutes ago.

I'm not sure how long I was sitting there. I was dimly aware that the crowd had thinned, that the room wasn't as loud or boisterous anymore. There was less soda in my glass as well, though I don't remember drinking any of it. Then I felt a hand on my shoulder, a gossamer touch, a gentle, tentative one.

"Excuse me," the voice said and I turned to it.

Melissa was staring at me curiously. She looked out toward the crowd and smiled professionally, then turned back to me and tilted her head. "Hi. We spoke a while ago. Your name is Ken, right?"

I moved to stand up, feeling the world swirl around me, wondering if my legs would hold me. "Yes, yes it is."

"Do we know each other? Have we met before?"

I took a deep breath and jammed my suddenly sweaty palms in my pockets. "It's possible." I wanted to sound casual. I didn't want to frighten her by letting her know how much it meant to me to talk to her.

"Your face seems awfully familiar, and I feel like I should know who you are. You will have to forgive me. I'm very bad at this."

"It's okay. You must meet millions of people."

She smiled. "I do. But this doesn't usually happen to me. *Do* we know each other?"

I began to warm to this moment. Suddenly I didn't feel like I was chasing after Melissa, but simply talking to her. Talking as we had thousands and thousands of times. "I think we might. Maybe we can go someplace and try to figure it out."

She hesitated.

"You're busy, I know," I said.

Melissa bit her lip and then nodded with a little smile. "That's okay. There's a private room down the hall where we can talk."

"Is it okay for you to leave? What about your adoring crowd?"

"This crowd?" she said, looking around. "I'm not sure anyone will miss me. They'll be perfectly happy adoring themselves."

We walked away together and I saw her catch the eye of someone in her entourage and nod subtly. The aide returned this with a somewhat confused glare, but Melissa didn't let it deter her. I followed her into a small room off a corridor, and she closed the door behind us, leaving it open just a crack.

She gestured me toward a chair and sat on the sofa next to it. She studied me silently and I bathed myself in her presence. In that moment, I realized that my memory of Melissa hadn't done her justice, as vivid as I believed it to be. Neither had the photos on her website or my perspective from an orchestra seat. This close, Melissa was more than beautiful. She was inspiring. If she hadn't spoken, I don't know that I ever would have. I was certain I could happily stay in this precise moment forever.

"So why do I think I know you, Ken?"

"We've been together before," I said. My voice seemed thick to me, as though time slowed. "I can't imagine you noticed me."

"At a concert?"

I nodded, not knowing what else to do. There was no chance I was going to mention our other meeting and risk driving Melissa away.

Her brow furrowed. Again, she tilted her head. From every angle, her face was magnificent. "By any chance, were you at my performance in Seattle a couple of weeks ago?"

The question stunned me. I couldn't help but laugh. "You saw me there?"

Melissa seemed absolutely baffled by this. "I don't usually notice faces in the audience. There are a lot of them, and light doesn't make it easy. But when I took my bows that night, I remember making eye contact with someone and getting this unusual sensation. A very, very unusual sensation. That was you, wasn't it?"

"That was me, but I can't believe you remember that. I thought you really saw me, but then I told myself it couldn't be possible. Sorry if I made you uncomfortable."

Melissa looked at the floor. "I didn't say it made me uncomfortable. It was just...unusual." She hesitated for a moment and seemed confused, as though she was try-ing to relive the experience.

"It didn't make you uncomfortable?"

"No," she said dreamily, "not uncomfortable." She smiled at me, though at the same time she seemed very far away. Then her eyes darted away and when she looked back at me, I could see she'd snapped out of whatever had taken her. "Did you like the show?"

"It was amazing. I didn't just enjoy the music, or even the musician. I enjoyed watching you. It was Me-lissa Argent the person who made the night sparkle."

Melissa's expression warmed. "I get many compliments for my work, but that's the first time anyone has said anything like that to me."

I leaned forward, so close I could have easily touched her if I had the nerve. "Would you like to have dinner with me sometime?" The words escaped my lips, propelled by sheer longing, even as logic screamed that I was acting too hastily.

I could tell from the look on Melissa's face that I'd gone too far too fast. "I'm sorry," she said, "I don't meet fans for dinner." Her tone was formal, her words automatic from long practice.

I tried to take a step back, to return us to the right path. "I'm sorry. I didn't mean to be too forward. But I felt something that night, and I'm feeling something now."

Melissa's expression softened again. "Kate's a good friend of yours?"

"We've known each other for years. She'll vouch for the fact that I'm completely harmless." I wondered if Kate would do anything of the sort, given my recent behavior.

"I'm not an impulsive person," she said carefully.

"Sometimes it's important to act on your impulses. Have dinner with me."

I had no idea how to read her at that moment. Had I overplayed my hand? Had I blundered the most perfect opportunity I'd ever have?

"I'm heading back west tomorrow night. But call me in the morning. I'll have Jackeline give you my private number. I'm staying at the Mandarin Oriental. Perhaps we could meet for lunch."

My heart surged, though I tried to maintain a modicum of calm. "I'll do that."

Melissa shook her head. I could tell she was wondering why she'd extended that invitation. She looked at the door.

"I have to be going. I really can only disappear for so long during these things."

She stood and I joined her. I extended my hand and she took it, allowing the touch to linger. "I'm very glad we met, Melissa."

She still seemed baffled. "So am I," she said softly. She let go of my hand and headed toward the door. I let her go alone, not wanting her to think I was attaching myself to her. I didn't want to do anything to make her think twice about taking my call tomorrow.

As she passed through the doorway, she turned back to me. There was a gleam in her eyes.

Chapter 23

Something Momentous

I skipped work the next day. It would have been pointless for me to go in, and maybe even a little dangerous for my clients. There was a lilt in Sharon's voice when I called her to cancel my meetings.

"This is so good for you," she said.

"What is?"

"Whatever you're doing instead of coming in to work."

"Why do you say that?"

"Because you almost never do it. That means it must be worth it."

I found this conversation a little befuddling, but the warmth in Sharon's voice moved me. I recognized it from another lifetime. "Sharon, if things go the way I hope they will today, there might be a few more days like this."

"That would also be a good thing."

Once I got off the phone with Sharon, I made two other calls. Kate, who still seemed stunned by what had happened the night before – she asked me to repeat my conversation with Melissa a half dozen times on the drive back home – seemed game for anything. Paul, on the other hand, required some coercion. His reticence and cynicism were something I hoped to see much less of in the future.

I drove down to Stephon's, halfway expecting him to be waiting for my arrival. Instead, he seemed pleasantly surprised to see me.

"Hello, Ken," he said, stepping around the counter to greet me, "how are things going?"

"Sensationally," I said brightly.

Stephon obviously wasn't anticipating that response. "Really?"

"Really. Now I just need my luck to hold. I met Melissa again. We have a date this afternoon."

Stephon smiled broadly and said, "Excellent." He clapped me on the shoulder and turned to go back behind the counter. "This calls for a celebration. I just received a shipment of Yinzhen Silver Needle tea. It'll only take a short while to brew."

It tickled me that he was so excited for me, and I laughed out loud. While Stephon busied himself with the samovar, I perused the new items in the store. I settled on a selection of pearlescent white stones delicately shaped into diamond, floral, and triangular designs. They were stunning.

"What are these?" I said to Stephon when he returned with our tea.

"Moonstone. Beautiful, aren't they?"

Stephon sipped his tea. I took a sip of mine and was transported by its sweet fragrance. "Really beautiful.

I don't think I've ever seen anything quite like them before."

Stephon grinned. "Well, I wouldn't want you to start thinking me ordinary, Ken."

"There's little chance of that." I took another sip of tea and continued to admire the moonstone.

"What brings you here today? I assume it wasn't only to share your good news with me."

"I did want you to know. But I also want to bring Melissa a present. You know how much she always loved this place."

"Indeed I do."

"I don't want to go too far over the top. It's supposed to be our *first date* and all. But I want to bring her something that says that this lunch means a lot to me."

"And your eye was drawn to the moonstone."

"My eye is drawn to *everything* here, but these moonstone pieces are remarkable. The tea is great by the way."

"I should hope so." Stephon held up a finger. "I have something you should see." He put his glass down behind the counter and walked into the back room. He returned less than a minute later holding a pendant from which hung a round stone larger than any he had on display, though still relatively small. "Isn't this magnificent?" he said, holding it out to me.

I held the pendant in my hands, running my fingers softly against the milky stone. "It's great."

"And extraordinarily rare. It is a perfect moonstone. Almost impossible to find in this size."

I looked up from the pendant to Stephon. His eyes were brighter than I'd ever seen them. "This would be perfect, wouldn't it?" I said.

"If you believe it's perfect, then it is."

I smiled. "I'll take it. I hope she won't feel that I'm going over the top here, but you've never steered me wrong before."

He offered me a meaningful glance. "I'm glad you feel that way."

I chuckled a little and Stephon boxed the pendant for me. When he finished, he handed me the box and I handed him my credit card. He brushed the card away.

"One of the privileges of owning one's own shop."

"I can't let you just give this to me."

He shrugged. "I'm not giving it to you. I'm giving it to Melissa."

I reached out my hand and Stephon gripped it firmly. "Have a good lunch, Ken," he said.

〜〜
〜〜

Melissa had made it subtly clear that she preferred meeting in an extremely public place, so we went to one of the dining rooms at the Mandarin Oriental. It was the sort of place where government and business icons met over studiously prepared meals served by impeccably groomed waiters. It was as safe and as public as I could imagine, and I hoped it was the last time we dined someplace this Old Money.

I arrived a half-hour early. Melissa was fifteen minutes late. I'd begun to wonder if she'd had second thoughts, deciding that even if I was a friend of Kate's and even if she remembered the connection we'd made in Seattle that this kind of thing was much too impetuous for her. When she came to the table, I was checking my cell phone for messages.

"I'm sorry I'm late," she said. "There were some complications booking musicians for Friday's session and I couldn't break away. Have you been waiting long?"

"Just a few minutes."

Melissa sat down before I could even rise out of my chair. She looked sensational. She was wearing a smart red outfit and I noticed that its cut was similar (though the color was not) to many of the business suits she'd worn in our other life.

"Well, again, I'm sorry. I hate it when people keep me waiting."

If she only knew how long I'd been waiting for her, she would have understood how insignificant the current delay was. "It's nothing," I said. "I'm glad you came."

"I have to say I was a little intrigued after last night. I don't usually do anything this spur-of-the-moment. Jackeline thought I was out of my mind. She insisted on coming with me, but I put my foot down. Don't be surprised if you see her peeking around a corner."

A waiter laid menus on the table ceremoniously. Melissa idly picked hers up, but she didn't look at it. I folded my hands over mine. "I promise you, I'm completely safe."

"I'm sure you are, Ken." She put her menu down, leaned forward a little, and smiled at me. "You have a trustworthy face."

"I do?"

"Does that surprise you?"

"No, not at all. It's just good to hear someone say it."

"You have a very nice face," she said and then seemed embarrassed that she'd done so.

"You have a nice face, too," I said, immediately scolding myself for saying something so lame.

Melissa cupped her chin in her hands. "Thanks. And you're such a smooth talker." She offered me a bemused smile.

I cringed. "I seem to be getting in touch with my inner junior high school boy at the moment."

Her smile grew wider. "I'm teasing you. Thank you for the compliment and thank you for inviting me to lunch. I've been looking forward to it all day."

I felt a tingle from her expression that I hadn't felt in much too long. What she looked like when she teased me was one of the things I'd allowed myself to forget in the time we were separated.

If I hadn't already been madly in love with Melissa, I would have started falling in love with her right then. We'd been sitting across from each other for less than five minutes and I was already feeling more alive than I had in weeks. It was intoxicating, and I was so thankful for it that I nearly wept. I promised myself I would remember every second of this exchange, that there would never be a time in my life when I couldn't call up the feelings I was feeling at this very moment.

Over the next several minutes, we traded stories. I told her about my career and my messy apartment, and left out little details like the reputation I'd developed as a party animal. That Ken Timian was so far removed from who I was now – who I planned to be for the rest of my life – it was as though he was a different person entirely. I suppose in some very real way he was.

Melissa told me about the course her career had taken, and provided a few anecdotes about her time at the conservatory and life on the road. She spoke with passion and excitement, and as she did so, I realized that she was everything I knew her to be but just a little lighter, a little less careworn, a little less worldly, even though she'd traveled the world. She dedicated herself almost entirely to her music, practicing from eight to ten hours every day, but she had no regrets about this, feeling that her time could hardly be spent in a better pursuit. I asked her as gently as I could about her rock star ex-boyfriend and she tossed it off as a media invention. Yes, they dated, even vacationing together once, but theirs was hardly a major romance and their breakup was nothing more than a decision to get on with the rest of their lives. I hoped I didn't seem too pleased when she told me this.

When the waiter came to take our order, we stopped talking only long enough to tell him what we wanted. The break, however, allowed Melissa to shift gears.

"So what's happening here?" she said.

"Here? As in right now?"

"As in right now, and last night, and in Seattle, and all of this. This certainly doesn't feel like a casual little lunch and you certainly don't seem to be looking at it that way." She eyed me carefully and I felt a little apprehensive.

She continued. "And neither am I. But why is that?"

I didn't want to blow it by saying too much, but I also knew that I needed – perhaps more than ever in my life – to say what I really felt. "From the first time I saw you, I knew that I would take every second with you seriously. I know that probably sounds ridiculous to you, but I felt it right from the start."

Melissa held my gaze for an eternal moment. Just then, the waiter came with our drinks, breaking the connection. When he left, I looked over at Melissa, but she was no longer looking at me. Instead, she was glancing down at the table. Then she picked up her glass.

"This is a total mystery to me," she said, "but I can't remember the last time being with someone felt this right." She raised her glass toward mine and we touched them together. "Here's to taking every second together seriously. Wherever this leads."

I wanted Melissa to decide that she needed to spend several more days in Washington. I imagined her calling her personal assistant and telling her to put her entire life on hold and then our staying in this restaurant until the waiters ganged up on us.

That fantasy lasted all of a minute and a half. Then her cellphone rang and Melissa pulled it out of her bag, moving to silence it.

"It's okay, Melissa," I said. "Take the call."

"Are you sure?"

"Of course."

Melissa got up from the table to take the call. I watched her walk away, praying that urgent business wasn't going to take her completely away from me just now. As time passed, I half expected a waiter to come by to say that Melissa was sending her regrets, but she had to run off. A couple of minutes later, though, she came back looking amused.

"Is everything okay?" I said.

"Everything is fine," she said, sitting down. She laughed. "That was Jackeline calling. She wanted to make sure I was all right. She's so ridiculously protective of me. She was offering me an opportunity to escape." Melissa leaned toward me. "I told her I wasn't to be bothered again the rest of the afternoon."

I smiled. "Thanks." I reached into my breast pocket and produced the jewelry box. "This is for you."

"Really?"

She seemed a bit apprehensive, so I moved quickly to minimize this gesture. "Just a little something. A getting-acquainted present."

I handed her the box and she ran her fingers over the top of it. "Stephon's," she said.

"You know the place?"

"I visit him every time I'm in town. He's my favorite jeweler in the entire world. I saw him yesterday and...."

Her voice trailed off and she looked baffled. "And?" I said.

"And he told me that something momentous was going to happen to me on this trip." She looked from the box to me, the light dancing in her eyes. "I think it has."

She looked down at the box again. Slowly, she opened it, removing the pendant and studying the gem carefully. "This is gorgeous. I don't recognize the stone."

"It's a moonstone. Stephon told me it's a rare perfect specimen."

She ran her finger over the pendant just as I had in Stephon's shop. "I can't believe you got this for me. I would have picked it out myself if I had seen it."

She had been in Stephon's shop yesterday and hadn't seen this display. I didn't think I was ever going to solve the mystery of that remarkable jeweler. "Try it on. It'll go beautifully with what you're wearing."

Melissa seemed a little unsure of herself but then took the pendant out of the box and tried it on. It looked as gorgeous on her as I imagined it would. "You have excellent taste in jewelry," she said. "Thank you." She looked down at the pendant for a long moment. "My head is spinning a little."

When she looked at me again, there was a glimmer in her eyes that could have lit the entire Kennedy Center. It was even more electrifying to my soul.

Chapter 24

I sat alone at the top of the mountain. Aspen in the early summer teemed with shoppers, tourists, and hikers striding challenging paths. Unlike in the winter, though, it was still possible to get a little part of it for yourself. The air was so different here from what it was in Washington. It was crisp even when it was warm. I lay back on the blanket and breathed deeply. It had taken me a few days to get accustomed to the altitude, but now it felt completely natural. Like my new life.

Three days ago, I'd shut down the apartment in Arlington. I supervised the loading of all of my belongings onto a moving van, picked up the cat's carrier, and headed to the airport. Colorado would be home now, but when one lived with Melissa Argent, one truly was a citizen of the world.

Warwick the Lesser almost seemed relieved when I handed in my resignation. We'd been going at it pretty hard lately. Over the course of two lifetimes, Melissa had taught me that truly caring about things meant more than simply paying lip service to them and I steadfastly refused to represent any client I didn't believe in. Since the firm seemed to specialize in attracting spoilers and despots, this lightened my workload considerably. I still billed major hours, but I'd clearly become less of a team player than Warwick desired. I don't think he'll ever understand how "that woman changed me." He'll always think I took my revised moral stance to remain in her good graces. What it really came down to for me was this: did I want to regale my grandchildren with stories of how I helped some rich people devastate the future for the sake of a buck or did I want to tell them how I negotiated fair deals for farmers all over the planet so they could make a decent living and we could enjoy the fruits of their labors? My new office would be ready in downtown Aspen when we got back.

Leaving Sharon behind was tougher than I'd expected. The divorce settlement turned out fine in the long run, but she still had some huge issues facing her raising two boys as a single parent, and her ex-husband took every opportunity he could to poison them against her. I nearly convinced her to move to Colorado and work with me again, but in the end she decided that she couldn't take her kids that far away from their father. There are no simple lives.

Paul took me to Dulles. He and Kate took me out to dinner to celebrate my last night in town. I got to choose the restaurant and I decided we should go back to the Neapolitan, the Italian place I went to with him and Angela right after I learned that Melissa was gone. He thought it was a strange choice, but I had my reasons. As I expected, the two of them spent a lot of time whispering to one another and swaying to the romantic Italian music. When Paul started singing Andrea Bocelli's "Per Amore," I nearly lost my appetite, but the contrast was still wonderful to watch. Introducing them had been one of my better inspirations.

"I'm gonna make the move," Paul said as we sat in traffic on the way to the airport. "I'm gonna ask Kate to marry me."

"Hey, that's great. I knew you had it in you."

"Yeah, I know you did. I'm not sure when you became such a great judge of character, but you were totally right. I just needed to be in the right relationship."

"I'm really happy for you."

"Thanks. I'm gonna do it in the plane on the way back from your wedding. I was going to ask her at your wedding, but I figured you and Melissa might have a little problem with that."

"Either way is great. Let the spirit move you."

His brow wrinkled. "She's gonna say yes, right?"

"I think there's a very good chance of that. You did notice her mooning over you while you were singing last night, didn't you? Kate wasn't the moony type until she met you."

"Wow, I had that effect on someone?"

"Imagine that. You'd better make sure to hold on to Kate, though. I'm not sure there are too many other women who would find your vocal stylings romantic."

Paul laughed. Even now it still tickled me to see him so easily amused. "Yeah, you're probably right about that."

Earlier that day, I'd gone to Stephon's to pick up the rings. They were platinum and gold and Stephon told me that they were based on a centuries-old design created by his family. I wondered if he created it himself centuries ago. Stephon was at least as much of a mystery to me today as he had been the afternoon he fulfilled my fantasy and turned my entire world upside down.

"I'll be back every time I come to D.C.," I said as I prepared to leave.

"I look forward to it. I would hate to lose a favorite customer."

"Not a chance. You know, you should have a website to allow people to shop your store online."

Stephon shook his head. "I don't believe in the Internet, Ken."

"You don't?"

"Not for the long term."

I wondered what he meant by that and how much he knew. I decided not to pursue the point. The world was probably safer that way.

As I lay on the blanket, the sun broke through a patch of clouds and I closed my eyes and let it warm me. I couldn't recall the last time I'd felt this relaxed. For as long as I could remember, my life whirled around me. Now it was time to slow things down.

I felt a presence above me and opened my eyes to see Melissa. She knelt down and kissed me softly and slowly.

"Is the album done?" I said.

"As done as it's going to be. I could work on it forever, you know, but I think this latest mix is as right as I can get it."

When we'd started dating, Melissa was halfway finished with her new album. After our lunch, she flew back to Aspen to work on it and then I flew out to see her for a remarkable weekend that confirmed everything I ever believed about the two of us. When she returned to work after that, she told me that she couldn't look at her new music the same way, that it didn't have the passion she now demanded from it. It didn't say who she was any longer. So she set about rebuilding it, making it more personal. The record company, who knew Melissa's star was on the rise, got very nervous when they found that she'd scrapped her sessions, but changed their minds when they heard some of the revised material. Still, it had taken her until this morning to get it just the way she wanted it.

"Congratulations," I said. "Does this mean we can honeymoon in peace?"

"We can honeymoon anywhere you want. We can honeymoon right on this blanket if you'd like."

"Don't tempt me. You know I have no will power."

"None?" she said, kissing me again.

"Really very little. If you're at all worried about paparazzi, you'll immediately start talking about your mother."

She laughed and sat up. The sun glinted in her eyes, though the sun was a poor substitute for their radiance. "So what did you bring me for lunch?"

I reached into the cooler pack and pulled out the sesame noodles I'd gotten for the two of us. "Chinese restaurants are much more expensive here than they are in D.C., and no one delivers. Are you sure we made the right decision?"

Melissa turned to glance off at the mountains and an eagle soaring in the clouds. "I'm pretty sure we made the right decision."

On Saturday, more than a hundred people (and certainly more than a few uninvited photographers) would gather on this mountainside to watch Melissa and me share our vows. I never imagined myself to be the kind of guy who would get married on a mountain. If the last year had taught me anything, though, it was that the unimaginable is always possible – and maybe even preferable. The Colonel, who was nearly as persnickety and set in his ways in this life as he had been in our other – even from the Argent retirement home in North Carolina – thought the entire thing was absurd and tried to prevail upon me to convince Melissa to do something more traditional. I asked him to tell me the last time someone had convinced Melissa to do something other than what her heart told her. "Trained her too well," he said morosely. Regardless, it was going to be a beautiful ceremony, complete with music provided by a world-class flautist and violinist.

When we finished our meal, Melissa leaned back against me. We had last-minute plans to orchestrate and travel itineraries to juggle, but all could be delayed for at least a few minutes.

"I had no idea what I was missing until you came around," she said. "Do you know how scary it seems to me that I could have gone through my whole life not knowing what was possible?"

I kissed the top of her head. "I think we always would have found each other."

"How? I mean I can still barely believe that it happened."

"We would have. I just know it."

Melissa turned to look at me and then shook her head. "Every now and then I still don't totally get you."

"You have plenty of time to figure me out."

She hugged my arm and then sat up. "I have something for you," she said as she reached into her shoulder bag. She pulled out the pocket watch I once wore proudly for such a short period.

"My mother gave this to me when I was sixteen." She held it up, letting it spin slow circles on its chain. "It was my grandfather's. I just got it back from the engraver. Give me your hand."

She lowered the watch into my palm, the chain sprawling across my outstretched fingers. I flipped it over and read the inscription: KEN + MELISSA FOREVER. I leaned over and kissed her.

"We are forever, right?" Melissa said.

"Absolutely forever. There is nothing that could ever take me away from you," I said with more certainty than I'd said anything in my life.

CPSIA information can be obtained at www.ICGtesting.com
Printed in the USA
BVOW061903060312

284554BV00001B/40/P